Anthony Gilbert and The Murder Room

>>> This title is part of The Murder Room, our series dedicated to making available out-of-print or hard-to-find titles by classic crime writers.

Crime fiction has always held up a mirror to society. The Victorians were fascinated by sensational murder and the emerging science of detection; now we are obsessed with the forensic detail of violent death. And no other genre has so captivated and enthralled readers.

Vast troves of classic crime writing have for a long time been unavailable to all but the most dedicated frequenters of second-hand bookshops. The advent of digital publishing means that we are now able to bring you the backlists of a huge range of titles by classic and contemporary crime writers, some of which have been out of print for decades.

From the genteel amateur private eyes of the Golden Age and the femmes fatales of pulp fiction, to the morally ambiguous hard-boiled detectives of mid twentieth-century America and their descendants who walk our twenty-first century streets, The Murder Room has it all. >>>

The Murder Room
Where Criminal Minds Meet

themurderroom.com

T0352015

Anthony Gilbert (1899–1973)

Anthony Gilbert was the pen name of Lucy Beatrice Malleson. Born in London, she spent all her life there, and her affection for the city is clear from the strong sense of character and place in evidence in her work. She published 69 crime novels, 51 of which featured her best known character, Arthur Crook, a vulgar London lawyer totally (and deliberately) unlike the aristocratic detectives, such as Lord Peter Wimsey, who dominated the mystery field at the time. She also wrote more than 25 radio plays, which were broadcast in Great Britain and overseas. Her thriller *The Woman in Red* (1941) was broadcast in the United States by CBS and made into a film in 1945 under the title *My Name is Julia Ross*. She was an early member of the British Detection Club, which, along with Dorothy L. Sayers, she prevented from disintegrating during World War II. Malleson published her autobiography, *Three-a-Penny,* in 1940, and wrote numerous short stories, which were published in several anthologies and in such periodicals as *Ellery Queen's Mystery Magazine* and *The Saint*. The short story 'You Can't Hang Twice' received a Queens award in 1946. She never married, and evidence of her feminism is elegantly expressed in much of her work.

By Anthony Gilbert

Scott Egerton series
Tragedy at Freyne (1927)
The Murder of Mrs
  Davenport (1928)
Death at Four Corners
  (1929)
The Mystery of the Open
  Window (1929)
The Night of the Fog (1930)
The Body on the Beam
  (1932)
The Long Shadow (1932)
The Musical Comedy
  Crime (1933)
An Old Lady Dies (1934)
The Man Who Was Too
  Clever (1935)

**Mr Crook Murder
  Mystery series**
Murder by Experts (1936)
The Man Who Wasn't
  There (1937)
Murder Has No Tongue
  (1937)
Treason in My Breast (1938)
The Bell of Death (1939)

Dear Dead Woman (1940)
  aka *Death Takes a
  Redhead*
The Vanishing Corpse (1941)
  aka *She Vanished in the
  Dawn*
The Woman in Red (1941)
  aka *The Mystery of the
  Woman in Red*
Death in the Blackout (1942)
  aka *The Case of the Tea-
  Cosy's Aunt*
Something Nasty in the
  Woodshed (1942)
  aka *Mystery in the
  Woodshed*
The Mouse Who Wouldn't
  Play Ball (1943)
  aka *30 Days to Live*
He Came by Night (1944)
  aka *Death at the Door*
The Scarlet Button (1944)
  aka *Murder Is Cheap*
A Spy for Mr Crook (1944)
The Black Stage (1945)
  aka *Murder Cheats the
  Bride*

Death in the Wrong Room

Anthony Gilbert

An Orion book

Copyright © Lucy Beatrice Malleson 1947

The right of Lucy Beatrice Malleson to be identified as the author of this
work has been asserted in accordance with the Copyright, Designs and
Patents Act 1988.

This edition published by
The Orion Publishing Group Ltd
Carmelite House,
50 Victoria Embankment
London EC4Y 0DZ

An Hachette UK Company
A CIP catalogue record for this book is available from the British Library.

ISBN 978 1 4719 0988 7

www.orionbooks.co.uk

For Comey
With my love

$\mathcal{C}$HAPTER $\mathcal{O}$NE

THE HOUSE stood on the side of a hill, with a windmill for background and behind that a wide expanse of pale sky with nothing to interrupt the view but a few trees and, in the far distance, a tall pointed spire white as limestone against the grayer clouds. It was clear that whoever chose the site had done so for a whim rather than with any sense of convenience, for it was isolation itself, and when it came to putting in a water supply two builders flatly refused to take on the job. They said it would cost as much as the house itself.

"Dammit!" exploded Colonel Anstruther, "are you being asked to pay for it or am I?"

He took his prospective custom away from them and approached a third man who, looking very long-faced, said it would be a job, a hell of a job.

"And what are you here for but to undertake jobs?" demanded the eccentric Colonel. "Upon my soul, if I'd shown as little initiative when I was in India holding my first commission I'd have been drummed out of the army double-quick and quite right, too. What you want in the army—and out of it for that matter—are men who can face up to a difficulty and find out how to tackle it. D'you suppose I'm paying you to tell me it's going to be a job to bring water here? D'you suppose I'm such a crack-brained flannel-footed oaf I can't see that for myself?"

This was precisely what the builder had thought, but he didn't dare say so. The Colonel was one of those long thin men with impressive moustaches, who look as though they

1

should suffer from low blood pressure, but if he did no one would have guessed it.

He got his water, of course, and as for electricity, he said that was a new-fangled idea—anything less than fifty years old was new-fangled to the Colonel—and only a fad to make life easier for a pack of lazy servants eating their heads off and getting machines to do their work for them. (But after Rose Anstruther came back electricity was installed as a matter of course.) In the background, but not too far away, was Jock, the Colonel's ex-soldier servant, a grizzled impassive creature with Scottish tenacity, sharing his master's view of the fuss and folly that is Woman. Rose didn't count as Woman; like her father, she was beyond normal rules and regulations in Jock's eyes and, as subsequent visitors were speedily to learn for themselves, it was Jock's word that counted.

It was after Rose made her surprising runaway match with Gerald Fleming that the Colonel built The Downs. He had fought against what he considered an absurdly fanciful title, but for once he suffered defeat. Having stood out for months against every suggestion his builder could offer from Seaview to Windmill House, he found that he had to have an address of some sort if any letters were to reach him, and down in the village it was invariably referred to as the house on the downs, so The Downs it became. The Colonel himself never used the name. My house, he would say, and, if pressed for a description of its situation, would add, "On the hill there. You can't miss it. There isn't another building for half a mile."

Rose Anstruther was twenty-eight when she ran away. She was one of those enigmatic Botticelli women, serene enough on the surface and lovely as something out of Primavera. Women openly wondered why she hadn't married before, and decided it was "that selfish father of hers." At that time the Anstruthers lived in a very pleasant house in the village, close to the sea; Rose never appeared to have servant trouble as other women did. Servants presumably left for the usual reasons and new ones took their place, but you never saw the stately Miss Anstruther in registry offices. In point of fact, Jock engaged the servants. Rose and the Colonel both thought this reasonable. It was Jock who would have to work with them. Perhaps it was living in India for so many years that gave them both their air of aloof dignity.

In Sunbridge naturally the household aroused a good deal of speculation. Women who had worked in the house said there were no photographs standing about, and neither the Colonel nor Rose ever mentioned the late Mrs. Anstruther. The Colonel belonged to a Club—Sunbridge is favored as a retiring-place for innumerable military men—and cherished a passion for maps. Miss Anstruther occupied herself with the flowers, a little ladylike gardening, her embroidery, and occasional visits to their few acquaintances. She was regularly At Home once a month, had select tennis parties in the summer, and it was a matter for congratulation to achieve the entree to any of her functions.

"What does she do with herself all day?" matrons asked one another, but a young man who had been infatuated with her at sight returned passionately, "People like Miss Anstruther don't have to do things. It is enough for them just to be."

It was the same young man who said of her that "she walked in beauty like the night," but when a certain Mrs. Pendlebury mentioned the young man's name to Rose, longing to know if anything was "likely to come of it," she turned her lovely, calm face to her companion, murmuring, "Mr. Bennett? Have I met him? I'm afraid I don't . . ."

Their exclusiveness and the fact that no one ever saw Rose moved by any transport of feeling started a rumour that she was—well, just a little, you know—and the ladies would nod and touch their foreheads and exchange experienced glances. No wonder the Colonel was so stiff and unyielding and shrank so obviously from feminine society, but though there were always ladies only too eager to prove to him that life might still be sweetened by human associations, he never took the hint. Morning by morning the stiff erect figure went down to the Club to read *The Times,* punctually at one o'clock he returned to lunch, and in the afternoon he and his daughter might often be seen together, apparently absorbed in one another's company.

3

Then, all of a sudden, Rose disappeared. Gerald Fleming was admittedly attractive, a year or so younger than Rose, a creature of impulsive charm and a delightful sophistication. Rose had always had admirers, and there were some, the Colonel among them, who couldn't see what he had to offer that made him more desirable than a score of other young nincompoops who had worshipped at his lovely Rose's shrine. But it seemed Rose had at last fallen in love and she proposed to marry her swain. The Colonel pooh-poohed the whole idea. The chap was unstable, he said, had no educated ideas about settlements, talked as if you could live on bread and cheese and kisses, in other words on his wife's income, and above and beyond all that, "a fellow doesn't marry to bring up a daughter to look after some other chap." Having expressed his views he appeared to consider the subject closed.

The affair differed from innumerable other romances in that there were no arguments, no wild pleas, accusations, broken-hearted Rose or frantic young man. All three participants were accustomed to having their own way; all intended to do so on this occasion. Rose for all her surface tranquillity was a creature of deep feeling, and it never occurred to her that she should not have what she so greatly desired. Since Papa was proving so unreasonable, and since open disagreement between them was unthinkable, she packed a trunk, told Jock to order a cab and drove away from the house one morning when the Colonel was at his club, to join her lover in London. She even left the traditional three-cornered note on her father's pincushion.

It was after this that the Colonel bought the site of The Downs and had the plans drawn up. Like his daughter, he wasn't used to defeat, and he went through the objections and hesitancies of builders and their allies like a hot knife going through butter. When they suggested other sites, he threw their plans on the floor and came back to his original notion. It must have been force of personality that got him his way, for he was not a rich man, nor was he an influential one. But the house went up at an astonishing rate, and carts and lorries climbed the hill and cranes came into position, and when the whole was finished it was a sight for the whole neighborhood. These came in admiring

4

groups to stand a little way off and tell one another in surprised tones that really it was staggering what the old boy had thought of. They themselves wouldn't have chosen that particular site—too expensive, too remote, any reason would serve; they wouldn't even have chosen that type of architecture—they supposed he'd got the idea from his Indian sojourns, they confided to one another, even those who had never been nearer India than Brightlingstone, the big seaside town that drew thousands from all over the country during the summer season—but one and all agreed that the finished article was extraordinarily attractive and stranger still, appropriate to its surroundings. Long and low—it stood on two floors only—with an unparalleled view across the Downs to the sea in the distance, it seemed to melt into its background, without ever becoming insignificant. However, their opportunities of admiring it were few, for after enduring the sightseers for about a week the Colonel stamped into his builder's establishment and demanded a board—at once. "Want it by Saturday," said the Colonel. "Here are the specifications."

The board read simply: This is a private house. Not open for inspection.

The next batch of curiosity-mongers laughed and said did the old man think we were living in the Middle Ages and he'd got something to learn, but all the same after its erection they stayed at a respectful distance. One of the wags, in fact, said the house was typical of its owner, and it would be luck to have him for a neighbor in hell, because he'd freeze even the purgatorial flames. All the same, the notice served its purpose, and the Colonel had all the privacy he needed.

The ladies of the community speculated on the size of the house. It was absurd, they said, to put up that barn of a place just for a widower, and they watched and wondered and confided to one another their suspicions about a new Mrs. Anstruther; they even tried to pump the servants, but they got short shrift here, for Jock was as unapproachable as his master and the only other member of the staff at that time was an enormous Scotswoman called Mrs. Mack, who contrived, for all her size, to remain practically invisible. So, for a time, the two elderly men rattled about in the place like a couple of peas. Then it leaked out that he had transported all his daughter's belongings to the new house, where he had had a complete suite arranged for her convenience with all her personal furnishings put in practically the same order as before. Her grand piano, her embroidery frame, her beautiful bedroom suite and curtains, her aubusson carpet, her china cabinet, pictures, knick-knacks, so that if she returned without warning at any time she could step straight into the life she had left.

And this, in fact, was precisely what Rose did.

Six years after her sensational elopement, she arrived at the door of The Downs in a hired car and a quantity of luggage, displaying no more hurry, secrecy or fear about this move than there had been about her flight. Out of the car stepped a tall auburn-haired Botticelli lady, beautifully dressed—her clothes had always been the envy of Sunbridge matrons—the driver alighted and rang the bell, and Jock answered the door. Rose said in composed tones, "Good afternoon, Jock. I've come home. Are my rooms ready? I should like a hot bath and some tea sent to my bedroom."

Jock said, "I knew ye'd be back anon," and that was the only comment he was ever known to make on the development. He and the driver carried up the luggage, a little later Rose had her bath and afterwards Jock himself took up her tea. He explained that the cook was a plain body, not much used to ladies, and Rose suggested the engagement of another woman to help in the house now that she herself was at home. Jock said, "I'll see to that first thing in the morning," and left Rose to drink her tea. Mrs. Mack lumbered up with offers of assistance, and between them the two women unpacked the boxes, which were then removed by Jock, and a few minutes later the Colonel came in. No one knew how he took the news, since no one saw the meeting of the two, but what he actually said when he saw his daughter again was, "Well, you've been some time making up your mind, but I knew you'd never stay with that flibbertigibbet. Now I hope you're going to settle down."

"Yes," said Rose gently. "I've come home, for good."

"That's fine," said the Colonel. "You'll find all your things here. Only one thing, Rose, I won't have that fellow here. He must understand that."

Rose said in the same dispassionate tone, "He won't come here. You see, he's dead."

"Dead, eh?" It seemed impossible to startle any of the members of this extraordinary household. "Probably the best day's work he ever did. How did it happen?"

"You were right about him, and I found that out within six months. Yet looking back, knowing as little as I did then, I believe I should do the same again. I don't think men understood it, but there was something very attractive about Gerald. Other women noticed it, too."

"Like that?" growled the Colonel.

"The real trouble was he was a natural gambler. Nothing could stop him. You know, he had no money except his retired pay."

"Chap of his age has no right to be retired," snapped the Colonel, "not unless he's got land to look after."

"Oh, I think there had been some trouble. He was always very lavish when he had money, spent it like a prince. But on the whole he was lucky. He gambled everything away..."

"Yours, too?" The Colonel's private opinion was the fellow looked like a pimp, but women seemed to have no discrimination.

"Everything he could touch."

"Thank God, your mother had the sense to tie some money up. Has everything else gone?"

She nodded. "Jewels, car.... The funny thing was I didn't mind at first, if he wanted it. Then I began to see how hopeless it was. It was like a drug. He didn't seem able to stop. He said he was writing a book on gambling. He took a villa at Monte Carlo so that he could have quiet to work..."

The Colonel looked at her sharply. She couldn't really be so green. Fellows didn't take villas in the Riviera to write books.... He saw that she wasn't deceived.

"That too?" he muttered.

Her next words shocked him. "It was there he shot himself," she said.

7

The Colonel was appalled. "My dear Rose! I had no notion . . ."

"Ever since it happened I've asked myself if it was my fault. He warned me he was at the end of his tether. He had done that before, but never with quite the same urgency. He said, 'If you don't help me now you may be sorry later on.' I explained that I had nothing left I could touch, but he said I could borrow on my security. I told him you had made me promise never to do that, but he said a husband's need ought to come before a promise that should never have been made. But oh!" She put out her hands in a gesture so weary yet so poignant that even the tough old man was moved. In spite of the atmosphere of tragedy in which she had returned, he could find nothing but joy in his heart at the sight of her. "What was the sense? It would all have gone in a few days and we should have been absolutely destitute. I asked him if he would come back to England, but he refused. I don't know whether he had some reason for not wanting to be seen there, but I think it was probably his passion for gambling that made him adamant. It was his life to him. He told me again that if I didn't help him this time he was ruined, but I had been through it all so often before, and I was hard. That night I felt exhausted and I went to bed soon after dinner. He said he was going back to the casino for a final fling. I never saw him again alive. Next morning he was found at the villa with his revolver by his side." She shivered. "The doctor said he must have been dead for hours."

Poor child, he thought, she must have known some passion of grief, of remorse, of anger, when it happened; but now her voice was dull as a gray day.

"His own revolver, of course?"

"Yes. He always had one. He used to say it was a gentleman's last friend. As a matter of fact . . ." she hesitated. "The police were very considerate and this never got into the papers, but I think he was expecting someone to meet him at the villa that night, perhaps someone who would have helped him. When they found him there was a tray on a sidetable with two glasses on it and some wine, that hadn't been touched. They thought he must

8

have waited until he realised whoever it was wasn't coming, and that was the end of his hope."

"May be a lot of speculation," growled the Colonel, hoping he was saying the right thing.

"They weren't very much moved by it," Rose acknowledged. "That sort of thing happens too often out there. Men gamble for fortunes, lose them and throw up the sponge. Gerald was just one of a great army, no personal significance at all. They were more interested to know if I could pay up his debts than anything else."

"You've left nothing outstanding?" The Colonel's voice was sharp.

"Nothing. I paid the hotel bill and I sold everything he left, his cigarette case and lighter, his watch, his clothes, everything. He wasn't on terms with any of his relations—I gather they broke off connections years ago, and there was no one left to write to. Two or three curious ghouls came to the funeral, but people out there are forgotten as you would forget a pheasant you shot last week. Living is very expensive, but life itself very cheap." She drew a deep breath and looked round her. "For nearly six years I've dreamed of coming home," she said. "It doesn't seem possible I'm really here."

They never talked of Gerald Fleming again.

The neighbors nearly split themselves trying to find out what had happened, but they were the kind that seldom goes abroad for a holiday and all they could learn was that he had died abroad. It was thought perfectly normal for Rose to return to her father's roof, and when, a year later, she unostentatiously changed her name by deed poll and was once again Rose Anstruther the Knows-Alls nodded significantly to one another and said it was a mercy the chap had died—all except those who didn't believe in the story of his death but imagined him gallivanting on the Continent with some bejewelled mistress.

After her return life at The Downs changed little. The staff was increased, every now and again large exquisite boxes bearing the names of famous *couturières* and milliners were delivered at the house, for Rose dressed as perfectly as ever, but the rigid ban on hospitality was not lifted, and now she was not even At

9

Home to her neighbors. A servant-girl said the lady did the most wonderful petit-point embroidery and spent hours reading and playing the piano. There were no photographs of the late Mr. Fleming anywhere and his name was never mentioned. For all the difference he had made to the household it seemed that he might never have existed.

About five years after Rose's return a new inmate came to The Downs. This was the Colonel's brother, Joseph Anstruther, a man of much the same build, only his hobby was crime instead of maps. He filled the shelves in his room with records of famous trials, autobiographies of detectives, treatises on crime in various countries, and delighted in the day-to-day crimes revealed in the press. When any such outrage had been committed, he was instantly on the trail, explaining to the tranquil Rose and the impatient Colonel, who was becoming a little deaf with increasing years, police methods and where, in his opinion, the authorities erred.

"If ever I commit a murder . . ." was a famous opening of his.

"You talk like a fool, Joseph," snapped the Colonel. "Of course you won't commit a murder. Haven't you ever noticed in all this multitudinous reading of yours that murders are never committed by gentlemen?"

When Joseph triumphantly instanced a famous murder by a soldier during the first World War the Colonel said, "Fellow was mad. They shut him up, didn't they? Well then, that disposes of your argument."

It was an odd household, the old Colonel living his detached life, Rose as apart from the things of everyday as if she had actually stepped out of the frame of an Old Master, Joseph Anstruther immersed in his hobby. He read innumerable detective stories, perpetually writing to authors to point out blunders, backing his opinion with actual judgments or cases in real life, and stressing the ideal location of The Downs as a scene for murder.

But it is improbable that he anticipated what lay ahead.

CHAPTER Two

IT WAS during the year that saw the end of World War No. 2 that the redoubtable Lady Bate (flour, snorted the Colonel) and her niece by marriage, Caroline, came to The Downs, and it was while they were there that Joseph Anstruther was justified in his claim that the house was ideally located for a crime. For it was during their tenancy that it suddenly sprang into a most unwelcome publicity. A few years earlier the Colonel would have been horrified at the notion of harboring strangers under his roof, but the war years affected the household in two ways. The first was financial. The Colonel had never been a rich man and he had put most of his capital into the house. In this he would have considered himself justified had it occurred to him that any justification was required. His tastes were simple and his expenditure microscopic. He had his pension and that was about all. Joseph also had a pension and no capital—he had, years earlier, married a most unsuitable wife, who had run through his substance and then run away with someone more entertaining. It was all such ancient history that even Joseph sometimes forgot he had ever been married. As for Rose, she had the small income bequeathed her by her mother, and the three of them, by pooling their resources, contrived to live without difficulty until about 1940, when rising taxes and increased cost of living drove all kinds of people, who had hitherto never thought of work, into the labor market. There could, of course, be no question of any of them taking what the authorities described as gainful employment. The kitchenmaid went into munitions and the housemaid,

11

who was old enough to know better, suddenly married a soldier, "and none too soon," commented Jock grimly.

Jock and cook agreed that, with the simplified living imposed by war conditions, they could manage without any other help. It never occurred to Rose that she should turn to, even to the extent of making her own bed, and this was done by the "girl" of the moment. She changed her identity so often that she was never counted as a member of the regular staff, and both Jock and the cook were surprised that anyone considered her as an asset.

It was one of Rose's talents that nobody ever thought of her as idle. To the two old men who relied on her, she represented a quality that the war practically killed, something beautiful and cool, with the element of mystery that their generation prized so highly. There was nothing mysterious about the modern young women with their revealing slacks and dangling hair and painted lips. But with all their simplifications it became steadily more difficult for the household at The Downs to meet their commitments. And then, to crown everything, came the air raids on London and the steady evacuation of the homeless and the helpless to the country.

It was Joseph who sounded the warning note. Joseph got about more than the others. His hobby took him into the town, and he observed with satisfaction that you could always count on a fair amount of crime in a seaside neighborhood. He used to sit in saloon bars, a thin eccentric old gentleman, and chat to anyone who turned up. Since that was the time when the writers of detective stories were reaping a rich harvest, and since he had a century's real crimes at his fingertips, he was never without an audience. It was there, in fact, that he first set eyes on Mr. Crook, long before Crook was officially involved in the affair.

Crook was down on one of the various cases that engaged his attention during those years, and he found the old man stimulating company. He was fond of explaining what he'd do if he committed a murder, and how he'd bamboozle the police.

"It's a matter of looking ahead," he explained. "Most chaps don't plan their murders."

But Crook asked him if he'd ever heard of the invisible witness, and said that the people to be afraid of weren't the police or the people directly connected with the crime, but hawkers, paper-sellers, old ladies exercising Pekineses, cripples whose main amusement was sitting at ground-floor windows and watching the street. Joseph took careful note of everything Crook told him.

"You've been around a bit," he would say, with some envy.

It was during his sojourns in the town that he realized what was likely to happen to the Colonel and Rose. Sunbridge had been selected by the authorities as an evacuation center. It seemed improbable that the Germans would bomb it, and, there being neither factories nor military camps in the immediate neighborhood, there was more accommodation there than in a good many other places. Of course, it was sea-coast, and if the promised invasion ever eventuated, it might imply a hurried exodus of the evacuees, but in 1940 the Government had its hands full with emergency measures—Dunkirk and the ravages wrought by bombs coming together was enough to try the most elastic Government, and so to Sunbridge came the trains from East and South London, all along the bank of the Thames where the first raids did the greatest harm, and mothers and children and old folk poured out on the platforms and were hurried away by distracted billeting officers to homes which weren't on the whole eager to have them, and where conditions were for the most part entirely foreign to the newcomers.

It was Sam, the barman at the Bird In Hand, who observed cheerfully to Joseph—he wouldn't have dared make a similar suggestion to the Colonel—"Suppose you'll be having your little lot from London any day now, sir?" and Joseph said, "Hey, what? Nonsense, nonsense. Can't park a lot of town brats on two old men and a widow."

But the observation had disturbed him. He put his developed gift for observation into more practical effect and realized that Sam was right. Any day now a billeting officer would arrive at the door, and although the combination of Jock and the Colonel would be enough to stagger Hitler, it was incredible what chaps could do in a war, with the Government behind them. It was difficult to make the Colonel appreciate the position, but Jock displayed unexpected common sense. Since it was inevitable that

13

part of so large a house would be commandeered, it seemed to his thrifty common sense that it might as well be done at a profit. There were two front staircases to The Downs, and there was no need for the family to see their unwelcome guests. It would mean, of course, some cramping. At present each member of the household had a personal suite, but fuel shortage was making it difficult in any case, and by rearranging some of the two old gentlemen's belongings it seemed to Jock that Miss Rose need hardly know the lodgers were in the house. Jock scorned the more polite description of "paying guests." To him they were lodgers and to the Colonel they remained boarders. It took even Jock some time to get round the various objections raised by the old autocrat, but eventually that half of the house where the rooms were slightly smaller and the views slightly less spacious, though, for that matter, every room had a view worth traveling miles to see, which had the inferior of the two bathrooms and contained the kitchen and the servants' quarters, was handed over for the invaders' use and the first party shortly arrived.

Joseph went round inspecting the arrangements. "Very nice," he approved. "Give 'em what's necessary, but don't make 'em too comfortable. Otherwise you'll have 'em here for life."

However, it was so quickly made obvious to the guests that they were an inferior form of life, who could only expect attention when the household proper had been attended to and their rare encounters with the family were so alarming that few of them stayed very long. The Government wouldn't allow them petrol, there were no adequate bus services—the Colonel had a special allowance, of course, for shopping and church. If you lived more than two miles from a church you got priority, and an official of the Fuel Ministry observed that it was amazing how many churches seemed situated on golf courses since the outbreak of war, while the number of golfers who suddenly took to religion might also justify an official inquiry. But naturally there was never room in the car for visitors, nor was Jock, who drove, amenable in the matter of executing small commissions.

"These silly women!" he remarked witheringly to his employer. "Do they no ken there's a war on? Mrs. Mack and the girl and myself have our hands full tending to them as it is, and instead of being grateful there they are asking will I fetch them some rubbishy paper or tobacco or some such fulishness. If it's so needful to their comfort, didn't the Almighty give them legs?"

To suggestions of breakfast in bed he had one reply. "This is a house, no' a hospital." He was very choosy, too, about lodgers, asking as many questions as a Government Department.

"For heaven's sake don't import a lot of these painted trollops," implored the Colonel, "or they'll think we're running a disorderly house and come down on me for income tax."

"You can't be too careful," added Joseph impressively. "Let them know there are two widowers here and we'll get such an influx of women who've missed their market we'd be better off with evacuees."

"Evacuees!" said Jock scornfully. "And how about me? I'm no a marrit man, and it's well known every woman sets her cap at a bachelor. The conceit of the creatures!"

The conceit, however, was by no means all on one side. All three men were convinced, after the manner of their sex and age, that they would be irresistible to any unattached female. As to the effect of any lodgers on Rose, this was not taken into account, it being agreed that Rose was not to be bothered with them. Once they saw a woman on the premises, opined Jock, they'd take the place for a boarding-house. The sort of women who became blind pigs were generally awed by a man-servant, and Jock, like the Almighty whom he frequently evoked, was no respecter of persons. A decent body lived in his or her own house. If they quitted it for any reason whatsoever, even though it had been blitzed over their heads, they sank unequivocally into that lower social stratum known as lodgers.

The comparative succession of strangers arriving at The Downs, being instantly enchanted by the view, writing to their friends that they really had struck it lucky this time, writing a week later in a slightly less enthusiastic strain that the whole position was a little peculiar, that you never saw anyone but the manservant, and all requests for an interview with Mrs. Anstruther were met with a blank refusal; these same lodgers' occasional glimpses of the two old gentlemen looking like an austerity version of Tweedledum and Tweedledee, but always a back view, always receding, never welcoming, their expressed conviction that there was something queer about the whole set-up—these became an accepted part of the house's routine. No one stayed for more than six months, most of them left after three or four. Some didn't stand the strain more than the first two or three weeks. The place was too isolated, they declared, and too much attention was paid to the family and too little to the guests.

Jock and Mrs. Mack agreed that one meal midday was all that could be expected of a single-handed cook, so at 12:30 a meal of sorts was planked on the table in the communal living-room, and immediately afterwards Jock brought the car round to the front door and the two old gentlemen and Rose got in and were driven down to the town, where they had a standing arrangement with the most exclusive restaurant for a permanent table—naturally, the best. Sometimes they returned at once, sometimes they drove into Brightlingstone, where the Colonel went to a cinema, a habit he had contracted since the war, Joseph browsed in bookshops, and Rose matched embroidery silks or bought wool, for she knitted with the same exquisite precision as she gave to every other activity that engaged her time, while Jock executed commissions for Mrs. Mack. At four o'clock they returned, at 4:15 they had tea, and at 4:30 Jock permitted the boarders to have theirs. No hints, no complaints even, moved him in the least. There was no compulsion on anyone to stay where he wasn't comfortable, he observed. And so the procession came and went until the arrival of old Lady Bate and young Caroline.

Lady Bate was probably the first person to come to The Downs who might be regarded as a match for Jock. She wrote from an hotel at Brightlingstone asking for details, and sent her niece to look at the rooms. Caroline was a shy, fair-haired girl who would have been much happier in the Services than dancing attendance on her alarming aunt. Her father had been a half-brother of the deceased Sir Charles Bate of flour fame, so that she was more like the old lady's granddaughter than her niece. Lady Bate, however, who was as accustomed as Rose Anstruther to having her own way, had mown down all the objections of the Ministry of Labor—she was an invalid, she insisted, and to prove it she bought an invalid chair that she made the luckless Caroline push around—she had made a home for the girl ever since the death of her parents when Caroline herself was five, Caroline was not very strong, she produced doctors' certificates right and left (dragged, as was subsequently proved, from reluctant acquaintances who could no more withstand the old lady's onslaughts than they could have withstood a robot bomb), and eventually the Ministry's harassed officials gave the old lady best, as Sir Charles had long ago learned to do. When Jock opened the door and saw this pretty creature in her plain dark coat and little dark hat trimmed with squirrel fur, his first impulse was to say that the rooms were let, but a second glance assured him that the girl wasn't outrageously painted and powdered, and when she spoke in a soft, appealing voice of "my aunt who is not very strong," he contented himself by making his time-honored remark about the house not being a hospital.

"I didn't mean she was delicate exactly," explained Caroline, "but it is rather a roundabout journey if you haven't a car, and if the rooms shouldn't prove suitable, though if they're anything like the outside of the house I should think they would be beautiful. . . . But she feels I should bring her a report because, having lived with her all my life, I know what she likes."

"If she's always had what she liked she's mair fortunate than most of us," returned Jock in his outspoken fashion.

What Caroline meant but naturally could not say was that the old lady was a tartar who had been requested by one hotel after another to leave at the end of the week.

"I don't know what the world's coming to," she would storm at Caroline. "No manners, no consideration, no respect for birth or for old age. Everybody thinking of themselves."

It was questionable if she had ever thought of anyone else in the whole of her long, selfish life. Even her adoption of Caroline had had a selfish motive. Her husband had recently died and she foresaw a wealthy but solitary, possibly helpless old age, and she had no fears of the girl leaving her to make some impracticable marriage just when she was most needed. The woman who had wheeled Sir Charles Bate into line would find

17

a girl child's play. Jock shared Lady Bate's opinion of Caroline. A puir saft body, he decided. He took her up to Lady Bate's prospective room, the best of the lodgers' apartments, with a dressing-room opening out of it. At Caroline's request he said grudgingly he could put up a camp bed in the dressing-room, but this room was really let as a double. He whipped open the door of the sitting-room, where the intimidated girl got a view of comfortable chairs—anyway two were comfortable—round a moderate fire.

"No private sitting-room?" she ventured.

"It was rooms, no' a flat that was offered," Jock pointed out.

Caroline nodded submissively. "I dare say Aunt Bate will make herself comfortable," she observed.

"There's others after the rooms," Jock informed her swiftly.

For the first time a gleam of humor shone in Caroline's eye. "That wouldn't affect her," she said.

Jock gave her a startled glance. "Mebbe her leddyship had best come herself to see," was his sour comment.

"I don't think that's necessary," said Caroline. "I shall tell her they're perfect. I," she added, "have always wanted to be in a room that looked over the Downs."

"Ye'll be on war-work? suggested Jock, but the girl shook her head.

"My aunt is war-work. Even the Ministry of Labor has agreed to that." Then she asked to see Mrs. Anstruther.

Jock stiffened like an iron rod. "Mrs. Anstruther is not seeing anyone this afternoon. She leaves the arrangements to me, ye ken. That suits the twa of us."

"I see," said the girl gravely, and again there was that betraying sparkle in her eye. "Oh well, Aunt Bate will probably be able to see Mrs. Anstruther when she comes. Will Monday be all right? I think the terms were settled."

So, on Monday, Lady Bate and Caroline arrived in a hired car with an incredible amount of luggage to be carried up to the first floor.

"Are you the porter?" she asked Jock.

"Ye've been misinformed," he assured her. "Butler is what we call it in a private house."

"I wasn't aware this was a private house," returned Lady Bate briskly. She was a formidable old dame, absurdly dressed in sealskin and sequins. Her luggage was old-fashioned but expensive. Jock made a feint of lifting one or two of the boxes, then turned to the chauffeur and asked him to lend a hand. The man looked as though he would refuse, and Caroline said quickly, in the manner of one used to stepping into the breach, "I can help you with the luggage."

"Nothing of the kind," snapped Lady Bate. "You're a guest here, not one of the servants. For what we are being charged I expect adequate service."

Jock turned and looked at her witheringly. "Ye must be a very disappointed leddy," he observed.

The chauffeur got down with the air of a man who knows that whatever else may be adequate his tip will not be, and between them the two men carried the boxes and bags upstairs. Lady Bate followed briskly. She remarked at once that she would prefer the bed in some other part of the room. Jock said, "Mrs. Anstruther doesna' like the furniture to be shifted about for a lot of giddy whims," and Lady Bate returned, "I will have a word with Mrs. Anstruther myself. In fact, I shall doubtless be seeing her shortly." Her manner intimated that it was surprising the lady herself had not been on the doorstep to greet the new arrival.

"Mrs. Anstruther can no' see anyone this afternoon." Jock was as firm as a granite gravestone.

"I am accustomed to seeing the lady in charge on arrival," said Lady Bate, not to be outdone.

"If there's anything else ye require ye should tell me," Jock invited her.

"This seems a most unusual establishment," remarked the old lady in her blunt fashion.

"Indeed it is," Jock agreed. "I dare say ye'll never have stayed in a house like this before."

Lady Bate glared. "I should like a cup of tea," she countered, but Jock had her there.

"Tea will be served at four-thairty. I should be getting it now but for bringing up these boxes."

19

"I'm fatigued," asserted Lady Bate. "I should prefer tea in my own room today, since you are not able to give me a private sitting-room."

"There's no meals served in bedrooms," Jock told her. "There's seven in the house including yourself, and no one but Mrs. Mack and me and the girl to ploy for them. And the girl's little enow use."

"Mrs. Anstruther . . ." began Lady Bate.

"Will be waiting. She and the Colonel don't like being kept waiting." He marched out.

"I never heard anything so outrageous," stormed Lady Bate who, in fact, made this remark so often that it would have saved time if she had had it recorded and just put on the record whenever the mood took her. "Who does he think we are?"

"Lodgers," said Caroline simply.

Her aunt swung round. "I intensely dislike that vulgar expression. We are paying guests and really, seeing they are only taking us for their own advantage, they might consider themselves exceedingly fortunate to have us on the premises."

"Oh, Aunt Bate," protested Caroline who, for all her years of experience of her aunt's irrational arguments, was still young enough to believe that she might be converted by pure reason, "you know no one likes having people in their house, and if they have us because they've got to, they'll like us all the less. You know what you say about Government compulsion, and . . ."

"If, instead of talking all that nonsense, you were to begin unpacking my things, you would be repaying me better for all I've done for you," remarked the tart old dame. "If it weren't for me you'd be sleeping 26 to a hut on Salisbury Plain by this time, and how would you like that?"

"I dare say I shouldn't like it at all," Caroline agreed meekly, "but then, as you've so often told me, life isn't for happiness, not only for happiness, I mean. And experience . . ."

"There are times when I wonder why Providence gave you a tongue, since you only seem able to use it for romantic rubbish. Caroline, *be careful of my linen*. You're crushing it in the most careless way. And you know how particular I am." She looked round. "Electricity. I see they have had the wit to put a plug in the wall. As soon as we've unpacked the electric iron you can start smoothing out the creases."

"Not before tea, Aunt Bate."

"Did I say before tea? At the present rate it'll be dinner-time before you've finished unpacking. And remember, some of my things are in that case of yours. I hope you put them all on the top, as I told you."

"Yes, Aunt Bate."

"Then stop wasting energy in idle talk and devote yourself to what you are doing. One thing at a time, Caroline. I've told you that so often."

$\mathcal{C}$HAPTER $\mathcal{T}$HREE

THE GONG for tea boomed before the harried girl had anything like finished arranging in the drawers her aunt's tremendous wardrobe. Lady Bate was not of those who complain bitterly that the President of the Board of Trade never considers women. Disliking most of her sex, she was inclined to back the President of the Board of Trade. Women, she said, only thought of their backs and complexions. Life was for higher things. Let them spend their spare time patching and darning instead of indulging in boogie-woogie. Then we should hear less about clothing shortages. She entirely overlooked (or ignored) the fact that at the outbreak of war she had a very considerable wardrobe of hand-made under-linen, and with the common sense and perspicacity that had so far always made her mistress of every situation, and had finally driven the luckless Sir Charles into the grateful tranquillity of the tomb, she had instantly sent for the "little woman," she habitually employed and ordered another dozen of everything, while materials and labor were still available. Caroline was an exquisite laundress—her aunt had seen to that, adding, "One of these days your husband will thank me for the way I've brought you up."

"I wonder if he will," mused Caroline incorrigibly. "I mean, if he only wants someone to wash his clothes, why not marry a professional laundry-hand? And if he only wants a decorative wife, he won't care if she can wash hand-embroidered pillow-cases or not."

"All men appreciate a wife who is careful of their pocket,"

enunciated Lady Bate, who would have argued the morality of the Ten Commandments with Moses, and had frequently done so with lesser personages. She would on this occasion have liked to leave her niece to finish the unpacking, but she was afraid that if she appeared late at the tea-table the best of everything would have gone, and after all she was paying full board for Caroline as well as for herself. So she said imperiously, "You can finish that afterwards. We had better go down now."

Not wishing, however, to give the impression, as she put it, that she was a lion in the Zoo waiting to be fed on carrion, she loitered along the passage looking at the pictures and commenting on the wallpapers. Distemper, she said, would be healthier and was washable. The Colonel had insisted on the best of everything, and the quality was excellent—indeed, the builders would not have dared give him anything less—and Lady Bate had to admire his taste, which was simple enough to have satisfied the late Sir Charles. A clock on the wall struck the three-quarters with a suddenness that made her jump, and she vented her annoyance on Caroline, who came hastily out of the bedroom and joined her.

"So here you are. We had better go down or we shall find the board swept clean. We've had enough experience of other people's greed to expect no consideration for late-comers." She turned and began to go down the stairs.

Caroline hesitated. "Aunt Bate."

"What is it? Come along, you stupid girl."

"This—this isn't the staircase we came up."

"What do you mean?"

"There are two staircases. I noticed when I came in. We came up the other one."

"What of it?" Her ladyship looked provoked. "They both lead down, I suppose."

"Yes, but . . ." Still the foolish creature lingered.

"Will you kindly do as I tell you, Caroline?"

"I mean, this may be private."

"Nonsense. You talk as if we were in a country house. This is simply a private hotel. . . ."

She was startled to hear a voice behind her exclaim, "No, on my sam, this is too much. Are we to have no privacy in our own home?"

She turned. A thin brown man was standing on the steps above her, his face twisted into an expression of concentrated fury.

Lady Bate put on her iciest manner. "Are you addressing me?" she inquired.

"Are you the new boarders?" Joseph Anstruther wasted no diplomacy on those whom he regarded as interlopers.

Lady Bate looked shocked and nearly as angry as her reluctant host.

"I am Lady Bate. I and my niece are on our way down to tea."

Joseph Anstruther came nearer. "I will speak to Jock," he said. "He has instructions to bring our boarders up the further staircase. This part of the house is reserved for the use of the family. Everything you require you will find in that half, which is set aside for your use and that of your fellow-boarders."

Lady Bate was not so easily put down. "We could hardly be expected to know your private regulations."

"If you had rung the bell in your room Jock would have shown you the way if you were uncertain."

"Your man-servant appears to be so overwhelmed by his duties that I should hesitate to bring him upstairs unnecessarily."

"Not unnecessary at all. You did lose your way. Besides, that's why women get such bad service. All this talk of consideration for the lower orders. What's the fellow here for but to take trouble?" He leaned over the well of the stairs and called peremptorily, "Hey, Jock. These ladies have lost their way."

Jock came up, stiff disapproval in every line of his grim face. "I thocht your leddyship would have the sense to come down the nearby staircase," he remarked, passing them and leading them back inexorably by the way they had come. "Maybe it would be as well to put a bow of ribbon or some such nonsense on the banisters."

"There is no need to be insolent," exclaimed Lady Bate, purple with fury. She turned to Joseph, who was already disappearing down the family stairs. "After tea, I should like to see Mrs. Anstruther."

Joseph stopped, twisted a malevolent face towards her and announced, "If you've any complaints already, make 'em to Jock, ma'am. He'll deal with them."

"This is most unusual . . ."

"Jock's here for the purpose, and in a military household like this one, men carry out their orders." He disappeared round the bend of the stairs.

Lady Bate turned to the waiting Jock. "Who is that?"

"Mr. Joseph. The Colonel's brother. I'll be glad of your ration books, leddies, if you please."

"I'll get them," said Caroline quickly, seeing her aunt was likely to break a blood-vessel. "I know just where they are."

"In the meantime perhaps you will be kind enough to show me where tea is served," the old woman continued.

But Jock said imperturbably, "If the young leddy knows just where they are she won't be above a minute fetching them," and Lady Bate, breathing flame so realistically that Jock would hardly have been surprised to see the banisters begin to smolder, had to wait until Caroline reappeared, rather pink but smiling, to hand the books over.

Jock glanced at them professionally. "Ye've been with dishonest folk," he told Lady Bate severely. "They've taken all yeer points and there's a week yet to run."

He looked as though he expected some reply. Lady Bate said, "You hardly expect me to do anything about that, I suppose?"

"Of course, the points cut out wadna be legal tender," Jock admitted, "but they should give me the equivalent. A nice tin of 10-point steak now."

"I wouldn't dare ask them," acknowledged Caroline with devastating frankness, and her aunt, more furious than ever, added, "I really cannot be expected to be troubled with these details. . . ."

"Them as caters for you has to be troubled," Jock pointed out, thrusting the book into the pocket of his coat and at last condescending to lead the way. In silence the three descended into the hall, where Jock showed them to a room looking across the Downs, where two ladies were having tea. The first was a large woman in the early fifties with a singularly unlined face and an expression like a page of blank paper—or a mirror, thought the more perceptive Caroline. She reflects what she sees. What does that mean? That there's nothing there? Or is she so clever she never tells you anything? She had a large blue-gray shawl over her shoulders and drawn over her head.

"Going thin on top?" wondered the uncharitable Lady Bate.

The creature looked out of its hood as the newcomers entered and smiled in what seemed to the old tyrant an unnecessarily familiar manner. After all, they were all paying their way, she reminded herself, and (having seen at a glance that this lady wore no wedding-ring, and probably was possessed of no distinction, mental or social) it was only reasonable that she should now give place to her superior. She was at this instant pouring tea from a trolley-table and dispensing the sandwiches as though she alone had paid for them.

The other occupant of the room was small, rotund and, as the astute Lady Bate perceived immediately, incurably vulgar. She sighed to think that to this level must she descend in the winter of her days.

Jock having closed the door and retired without a word, Lady Bate and her companion were left standing in the middle of the floor. The tea-pouring female said pleasantly, "Tea?" as though she were the hostess. Lady Bate looked round as if she expected a chair to glide up and put itself in position for her. Caroline picked out the most comfortable of those not occupied and brought it to her aunt's side. Lady Bate sat down.

"I am Lady Bate," she said. "This is my niece, Caroline."

The pseudo-hostess said nothing, but the cheerful little nonentity in the opposite chair announced, "That's Miss Twiss, our oldest inhabitant." She laughed to show that this was a joke. "That's why she wields the teapot. Otherwise I'm afraid I should be inclined to claim my rights. Married ladies first, my mother always taught me, and a mistress at the school I went to said the unmarried would be first in the Kingdom of Heaven. Well, I told her, it's nice to have something to look forward to if you've nothing to look back on. It's all right about Miss Twiss. She's as deaf as a post, hard of hearing she calls it. You can say anything you like."

26

"Anyone would be hard of hearing wearing that plate-armor," returned Lady Bate coldly. "Caroline, I think I see a footstool there. . . ."

"Old dragon," thought Mrs. Hunter. "Thinks she's bought the girl body and soul, I suppose."

"Is that comfortable, Aunt Bate?" asked Caroline.

"I should tell you if it were not. Don't fuss, my dear. You'll never get a husband if you fuss."

"Mr. Hunter—my late"—explained the garrulous little lady, "used to say any girl could get a husband if she wanted to. He traveled in biscuits. That gives me an advantage, of course." She held out a plate of sandwiches. "These are quite good. I must say they do do you quite well here. When I think of some of the places I've been in—but there, I dare say you know for yourself. What I say is there's a great deal of bare-faced robbery going on within the limits of the law. All very well for Cabinet Ministers, no doubt. They've no idea what we put up with. I always say people like us are just the P.B.I."—she smiled roguishly at Caroline—"of the population. Put up with everything and get nothing. Where were you last?"

Lady Bate looked as if she couldn't believe her ears. Miss Twiss leaned forward holding out a second cup of tea.

"It's rather strong," she said in a deep voice, "but you won't mind. The young never do."

Caroline, who was trained to watch for trouble and dodge it, took the cup and said quickly to Mrs. Hunter, "Do tell me what you meant when you said it was an advantage having a husband who traveled in biscuits."

"Really, Caroline!" Lady Bate sounded outraged. "We are not concerned with this lady's personal affairs."

"I just wanted to know," explained Caroline.

"I'm sure the young lady hasn't done any harm," expostulated Mrs. Hunter. "It's like this, dear. Take one of those sandwiches before your Grannie's had the lot," she added. (It seems a moot point whether Lady Bate or the girl would choke first.) "My hubby was connected with the biscuit trade all his life, and he was one of those live-and-let-live men. He used to say Government controls are all right in a war, but it's important to know when to make exceptions. Everyone," she added sweepingly, "liked Alfred—even his wife." She laughed again.

Lady Bate said, "I've often wondered how the Black Market operated," and this time it looked as though it would be Mrs. Hunter who would choke; but at the eleventh hour she changed her mind and said, "You know what they say about a friend at court, and when your friend's your husband too . . ."

Lady Bate, having given her cup of tea a glance that would have chilled it if it hadn't been cold already, was lifting it to her lips when a sudden exclamation caused her hand to jerk and a little of the tea to spill on her dress.

"Oh dear, that's unlucky," chattered the vivacious Mrs. Hunter. "Still, I don't suppose there was much milk in it, they're careful with the milk here, and if your granddaughter will just scrub it off for you . . ."

"I may be 76 but I am not an imbecile," announced Lady Bate.

Mrs. Hunter laughed heartily. "I'll say you're not, though as a matter of fact Alfred always said that people who really are a bit—you know—are always the first to say they're all right."

Miss Twiss, quite regardless of the trouble she had caused, was leaning forward, her face transfigured and at the same time twisted by an odd emotion.

"That," she said in her deep masculine voice, "is a very beautiful ring."

It was certainly strange, unusual, striking—a great slab of cornelian set in a marquisette frame. The combination was unexpected, and there was a fire about the stone itself, like a miniature river of gold running through it.

"Stones have a vitality of their own," announced Miss Twiss, and Mrs. Hunter sighed good-naturedly and said, "Oh dear, now she's off again. Jewels are her passion. Stands outside shops staring through the windows like someone bewitched."

"My mother married a man in the jewelry business when I was a little girl," explained Miss Twiss, with the air of having heard nothing Mrs. Hunter had said, as indeed might have been the case. "That probably accounts for my interest. Have you a great many jewels?" she added, smiling.

Not many people could boast that they had flummoxed Lady Bate, but in that instant Miss Twiss added herself to their number.

"I—really——"

"If so, you are most fortunate," Miss Twiss continued. "I have always thought that owning precious stones must be like owning a rainbow, give one quite a supernatural sense."

"I really don't consider, remembering what we pay, that we should be expected to put up with lunatics," reflected Lady Bate, and made an inward resolution to keep her eyes on her jewel-case.

Having tasted the tea, she set down her cup with a bang that would have broken more delicate china.

"Good china?" Jock had ejaculated, when supplies were being laid in for the visitors. "If they get what I'm buying it'll be as good as they're used to." Which was an error of judgment of the first water. As Mrs. Hunter used to say, "In Alfred's time my table was as good as a lord's, and I don't only mean the food."

"This tea is undrinkable," next announced the old tyrant.

"You were late, you see," Mrs. Hunter explained. "Jock's a great autocrat. Nothing a minute late and nothing kept for anyone."

"I shall certainly speak to Mrs. Anstruther," said Lady Bate.

Mrs. Hunter picked up the new scent with delight. "Do tell me if you manage it," she begged. "I mean, we've all wanted just to have a word with her ever since we came, but it seems she never sees anyone. I think myself she's a screw loose, the way those two old men look after her. It's a funny house altogether," she added casually.

Lady Bate wore her "This is insufferable to one of my breeding" air, but Caroline once more spoilt the effect by asking, "What do you mean by funny?"

"We—ell, the way she's never allowed out alone, and they don't have letters—I asked the postman—and no one's ever allowed to talk to her or have meals with her. Why, they go out to lunch every day."

"Now we know what to expect," returned Lady Bate dryly.

"No, thank you, no more tea. This is quite cold. Surely the management can supply a pot of tea for each party."

"Well, my dear," Mrs. Hunter settled comfortably back against the cushions (it looked as though life was going to be more interesting than it had been for a long time), "if you can persuade Jock to do anything he doesn't choose you'll have broken his record. His will's law here. And that's another funny thing." She leaned forward again. An enviable woman, thought Lady Bate disdainfully, entertained and enthralled by such poor devices. "Why is he the boss here? Because he is. What he says goes, even with the Colonel. If you ask me, there's a mystery."

Lady Bate decided that the entire household must be intolerably incompetent if they let that gawky piece of Scotch insolence rule the roost. As for mystery, she thought it vulgar. She rose, having had an unfreshing and unpleasant tea.

"Come, Caroline, it is time we finished unpacking. I shall make a point of seeing Mrs. Anstruther myself and informing her that four people cannot be expected to share one pot. After all, they have two ration books for us." She swept out.

Mrs. Hunter grinned vulgarly at Miss Twiss. "Bit of a tartar," she remarked. "I'm sorry for that girl. Still, if she's got any spirit about her, and I think she has, she'll know how to get a bit of fun on the side. My mother was just the same. Do your duty and teach in the Sunday-school and you'll get all the pleasure God means you to have. she'd tell me. But either she was wrong, or I bested Providence."

Miss Twiss smiled. "A lovely afternoon," she said, and "I wonder if you're really as batty as you seem," reflected Mrs. Hunter. "My word, Alfred would have thought this place a queer tin of biscuits. Easy to see why Lady Vere de Vere's here. Been chucked out of every other hotel in the place." She dropped the knitting she had picked up a moment earlier, and putting up her three round chins she observed, "I shall make a point of having a word with Mrs. Anstruther myself. H'm." She let her chins drop to their normal level. "I'd like to be behind the curtain."

She picked up the knitting once more and went on with her work. She dropped a stitch or two, but she was doing it for some anonymous heathen who wouldn't notice anyway. It didn't matter to her that everybody on the premises except herself was either already qualified or in a rapid process of qualifying for an asylum, according to her view. She hated life to be humdrum. It hadn't been humdrum when she lived with Alfred. He'd been one of those men who create fun out of the air. That was a pretty girl; she hoped she wasn't one of these downtrodden ninnies who let the old get away with anything. She looked across at Miss Twiss and found her watching her.

"Sly—that's your middle name," she said to herself, and aloud she asked, "What do you think of the new arrivals?" She shouted the words so that even a deaf woman would hear them.

"A pretty girl," said Miss Twiss equably. "I had fair hair when I was a girl."

"So had I," agreed Mrs. Hunter, who was a bright cheerful red. "Sort of ash-color, but I wasn't going to have anyone dictating to me about the color of my hair." She put down the unfortunate knitting again (she never knew what she was making. "Wait till it's done and then we'll see," she'd say.) "Tell me, Miss Twiss, if you don't mind me asking, have they raised your rent?"

Miss Twiss looked for a minute as if she wasn't going to have heard, but Mrs. Hunter's bright eyes and nodding head were oddly imperative.

"I have an arrangement," she answered vaguely, and Mrs. Hunter sat back so suddenly that one of the knitting needles snapped in two. "I'll say you have," she commented in a low voice, much too low for a deaf woman to hear. "So that's their little game. Think they can clear me out by putting up the rent. Well, they don't know Winnie Hunter." She fell to wondering why they should want her to go. She paid on the nail, she made her own bed, she didn't complain. She always had a pleasant word for Jock, complimented the Colonel on his garden whenever she saw him, called out cheerily, "Any more local murders?" to Joseph as opportunity offered, never had words with any of the other guests, even let an old maid like Miss Twiss take charge of the teapot—if they wanted her out of the way you could depend upon it there was something wrong. As for the

new-comers, how did they fit in? Paying through the nose perhaps, or Mrs. A. with her haughty ways might cotton to a title.
If Alfred had lived ten years longer he might have had a handle
to his name, too. Sir Alfred Hunter. Alfred used to shake his
head. Too common, he said. Have to wait till they give me a
barony. Lord Hunter of Potters Bar, that's who we'll be. She
sighed a little. She missed Alfie more than anyone would ever
guess. Still, life went on being exciting, you couldn't deny that.
This Miss Twiss now—had she got a hold over them the same
as Jock had? What awful secret was there in their past? Goodness knew the two old men were ancient enough to have betrayed
their country in the Indian Mutiny or something precious like it.
And how was it that Colonel Anstruther's daughter should be
Mrs. Anstruther, unless she married a cousin? But there was
some rumor in the village about her changing back to her maiden
name. "Divorce—juicy, I dare say," thought happy, vulgar Mrs.
Hunter. "That's what Jock knows, I shouldn't wonder, though
it must be pretty bad if he can dominate 'em all. P'raps it was
worse than that, though. P'raps she murdered Whatsisname.
P'raps she'll murder all of us in our beds one of these days."
The idea might have alarmed a less robust woman, but to Mrs.
Hunter it gave an enticement about going to bed she hadn't
known since she became a widow.

Now, turning back to Miss Twiss, she said, "Well, you're
lucky. They've put me up and they know I'll pay, because it's so
difficult to find anything. But if I didn't they'd have me out in a
week. I know them. But what I don't know," she added mysteriously, "and what I mean to find out, is why."

She rolled up her knitting and went upstairs. By leaving her
door open and walking once or twice down the passage to the
bathroom she might be able to overhear a bit of what the old
tartar was saying to the girl. After she had gone Jock came in
and, piling the cups on the trolley, prepared to wheel it away.
Miss Twiss looked up from her book.

"A beautiful afternoon," she said.

"Depends where you're seeing it from," returned Jock. He
turned and gave her a sharp glance.

Miss Twiss smiled.

CHAPTER FOUR

IN SPITE of her expectation of getting her own way immediately it was a week before Lady Bate actually came to face with Rose Anstruther. During that week she was like the beasts in the Revelations, she had eyes before and behind, spying out the land for possible weak lines of approach, making up her mind as to the best course to adopt with her fellow-boarders. She had hoped that when she both saw and heard her title Miss Twiss, that most contemptible of all things, an elderly spinster, would see the fitness of handing over the guardianship of the teapot, but though Miss Twiss was amiability itself it did not seem to occur to her that any change in the regular routine was called for. As for Mrs. Hunter, she was just a sunny little vulgarian upon whom no social graces would have any effect. She still talked in the most open and shameless way about her departed husband, and she would say, with Miss Twiss not a yard away from her, "Poor thing! I do feel sorry for spinsters, don't you? I mean, they may have been saved a lot of trouble, but you do feel they only get the small change of human relationships, don't you? Even the really successful ones, and I don't see how you could call Miss Twiss successful. Not that she talks about herself much, partly being deaf, I suppose, though sometimes I wonder if she's as deaf as she makes out. D'you know what I've thought? That she's a sort of spy of the family, watching all of us and reporting."

"What a nonsensical notion," said Lady Bate. "There can be no conceivable reason..."

"Ah, but can't there? That's just what we don't know. What's

33

the mystery, Lady Bate? What's the mystery? I've been trying to find out ever since I got here, and that's more than eight months ago, and except that it's to do with Mrs. Anstruther—that I'm quite sure of—I'm no further on than I was when I arrived."

Contrary to all their expectations it was Lady Bate who discovered its nature and gravity.

Living at such a distance from the nearest shop, she often sent Caroline out to execute various small commissions while she herself sat in the big guests' parlor, doing a little perfunctory sewing or glancing through some trashy library book—the author was not living who could satisfy her, and Caroline once remarked it was a good thing that the people who wrote the Bible were dead and thereby rescued from her aunt's universal contempt—and always agog, eyes and ears wide open for any hint she could gather. Mrs. Hunter was a lively little body. Soon after breakfast she took herself off to have a look at the shops and the sea and go to Boots to change her book—she changed one practically every day—and to Moons for a morning cup of coffee and the most sickly cake she could find—elevenses she called that, and "I have previously understood that only servants use that expression," said Lady Bate to her niece.

"Oh no, Aunt Bate, everyone does now," returned Caroline blithely. "We're living in a democratic age."

"It may suit you and your contemporaries," was her aunt's frigid reply, "but those of us who remember a better way of living deplore the free-and-easiness, the lack of any sense of responsibility, the notion that there's no need to preserve any self-respect because you can get it on a coupon from the State like everything else. . . ."

Caroline, whose spirits had mysteriously improved since her arrival at The Downs, said, "Oh well, if you can't get more on that coupon than you can on most of the others it won't go far," put on a blue pixie hood and a mackintosh of the same shade and went gaily out. From her comfortable chair in the parlor—it was Lady Bate's conviction that the woman never left it except for meals and bed—Miss Twiss watched her go.

"Such a pretty girl," she babbled to Lady Bate, "so nice for

34

us to have her here. Like having spring in the house all the year round."

Lady Bate said emphatically, "I have brought Caroline up since she was out of swaddling clothes or very nearly."

Miss Twiss appeared not to have heard. That was one advantage of being deaf, you never had to hear anything you didn't want to, or answer inconvenient questions.

"It's rather dull for her, I'm afraid. I do think the war was a godsend to young people, bringing them together, giving them experiences they would never have had otherwise."

"And other things that will last into the peace that one hopes they wouldn't have had otherwise," rejoined Lady Bate, grimly. It was fortunate for Caroline that she'd been preserved from life in the services and what her housemaid would have called goings-on. She'd never trusted Caroline's mother—one of those gay, irresponsible young women. If she hadn't been irresponsible she would never have caught a chill and died when her daughter was five years old. She'd have kept herself in good health for the child's sake. Lucky for her that she, Lady Bate, had been prepared to step into the breach. Then Mrs. Hunter came bustling into the parlor, stopped a moment when she saw that the old termagant had got her special chair, laughed good-naturedly and said, "Beaten at the post," and pulled up another chair quite close to the old lady. Lady Bate almost groaned. A whole morning of Mrs. Hunter was more than she had bargained for. She talked incessantly about food, telling you, as if you were interested, about Alfred's tastes. Don't save and skimp, had been Alfred's motto. Have a good time while you can. Otherwise you'll find someone else enjoying your savings.

"Quite a change in the weather," said Miss Twiss with her usual bland smile to the new arrival. "I shall soon be able to discard my shawl."

"The farmers need rain, I understand," remarked Lady Bate, hoping that would be the end of it. But she had reckoned without Mrs. Hunter.

"I dare say they do, but I can't help feeling Providence might remember there are some of us who aren't farmers. I'd planned to try that new café this morning—the Devonshire Tea House, they call it, though why Devonshire in Sussex, I can't imagine. But these places usually begin very well just to get fresh custom, you know, though Alfred always said the public can be counted on to try something new and that showed that private enterprise was really part of our national make-up. Alfred was great on politics, he taught me all I know."

"That must have been an easy spare-time job," muttered Lady Bate inaudibly.

"Your girl gone out?" Mrs. Hunter rattled on.

"My niece is doing my personal shopping," replied Lady Bate, icily.

"Must be a bit dull for her." (The impertinence of the creatures, thought the old lady. Two of them within half an hour.) "I mean, this may be cosy enough for three old fogies like us, but a girl like that wants a bit of fun. You tell her," she leaned towards Lady Bate in an odiously familiar way, "not to make the mistake too many girls make, think that when they're ready a husband will fall into their laps as surely as the income tax demand coming through the letter-box. Husbands aren't like that, specially nowadays, and it's my belief they never were. Look at her," she nodded towards the unconscious Miss Twiss, "must have been a pretty girl once, and a spinster all her days. No, no, you tell Caroline, Lady Bate, that husbands are like jobs and houses and everything worth having. You have to put your name on a list and call in at the office every few days to make sure you're not being overlooked."

Lady Bate stared as if she couldn't believe her ears; she turned to look at Miss Twiss, but the spinster was smiling at her work. How much had she heard, thought the old termagant, how much truth was there in Mrs. Hunter's suspicion that she wasn't as deaf as she made out to be?

"My niece, I am glad to say, will have no cause to feel anxiety about her future," she said in her most forbidding voice.

Mrs. Hunter laughed. "Get along with you," she said. "Every woman's got cause for anxiety till she's found her Mr. Right. Still, a girl like that shouldn't find it too difficult. I dare say she has her little secrets like all the rest of us—including Mrs. Anstruther," she added.

"How vulgar!" reflected Lady Bate.

Whether by instinct or because some of this conversation did actually penetrate her thickened ear-drums, Miss Twiss changed the subject.

"How extraordinary!" she exclaimed. "You would expect them to catch their death on a morning like this, but they belong to the old school that go bathing in the Serpentine in all weathers, and perhaps living in the East makes people hardy, though that isn't what we're told."

Lady Bate said nothing, but Mrs. Hunter, poor little snipe, rose at once to the new bait.

"Why, Miss Twiss, what is it?" she yelled.

"The Colonel and his brother are going over the moors in this rain. It seems very rash to me."

"Perhaps it's someone else. Have you ever noticed how much alike men's back views are?" Without waiting for an answer she popped up, lively as a robin, and ran across to the window. It was quite true. The two tall thin old figures could be seen marching away shoulder to shoulder up to the peak of the downs. Both wore raincoats and tweed caps. Although the Colonel was 80 and his brother not much less, they seemed entirely undeterred by the inclemency of the weather.

"You'd think they'd have gone out with Jock in the car, wouldn't you, on a day like this? He went off half an hour ago. But it's my belief everyone in this house is a bit daft." She looked up chuckling. "Present company always excepted, of course."

Lady Bate stood up, as though she could endure no more, and marched out of the room.

"Now, what's come over her?" marveled Mrs. Hunter. "She can't be setting her cap at either of them, not at her age. My goodness!" Her podgy little figure doubled up in honest mirth. "It would be worth paying the extra rent to watch her. What do you say, Miss Twiss?"

But Miss Twiss as usual made no comment. She continued to smile at her work as though she hadn't heard. After a minute she said, "I'm sure it's ungrateful of us to grudge the farmers their rain, seeing what they've done for us all through the war."

37

When she left the parlor Lady Bate went upstairs and into her room as though to fetch a handkerchief. This room had the same view as the parlor and she was able to verify Mrs. Hunter's statement that the two old gentlemen had set out for some reason best known to themselves for a stiff walk on this wet spring morning. She waited a moment, then came out of her room, stood still as if expecting someone or something to be hiding behind the wall-paper, and when there was not a sound from anywhere, walked deliberately past the head of the guests' staircase and down the second staircase, the one reserved for the household. No one seemed astir; but that was hardly surprising, since the three men were out and Mrs. Mack seldom emerged from her kitchen. As for the girl, she seemed to spend most of her time brewing tea and then drinking it, and in any case was negligible. Lady Bate went through the hall and, making the merest feint of rapping on the door, entered the room she had discovered belonged to Mrs. Anstruther. Rose had been arranging flowers at a table facing the door; the knock had been so slight she was not even sure she had really heard it, and when she saw the door open and Lady Bate's tall, emaciated figure on the threshold, an expression of extreme displeasure crossed her face. This was significant because she so seldom registered any change of mood; but what happened a moment later was more significant still. The look of anger passed and one of incredulity changing to alarm crossed those tranquil features. After all, it wasn't really surprising; Lady Bate was unforgettable.

Nor, it appeared, did *her* memory fail her. Closing the door, she moved with great composure towards an armchair. Seating herself she said, "But how delightful this is! And how exceedingly interesting. Of course, if I had realized who you were . . ."

Rose found her voice. "I'm afraid I don't understand this intrusion," she said, and her manner was perfectly under control. "It is arranged that this part of the house is entirely private."

"I don't blame you at all," agreed Lady Bate, almost cordially. "One can't be too careful, though it is stretching coincidence rather a long way to imagine that after so many years another visitor from that hotel at Monte Carlo would come here as a guest. Still, there's a saying about it being a small world, and

38

personally I have always believed that life works to a pattern."

Rose, who remained standing by the table, asked in her even voice, "Will you please tell me why you are here and what there is I can do for you? My servant, Jock, has instructions . . ."

"Ah yes," interrupted Lady Bate smoothly, "that would explain so much authority being delegated to a servant. Naturally, your father and uncle are too old to be expected to play any active part in the running of a boarding-house, but I must confess that I was surprised to find no hostess in charge. Now, of course, I understand."

"I must repeat," said Rose more sharply, "that is more than I do."

Lady Bate spread her long arms with their thin blue-veined hands like elegant spiders along the supports of the chair.

"Since you came back to England," she inquired softly, "have you told anyone exactly what did happen on the night that Gerald Fleming died?"

*C*HAPTER *F*IVE

CAROLINE BATE, unaware of the extreme importance of the day in the lives of her small circle, swung happily through the rain towards the town. Had she seen the old gentlemen setting forth she would not have experienced one half of the surprise of the rest of the household at The Downs, for this was one of those days of early spring when it was a joy to be out of doors. Even the rain had a caressing effect. On such a morning Lady Bate would not expect to leave the house. It was a little after ten; lunch was at half-past twelve. She had two clear hours in which to enjoy herself and few commissions to execute. These accomplished, she turned towards the sea-front, but a case of hand-printed advertisements caught her eye and she paused to read. They seemed to give her a glimpse into the lives of a number of of strangers who wanted home helps, refined nannies to walk out their children, or who wished to dispose of fascinating white elephants in the shape of bath-chairs, push-carts, outworn vacuum cleaners, outgrown clothes.... How could anyone bear to part with clothes at the present time, she wondered? Or were these the wardrobes of the recently deceased, whose relatives could make no use of them themselves? From Articles for Sale she passed to Help Required, and so to the separate board marked Personal. She was reading an announcement of an elderly man anxious to obtain a lucrative position of trust in a widow's establishment when she was aware of someone standing near by and watching her intently. He was a tall, fair young man in a shabby raincoat, hatless but apparently quite unconcerned, and when he realized that she had noticed him he smiled frankly.

"Looking for a job?" he asked in a way that would have made Lady Bate class him as suspicious.

Caroline laughed. "Oh no. I have one. That is, I don't need one."

His fair brows lifted; he had a long curly mouth and when he smiled it seemed to stretch half across his face.

"One of the idle rich? Take care, you're meat for the authorities. No one's going to enjoy the pleasures of idleness so long as they're in power."

"I'm not idle exactly. I—I live with my aunt—only she's generally taken for my grandmother."

"St. George and the Dragon, 1946 version. Women are getting all the men's jobs these days, they tell me. How long before you slay her?"

She looked delightedly scandalized. "It's more likely to be the other way round."

"That's very difficult to believe. What use would you be to her dead? Or are you that *rara avis,* an heiress disguised in a pixie hood?"

It was ridiculous; her aunt would have said it was shameless. She'd have said he was up to no good, and for all Caroline knew she would be right. All the same, she continued the conversation.

"Oh no. I hope you aren't disappointed."

"Cut to the heart. I've been looking for an heiress ever since I was demobbed."

"Haven't you got a job?" asked Caroline. Wonderful, she was thinking, to be out in the world on your own account, no Aunt Bate to give you orders and command your comings and goings, to live in a combined room and go out to work every day, stand in the bus queue, take your pay packet home on Friday and spend it how you like, have your own friends....

The young man was laughing again. "I live by my wits. What are you thinking? That I have designs on you? But you've just told me you're not an heiress. Or do you think, if I live by my wits I must make a pretty poor thing out of it?"

Caroline laughed too. "Of course not. I was thinking what fun to have a real job, never mind what it is."

He came a little nearer. "You're getting wet," he pointed out. "Isn't it time you had your elevenses?"

"Oh dear. That's what Mrs. Hunter calls them."

"I thought it was what everyone called them."

"Everyone except Aunt Bate."

"What's her name for mid-morning cup of tea?"

"She doesn't have one. She thinks its effete, except for invalids."

"Doesn't she realize it's a delightful excuse to stop work for fifteen minutes? But I suppose she doesn't work."

"I suppose not, though she's always busy."

"That's different." He took her arm and led her into Moons, the acknowledged coffee-house, where the air was delicious with the fragrance of roasting coffee. "You can see for yourself we aren't the first. There's a table there." He took off her wet raincoat and his own and hung them up together. "Now tell me your name."

"Caroline," said the girl in a dazed voice. She was wondering what on earth her aunt would say to see her now. There was no need to speculate what Mrs. Hunter would say. "Looks as if butter wouldn't melt in your mouth, but I dare say you have your bit of fun just the same." She'd said that no longer ago than yesterday.

"I'm Roger Carlton. Not my fault. My father's. I was called after my god-father in the hope he'd be flattered."

"And was he?"

"He didn't have time. He died the following year in a train accident, so I might just as well have been Charles or Edward for all the good it's done me."

A waitress brought them coffee and cakes, and the young man went on, "Tell me about your aunt."

"She— I've heard her described as a typical Edwardian, whatever that may be."

The young man nodded. "Overbearing. Keeps people in their proper places. Dignified." He suddenly drew his expressive face into so true a parody of the old lady that Caroline stared, her cup poised in mid-air.

"I believe you know her."

"She's not unique. And I was on the stage once, though only just on it, if you get me."

"I wonder if I could be an actress. If—if anything happened to Aunt Bate, that is."

"Much better be a children's nurse or a stenographer or anything that brings in a weekly wage—unless, of course, Aunt Bate's going to leave you comfortably provided for."

"I don't know. She's never said anything definite, but she does say she hopes she knows her duty."

"Hope," quoted the young man dryly, "is not yet taxed."

"I should like to have a job," continued the girl in wistful tones.

"What do you do with yourself all day now?"

Caroline tried to explain; it didn't seem to amount to much but when she had finished Roger said, "And then you say you don't earn your keep. My good girl, it's time you asked for a raise."

"What do you really do?" she went on, "or is it rude to ask?"

"I might tell you I have a most lucrative position with excellent prospects, but then you'd very properly ask me what I was doing picking up lovely girls at half-past ten in the morning. As a matter of fact, I stand for the ancient ashibboleth of private enterprise."

"I had noticed that," agreed Caroline. "Do you think I could have a second bun?"

"Does she starve as well as beat you? Have another plateful of buns."

"She's really very good to me," Caroline pointed out, but her voice was doubtful. "I'm really not a proper relation at all."

"Don't overdo the gratitude," begged the young man. "From all you've told me she isn't doing this without an underlying motive."

"She doesn't really like girls. She always says she hoped she'd have sons. She'd have been wonderful to a son," added Caroline. "No, I mean it. He'd never have done wrong in her eyes."

43

"You must introduce her to me," said Roger cordially. "She's just the sort of old lady I'm looking for." (And how was she to guess that she was meant to take that at its face value?) "How long are you staying?"

"Till Aunt Bate's exhausted all the hotels in the neighborhood. She's at the end of the local list now."

"And then?"

"We shall move to another neighborhood."

"No time to lose," reflected the young man. "We'll cook up a plan between us, Caroline, you and I."

"Then perhaps she'd stay here a bit longer. I believe she can be terribly nice when she likes."

"You mean, you know it by hearsay. Poor girl. I'm not surprised the Fairy Prince fell for Cinderella if she looked anything like you. Have some more coffee. Yes, do. What else is there to do on a wet morning?"

"It would be nice if we did stay," pursued the single minded Caroline. "Moving about as we do you never get to know anyone well."

"Another way of putting it would be that some people get to know her too well. I suppose she's the kind that's all set to be a centenarian?"

"She always boasts she's never known a day's illness."

"I bet she's known years of them by proxy. What are you going to do about it?"

"It's a good thing the police aren't here. It sounds as if you were urging me to push her off the edge of a cliff."

"Could you?" He helped himself to a third bun.

"I could take her out in the folding chair and take my hands off the handles as we were going downhill."

He smiled approvingly. "I can see you believe in private enterprise, too," he said. "Seriously, are you really going to stay with that living death?"

"Are you sure you don't write novels as well as act?" Caroline inquired.

He threw up his hand. "One man in his time plays many parts. I'm a fatalist. What will be will be, but there's no harm helping fate. Do you often come to town by yourself?"

"Only when it rains."

"Thank God for the farmers. They're a stubborn crowd and know what they want. Just now they want rain. Are you ready? Put on your pixie hat, my dove, and we'll walk along the front while I tell you the rest of my enthralling life-story."

They walked up and down the front and he talked. Living on one's wits seemed to embrace a number of occupations and to take you over a large part of the world. He was an excellent raconteur and he held her attention so closely that she was shocked to discover in no time at all that it was time to return to The Downs. In fact, she had to run part of the way, and arrived breathless and apprehensive. In the delight of this novel companionship she had forgotten how alarming Aunt Bate could be, and although she might tell herself, as Roger had already told her, that there was work for all and she needn't follow the example of the early Christian virgins sacrificed to dragons, things looked less rosy when she began to add up her list of accomplishments. For these were virtually nil.

She couldn't shorthand or type, couldn't sew or darn really well, had no diplomas for any subject under the sun, couldn't even drive a car.

"Why, I'm only fit to be an old lady's companion," she exclaimed in dismay as she pushed open the gate of The Downs. In the hall she twitched off the pixie hood, hung up the mackintosh, realized with a shock of surprise that the rain had stopped and the sun was struggling out and nerved herself to peer into the parlor. Here she found Miss Twiss preparing to go into lunch.

"Have you seen my aunt just lately?" shouted Caroline.

But Miss Twiss smiled at her anxious face. "The sun's out," she said. "There should be a rainbow soon. Like life, isn't it?"

She rolled up her sewing and put it into a lavishly embroidered bag. Caroline smiled back. Now what does that mean? she thought, hurrying up the stairs. Is it an omen that Aunt Bate will be in a good mood?

Apparently it was. The old lady had just patted her fine gray hair into perfection and was turning from the glass as the girl entered the room.

45

"Have you had a nice walk, my dear?" she inquired. "When I was a girl (she pronounced it gairl) we used to be told that rain improved the complexion. I can remember getting up early in the morning to collect rain water to wash my face. Ah, that surprises you, does it? The trouble with you young people is that you forget we were twenty-one once. But when you're my age you won't forget it."

Caroline, startled out of her usual carefulness by the old lady's unusual affability, asked suddenly, "Would you go back and be twenty-one again, if you could?"

Aunt Bate smiled. "All the years have their harvest. Sometimes of course one waits a very long time and one begins to think that that particular crop is going to prove barren, and then when one least expects it the harvest begins to roll in. I had such a delightful surprise this morning," she continued in the same animated voice. "I found that I had met Mrs. Anstruther before, though she wasn't calling herself Mrs. Anstruther then. She took her maiden name again, to please her father, she says, after her husband's death."

"Where did you meet her, Aunt Bate? I've never seen her close to, but I have had glimpses and there's something secret and romantic about her."

"Secret. And romantic." The old lady seemed to turn the words over like sweets on her tongue. "Perhaps. It was a long time ago that we met, but we knew one another at once. It was in 1935 when I was staying at Monte Carlo with Sir Charles (she always referred to her late husband in this formal way). Mrs. Anstruther and her husband were there, too. Mr. and Mrs.—no, Captain and Mrs. Gerald Fleming. Quite a striking couple, they were. It was a queer coincidence that we should both have been widowed within six months of one another. I'm sure, watching Sir Charles on that holiday, no one would have believed he had a weak heart. I remember how he insisted on coming back during the first week of September because of some absurd board meeting in Manchester. I didn't stay on without him, of course. Wives didn't, in my world. And it was just as well I did come, because the following year your mother so inconsiderately died of pneumonia—well, Sir Charles had always wanted a daughter, used to talk of adopting one, so I felt it my duty . . ."

"But he was dead," murmured Caroline, bewildered.

"Do you think I would take advantage of that fact? He wanted to adopt a daughter. Was it my fault that no suitable daughter presented herself until after he died?"

She sounded so violent, gave so much evidence of thunder clouds rolling up to obscure the rainbow, that Caroline asked hurriedly, "Did Mrs. Anstruther have any children?"

"I never heard of any. She must have come back soon after we left and come straight here."

Caroline thought for a moment. Then she said, "She must have been very unhappy about losing her husband to live like a nun ever since."

"Yes, I think she was—desperate. I happened to mention him to her a short time ago and she made it quite clear that she couldn't even endure to hear his name. 'I regard that as a closed chapter in my life,' she said."

"Is she as beautiful near to as she looks if you only see her at a distance?" persisted Caroline unwisely.

"Beautiful?" The old autocratic brows drew together. "I should say she was always more striking than beautiful. Of course, she's aged a great deal in twenty years, but she's quite unmistakable. I remember Sir Charles saying it would be difficult to forget a woman who looked like that. It wasn't thought good taste to be so noticeable when I was a gairl."

Was Sir Charles secretly in love with her? reflected Caroline. But in that case Aunt Bate wouldn't want to stay here. "I suppose Mrs. Anstruther is glad to have someone she used to know instead of a perpetual round of strangers." But somehow Lady Bate seemed more triumphant than pleased.

At that instant the gong sounded for lunch and the two ladies descended the stairs. On the way down the old woman said carelessly, "I must say it will be very pleasant being able to sit with one's own equals for part of the day, instead of having to rub shoulders with that vulgar little nonentity, Mrs. Hunter."

"I rather like her," confessed Caroline.

"My dear, your generation was born without a palate. You

47

know nothing of quality. I am told that young men nowadays will order wine, *tout court*. In my day a young man who could speak of wine in that farouche fashion would never have been found at any but middle-class tables. And it's the same with people. You can't differentiate. I dare say to you there is little to choose between a gentlewoman like Rose Anstruther and a tedious little nobody like Mrs. Hunter, and by the time the next generation makes its appearance the difference will have ceased to exist. But for myself I must admit I am thankful to have been born in an age of discrimination."

The afternoon remained wet and Lady Bate announced that she had no intention of contracting pneumonia, so she established herself by the fire in the parlor with a large leather-covered album furnished with a handsome brass lock. "I call this My Autobiography," she announced. "It contains the story of my married life. Sir Charles was a very distinguished man. He was constantly mentioned in the press. I kept a cutting-book and I put in every reference to him, complimentary or no."

"Were there ever any that weren't—complimentary, I mean?" inquired Caroline.

Her aunt regarded her coldly. "You cannot be a *person* without having enemies," she observed. "When I hear anyone—generally a woman—foolish enough to say that all the world is her friend, I know she can't be worth an instant's consideration. All great men and women all down the ages have had their detractors and Sir Charles was no exception."

"I know," agreed Caroline. "The man who never makes a mistake never makes anything."

Lady Bate's brows beetled. There was no other word for it.

"It doesn't become a young girl like you to talk about mistakes made by prominent men. Errors of judgment may be made by anyone, and your uncle (she was deeply moved to refer to him in this familiar phrase) had a most generous nature. He was always prepared to find the best in everyone. Naturally, he was sometimes deceived. A more suspicious man might have been infallible, but in that case he might have done injustice—or something less than justice—to perfectly innocent people."

48

"I'm sure he was wonderful," agreed Caroline. "I always wish I'd met him."

Lady Bate said nothing to that. She continued to turn the pages with an absorbed air, and Caroline slipped away; she thought it a good opportunity to wash her aunt's silver-backed brushes and comb, and dream about the morning's adventures. Mrs. Hunter, whom she met on the stairs, wearing a red pixie hood edged with fur, said it was enough to depress a cat sitting in the lounge all day and she was going to the pictures. When Caroline returned only her aunt and Miss Twiss, the inevitable blue shawl humped over her shoulders, occupied the sitting-room. Lady Bate was still deep in the closely-printed columns.

"If Sir Charles were alive now," she said, "we shouldn't have this ridiculous Government in power," a statement so sweeping that Caroline felt even the indomitable Mrs. Hunter could have found no adequate retort.

After this incident Lady Bate made a point of traipsing through into the private part of the house at least every second day. She also achieved other favors, such as a separate table for meals for Caroline and herself, and early morning tea in her room. Mrs. Hunter was loud in her disapproval of these developments.

"It ought to be the same for everyone," she proclaimed.

"But why?" inquired Lady Bate, to whom she had the temerity to voice this opinion. "We aren't all alike."

But if Lady Bate was pleased by the change it satisfied no one else. Neither of the Anstruthers liked her. Joseph expected women to be curved and affable, and said he'd as soon spend his time with a darning-needle. The Colonel protested violently at her invasions the instant she was out of the room.

"My dear Rose, I thought it was distinctly understood that our visitors should keep to their part of the house. Life is going to be intolerable if they can stray into our rooms. Can you not tell the Bate woman that we feel bound to abide by our regulations? Otherwise we shall have the whole menagerie of them in here. I know we are compelled to endure some discomforts in a peace, but even so we have a few rights left."

Joseph was more outspoken still. "She's a pusher. I saw that at once. A woman of breeding would see where she wasn't wanted and would stay away. If you're afraid of hurting the lady's feelings, let me have a word with her. I fancy I can make her appreciate the position."

To his amazement Rose said, "I hope you won't do anything of the kind, Uncle Joseph. I know it's tiresome, but I'm afraid we can't refuse to let her sit with us sometimes if she wants to. After all, we are old acquaintances. If she sees that we dislike her, then she'll push herself at every conceivable opportunity. If we are pleasant, the novelty will soon wear off. At least one hopes so."

"I wish you women would curb your philanthropic impulses," grumbled the Colonel. "After all, if she comes here we either have to stay away or put up with her too." He went out of the room.

But Joseph, more observant if more talkative than his brother, said slowly, "What have you got up your sleeve, Rose? Do you mean we've *got* to put up with this woman here?"

Rose lifted a haggard face. "Uncle Joseph, you're right. It's horrible for you, and I'm sorry, but—for the time being we've got to put up with it. Please, please don't ask me any questions. We must only hope it won't be for long."

"I know her type. Finds herself with an advantage in hand and sticks to it like glue. Couldn't spell scruple. Never forgave me for telling her the family liked its privacy. Where did you meet her?"

"Years ago—when I was abroad. I can't pretend not to recognize her, and if I do then I can't refuse to let her come in and sit with me from time to time."

"Throw her out," suggested Joseph, but she said quickly no, she couldn't do that.

"She wants to stay. Of course, if I were to go away—Uncle Joseph, that would be the solution. If I were to go . . ."

His thin friendly hand gripped her arm. "Ever heard of cowardice in the face of the enemy? I never knew you to be afraid, Rose."

He didn't understand the expression that crossed her face

50

then. How simple it is to deceive even those with whom you live, she was reflecting. She a stranger to fear, she who within a few weeks of leaving her home to marry Gerald Fleming had felt its ruthless grip on her life, who felt it still, petrifying and immobilizing her from every normal activity?

Joseph Anstruther was watching her keenly. He perceived that she would say nothing further. Afterwards he realized that that was the first time that the thought of murder entered his mind.

CHAPTER SIX

IF ANYONE had told Lady Bate she was resorting to blackmail she would have been horrified. She was so much accustomed to cutting her thoughts to fit the particular pattern of her life that even to herself she seemed to be merely taking advantage of an earlier acquaintance that, fruitless enough at first sight, was now proving profitable. She was by no means dense; she knew that both the Anstruther males disliked her, and she had no intention of making her position in the household intolerable. Her ambitions were petty in the extreme. She wished to assert her right to see Rose Anstruther about minor details instead of using Jock as liaison officer. She liked to be the only guest in the house able to use the family staircase and enter Rose Anstruther's sitting-room. In short, she wished to assert her superiority over her companions, to show that she was of a different clay. She felt secure enough; Rose would neither give her notice to quit nor resort to that other equally potent alternative, an increase of rent. That, however, was the height of her ambitions. To cast her net wider and make actual material profit out of what she knew never entered her head.

Caroline, who had been at first a little curious about the situation, was soon too much engrossed in her new interests to think about her aunt's position. She and Roger met daily and the girl thanked her stars for release from the customary routine of hearing that the rooms were unsuitable, the landlady insufferable, the food atrocious, the rest of the company common to a degree, all this closing with a command to herself to look for other, more suitable accommodation. Caroline by this time knew that even Buckingham Palace wouldn't provide all the amenities the old lady would consider her due, and if she thought about Rose Anstruther at all it was to be grateful that she and Aunt Bate should have had that chance encounter years ago. Later when Crook said, "Don't you use your headpiece in your home life?" she colored and said, "I'd done enough thinking about Aunt Bate to last a lifetime, and just then I had pleasanter things to think about." But, of course, she saw his point. If her attention hadn't been distracted she would have seen that something very queer indeed was in the wind. Day after day she contrived to meet Roger in the town, and with the whole-heartedness of youth abandoned herself heart and soul to this new adventure. Her life with her aunt had kept her clear of all emotional entanglements—it would take a brave man to run Lady Bate's gauntlet—and how she had yearned to suffer and adore with her contemporaries! It was small wonder that she was completely infatuated with the young man, his hit-or-miss attitude towards life, the aura of mystery that hung about him, his apparent ability to exist on air.

"Not air, my wits," he corrected her firmly when she expressed her surprise. "By the way, when are you going to introduce me to the Gorgon?"

Caroline was so much taken aback that for the moment she was reduced to speechlessness.

"To Aunt Bate?" she gasped at length. "You're not serious?"

"Of course. Didn't I tell you the first day we met she's the Fairy Godmother I've been looking for all my life."

"I've heard about angels in disguise, but fairy godmothers looking like Aunt Bate—oh no!"

"I believe you're ashamed of me," he turned her.

"Of course I'm not." But he saw the quick color come into her cheeks.

"Then why? Or are you afraid she'll send you to bed on bread and water for deceit?"

"It's not that either. The fact is—I don't want to share you with her," acknowledged Caroline with adorable simplicity. "She's my aunt and I suppose you could say she was my benefactress if you wanted to be old-fashioned, but as soon as she has any part in a situation she dominates it—I should get pushed out. . . ."

"I believe you're really in earnest. Oh, 'Caroline, what a heavenly fool you are. My only fear is that she'll hate me on sight, and that wouldn't suit my book at all. You won't let her disapproval influence you, will you, Caroline?"

"I think I'm what they call shameless," Caroline confessed. "If you suddenly disappeared to London, say, I should run away from Aunt Bate and follow you till I found you."

"I knew you were an angel the minute I set eyes on you. Now, I've got a plan, very simple for an intelligent girl to follow but one that will do away with the necessity for tiresome explanations. You take the old lady around in a pushchair, don't you?"

Caroline nodded grimly. "Every morning when it's fine."

"And I don't doubt that she sticks to the old rhyme about casting clouts, which means she'll be wearing that wolf-hide she seems so fond of."

Caroline stared. "How did you know about her fur?"

"You don't suppose I've left a stone unturned to find out as much about you as I can. I've seen you meekly pushing the old dame round. Now this is what you have to do. It's quite warm really, and your Aunt Bate is pretty sure to push the fur off her shoulders sooner or later."

"And then?" prompted Caroline.

"Then you're not half the girl I think you are if you can't manage to give it one more push and leave it lying forlornly on the pavement to be rescued by Knight-errant in modern dress."

"I see," said Caroline, but she sounded dubious.

"Don't look sour, Caroline," he begged. "You'll see, she'll be eating out of my hand in a week."

Caroline didn't believe it, but she couldn't withstand Roger. He, experienced youth, could have taught her a good deal about human nature she didn't even suspect. The very *naiveté* of the plot ensured its success. Aunt Bate was feeling triumphant, which was also a help. She had bested Jock, thanks to unwilling but unmistakable support from Rose Anstruther, and it was now agreed that she should have a particular armchair she fancied moved from Rose's private sitting-room to the parlor for the exacting old lady's personal use. Jock looked as black as a thunder cloud; the two Anstruther brothers by common consent now kept out of the way whenever Lady Bate was on the war-path. She noticed it with delight; on her first day at The Downs Joseph had humiliated her. Now she was making both old men feel ill-at-ease in their own home. Few things could have given her greater pleasure. As for Rose, she put up no fight at all. Lady Bate held all the aces and she wasn't in the least above stacking the cards. Rose had spoken of going away but there was nowhere where she could go. The Downs was her last home and refuge; she had left what it represented for a short period, only to return like a homing pigeon, and sooner than be driven from its gates she would endure all manner of petty persecution and encroachment. All one could hope for was that Providence or someone equally obliging would remove the source of all the sting and distress before it became intolerable.

Roger Carlton was a quick worker. Having explained his plan to Caroline, he persuaded her to put it into force the following day. Events were propitious, Lady Bate so full of her minor triumph that she never noticed they were being casually accompanied on the other side of the road by a most personable young man. Caroline was aware of little else, and her replies to her aunt's sharp questions lacked point and even sense.

"What on earth's come over you?" Lady Bate demanded. "Day-dreaming like a green girl."

"It's the spring," explained Caroline foolishly. "You feel anything might happen on a day like this."

"All that will happen if you go on mooning as you're doing at present is that you'll overturn my chair and have to answer some very unpleasant questions at the inquest. Very unpleasant indeed they'd be," she added in the tone of one enjoying herself. "Heiresses shouldn't be in the picture when their benefactresses die. It looks bad."

"Heiresses?" stammered Caroline.

"Well, I don't mind telling you you'll find yourself very nicely provided for when I'm gone. Not that I mean to go for a good many years yet and don't you think it, but if you do your duty by me you won't be the loser. Quite a prize for some man you'll be then, and if you aren't fool enough to be married for your money you can live a very comfortable life of independence, if you play your cards well."

Caroline envisaged it; the well-off spinster, getting an occasional proposal for the sake of what she had rather than what she was; and if Aunt Bate was right it would be another dozen years at least before her poor relation could hope for her independence.

"Would you cut me out of your will if I married and left you?" she asked, trying to sound light-hearted and casual.

"If you had a husband to support you you wouldn't need my money, would you? And I'm not such a philanthropist that I should want to see my money frittered away by a man who couldn't even keep a wife."

Caroline was so much obsessed by this vision that she quite forgot her plot with Roger who, however, proved his devotion to private enterprise by crossing the road behind the wheelchair, filching the wolf tippet and coming hurriedly into sight of its owner with the observation, "I believe this dropped off your chair just now. I'm sure you'd hate to lose it."

"There, Caroline, I told you how it would be, mooning away like that. My wolf stole. Immensely valuable. You wouldn't believe me if I told you what I had it insured for. And if it hadn't been for this young man—though how you could let it fall without even noticing it passes my comprehension."

Roger glossed that over with some compliment about the quality of the fur and the pair slipped easily into an animated conversation. Caroline's admiration of Roger's adroitness changed presently to resentment at what appeared to her her deliberate exclusion from the talk, but she could not easily intervene since she and Roger were supposed to be strangers.

"I knew it would be like this," she told herself. "My instinct not to let them meet was the right one." Yet, if Roger meant anything serious by his words, his expressions, his casual endearments, sooner or later the introduction must have taken place.

"But he hasn't said anything," she told herself desperately, and was cast down to reflect how little she really knew about him. When she tried to get some definite statement from him about his job he had only said he was rather keen on writing and would surprise her one of these days, which got her no further. At the end of a quarter of an hour Lady Bate was telling her young cavalier that he must come and have tea with her one day soon, to which Roger replied heartily, "Like Mr. Mell, I say there's no time like the present," and was invited for that afternoon. During this time his manner towards Caroline had been irreproachable from the old lady's point of view. He had acknowledged the introduction with a pleasantly casual air and after that had behaved as though Lady Bate were the only woman in the world. The old tyrant was in high good humor when they reached The Downs and said coolly, "I must let Jock know we have a visitor this afternoon. It would have been nice if we could have had a private sitting-room. I really think I shall have to speak to Mrs. Anstruther about it."

However, she did not press the point for the moment, but contented herself by ringing and informing Jock that there would be one extra for tea. If Jock looked disgruntled, no one else did. Mrs. Hunter was flagrantly delighted at the presence of a young man, and when he arrived looked meaningly from him to Caroline so often that the unhappy girl was a mass of blushes before the teapot was brought in. Miss Twiss, on the other hand, behaved as though Roger were invisible. She drank her tea quickly, pulled her shawl round her and walked out of the room. Mrs. Hunter, who hadn't been introduced, dropped her knitting on the floor and waited for Roger to retrieve it. As he handed it back she laughed gaily and asked him if he knew what she was making. Roger said promptly he didn't, and she laughed more loudly than ever and said, "Would you believe it, I don't even know myself. It all depends whether it looks more like bedsocks or a Balaclava helmet when it's finished."

"You remind me of my Aunt Susan," said the young man readily. "She came to see me once when I had a couple of dogs on the premises, a fox-terrier and a Scottie. When she'd looked at them for some time she said she liked the fox-terrier best because he was more like a fox-terrier than the other."

Mrs. Hunter laughed heartily. "I can see you've a sense of

humor," she said. "My husband was the same. Ever such a man for his joke. I believe in laughing. It may make you fat, but it does keep you young. I can't think how these women who live alone get on at all. Unnatural I call it. Now I enjoy being here, seeing the people come and go. It does me good to see a pretty girl and a nice young man having tea in the same room as me."

Lady Bate was furious, but helpless. Mrs. Hunter ran on like Tennyson's brook.

"Mystery House, I call this. Don't you agree, Lady Bate? Take our hostess now. There's a mystery about her all right. But it's all come out one of these days. That Miss Twiss too. Makes out she's deaf. I wonder. I've got an idea she's a spy, put in by the management. Or else she knows something too."

"This makes up my mind once and for all," announced Lady Bate emphatically that evening while Caroline was brushing her hair before bed. "I shall demand a private sitting-room. It's absurd that we can't have people to tea without that vulgar woman butting in. And I must say," she added, with her rare smile, "that's a very attractive young man. Lives on his wits he tells me. And if that's so he ought to make an excellent living. Alone in the world, apparently. He wouldn't say much about what he was doing during the war, but I imagine it was something quite outstanding. He doesn't seem to have very good prospects for the peace. It's what I've always said. A young man of parts needs someone behind him to get him started."

"I thought you believed in young men fending for themselves," murmured Caroline.

"What I have always said—take care, girl, my hair is actually attached to my head even if mischief-makers have sometimes hinted it wasn't—what I say is that outstanding young men should have some backing. The rank and file don't matter. They're as alike one another as lead soldiers anyway. But this young man makes one feel he oughtn't to be wasted."

Caroline knew she should be delighted at Lady Bate's enthusiastic reception of Roger Carlton, yet her heart felt chilled. She remembered what the young man had told her about living on his wits, how he had acknowledged that he had watched her wheeling the old lady out in the push-chair.

"And how," thought Caroline, "can I be sure that he didn't see her before he saw me? Suppose I'm just a catspaw? He said she was just the sort of old lady he'd been looking for? And that she would soon be eating out of his hand. We don't know anything about him, and he may just be making fools of us both. He hasn't said anything to me about love or marriage and perhaps he never means to." And as the days passed and Lady Bate showered more and more approval on the young man her fears grew.

There were, however, diversions to distract her attention from her own troubles, and the first was a hint of the nature of the hold Lady Bate so clearly had over their hostess. Coming in one afternoon a few days after Roger's introduction into the circle, she was arrested by the sound of voices on the floor below. She was almost at the head of the visitors' staircase and the voices sounded from the hall of the Anstruthers' half of the house. One was unmistakably that of Lady Bate, the other must, she supposed, be Mrs. Anstruther, whom to date she had not met. Instinctively she mounted the rest of the stairs, tiptoed along the passage and leaned over the well of the stairs. Seen from above, Lady Bate had a curiously squat appearance, her abundant gray hair fanning out above her large ears. Mrs. Anstruther by contrast looked delicate and aloof, but even from that position Caroline could see that she must once have possessed great beauty. Lady Bate was speaking. Caroline caught the word "husband" uttered in a menacing tone.

"So there is some mystery about the late Captain Fleming," she thought. "Was he a criminal, an embezzler, something shameful?"

And then Mrs. Anstruther spoke. Her voice was slow, almost contemplative, yet it had a vigor that was terrifying.

"You will never forgive that, will you?" she said. "I thought when I came here I could say farewell to my unhappy past."

"If they had known the truth," said Lady Bate, swaying slightly to and fro, so that voice and posture alike reminded one of a serpent, "you would have had a much harder time. Your husband's record..."

"I see you are determined to balance the scales," agreed Mrs. Anstruther.

But Lady Bate vigorously disagreed. "That's an absurd thing to say. You know that's out of the question. In any case, I'm not looking for trouble, and I believe you when you say you would like to forget the past. All I am suggesting is that you should be ready to extend to me the normal courtesies to be expected from one gentlewoman to another. Consider the position I am accustomed to occupy, I don't think I am making any very great demands."

"Only the indirect control of my household," agreed Mrs. Anstruther. "There's a poem by Arthur Hugh Clough . . ." and to Caroline's surprise and Lady Bate's obvious disgust she quoted it.

> " 'For while the tired waves, vainly breaking,
>   Seem here no painful inch to gain,
>   Far back, through creeks and inlets making,
>   Comes silent, flooding in, the main.' "

"But suppose I don't agree? What then?"

Lady Bate considered for a moment. Then she said, "Even the English read newspapers, Mrs. Anstruther, though I admit that a good many of them seem incapable of reading anything else. I feel sure you wouldn't want the mists of obscurity that surround your past and that of your husband to be dispersed."

"Were you looking for someone, miss?" inquired a steely voice at Caroline's elbow, and she straightened herself, scarlet with embarrassment, to meet Jock's inimical stare.

"I was watching Mrs. Anstruther," she stammered. "I've never met her, you know. It seems so queer. How beautiful she must have been."

Jock, who had his own conception of his place in the household and who allowed no one to budge him from it, said in a blunt voice, "It's no the kind of thing ye'd like to have happen in your ain house. Young leddies leaning over balconies. One of these days you'll maybe lean a bit too far and be picked up with a broken neck."

60

Thoroughly crushed, Caroline crawled into her room, but presently she forgot Jock's strictures and began to wonder at the extraordinary scrap of conversation she had overheard. Clearly Mrs. Anstruther was in some way in Lady Bate's power, as she had hitherto suspected. She had spoken of the general reaction should the truth be known, had mentioned newspapers, and something about a husband. And linked to all that was Lady Bate's grim smile on an earlier occasion when she had said that Sir Charles had admired Mrs. Anstruther, adding, "It wasn't thought good taste to be so noticeable when I was a gairl."

A few days after this incident there occurred another that threatened to set the whole house by the ears. Lady Bate missed a ring, not the cornelian one so much admired by Miss Twiss, but a diamond ring that had been given to the old lady by her husband many years before. Instantly all was pandemonium.

"I distinctly remember wearing it on Tuesday," she stormed at Caroline. "You should have put it away in my jewel-box that night but you're always so careless with other people's things. If it were your ring you wouldn't be so casual."

"I always put your rings away when you take them off," protested the unhappy Caroline.

Lady Bate flew into an instant rage. "Are you suggesting it is my fault?"

"I'm not suggesting anything, except that I always put your rings away when you take them off."

"If you counted my jewels each night you'd have noticed it was missing. Very well then, if you're telling the truth and it isn't just carelessness on your part, it must have been stolen. Though if you hadn't left it lying out no one could have got hold of it. I keep my jewel-case locked, as you know."

"Perhaps it's only fallen behind something," suggested Caroline weakly.

"I understand that this room is cleaned and put to rights every day. If it had fallen down it must have been found. No, it is perfectly clear to me that we have a thief on the premises."

"But in that case why only that ring? You have so many other valuable jewels..."

"I've been trying to make you understand that obviously you

61

failed in your duty and didn't return it to my jewel-case, and I suppose it was too much for that half-witted girl who brings up my morning tea. No more sense of right than a jackdaw. You've only got to look at her. She'd never have been taken in a decent house a generation ago. I shall speak to Mrs. Anstruther after breakfast."

"You can't accuse the girl," began Caroline, but her aunt interrupted fiercely, "I suppose, according to your milk-and-water code, I should be satisfied to lose the ring. Well, I'm not. Your uncle would turn in his grave at the thought I should let a valuable possession like that disappear without making every conceivable effort to get it back. You've no backbone, you young people. The easy road, that's what you're all looking for."

"Considering the worst war in the world has just been won by young people," began Caroline, as fiery for once as her aunt, but once more Lady Bate scored with, "I wasn't aware that you did anything very strenuous to bring about that victory. Now brush round the hem of my skirt (for Lady Bate wasn't one of these skittish widows who believe in showing a lot of leg, in which she was wise) and we'll go down to breakfast. I'd speak to Mrs. Anstruther before breakfast, if it weren't that I know those two insufferable women would have eaten our share as well as their own if we gave them the chance."

Mrs. Anstruther, acquainted with the loss, was horrified. She said that obviously the ring must have slipped into a crevice, her servants were completely trustworthy, and so on and so forth.

"Perhaps it's your guests' records that require investigation," snapped Lady Bate, looking like a grenadier's nightmare against Mrs. Anstruther's more feminine and even voluptuous curves.

"You really cannot be suggesting examining my guests' belongings."

"It's what the police would do," rapped back Lady Bate.

"Are you proposing to call in the police?"

"Not if I get my ring back. I'm prepared to wait twenty-four hours."

Eventually the harassed Mrs. Anstruther agreed to question Gladys, who was as antagonistic as possible, and said she'd never had a word against her yet, and there was a thing called defamation of character.

Mrs. Anstruther unexpectedly rose to the occasion. "There is no need for this very unpleasant scene, Gladys," she observed coldly. "I merely sent for you to ask you whether you had noticed the ring when you were cleaning the room."

"Well, I haven't," returned Gladys sulkily. "She never leaves so much as a postage-stamp about."

The tension during the remainder of the day was intense. Even Jock was affected by it. At lunch he looked as though he would like to pour the sauce down the old lady's neck instead of handing it in the usual manner. Only Miss Twiss seemed unperturbed, but, as Lady Bate said viciously, it would take another world war to move her.

The evening was most uncomfortable. Lady Bate looked like Edgar Allan Poe's famous raven—grim, ghastly, gaunt and ominous—Caroline was nervous, Mrs. Hunter openly entertained.

"I'm sure anyone can go through my belongings with a toothcomb," she proclaimed to anyone who cared to listen.

Miss Twiss was unperturbed as always. Presently she and Mrs. Hunter settled down to play Demon Patience, for which Miss Twiss had what she called a passion; they played for stakes so small that Lady Bate once observed scornfully they couldn't pay them for the energy involved. Mrs. Hunter played like lightning, Miss Twiss like the child in the nursery rhyme—one step forward and two steps back—but Mrs. Hunter invariably won. They made a point of settling their accounts every evening, and tonight, as Miss Twiss opened her bag, it slipped from her knee and the contents were spilled on the carpet.

"Dear me!" said Miss Twiss, as unflurried as ever. "How careless!"

"Gracious goodness!" exclaimed Mrs. Hunter, diving for the scattered treasure and giving the impression that she was an octopus. "Lady Bate, isn't this your ring? How on earth did it get there?"

She came up flushed, smiling, delighted at the new turn of events. Instantly Lady Bate was on her feet, Caroline followed her example, trembling and uncertain; even the indomitable Mrs. Hunter, realizing the implications of the situation, began to look a shade apprehensive. Only Miss Twiss remained unmoved.

"I knew there was some reason why I tied that knot in my handkerchief," she said. "Of course—your ring, Lady Bate. You left it in the bathroom."

Lady Bate recovered her voice. "I did nothing of the sort," she declaimed.

"I found it in the bathroom," insisted Miss Twiss. "And knowing it might be a temptation . . ."

"Who to?" snapped Lady Bate.

"My dear mother used to say it was quite wrong to leave valuable things lying about, because what was perhaps no temptation to oneself might be a great temptation to someone else."

"If you mean me," began Mrs. Hunter, turning rather pink . . .

"One has to consider servants," explained Miss Twiss. "In any case, it seemed wiser to take charge of it."

"And why," demanded Lady Bate, controlling herself with difficulty, but pale with the rage that consumed her, "did you say nothing—*nothing*—of this when you knew the whole house was being ransacked for my ring?"

"Was it?" enquired Miss Twiss, looking astounded. "Dear me, I had no notion. But if only I had been asked. It's my affliction, you see."

"Nothing will make me believe you didn't know my ring was missing," insisted Lady Bate, flatly. "It's my belief you took it deliberately, and if you hadn't happened to drop your bag just now it would never have been recovered."

Miss Twiss turned to Mrs. Hunter. "Does she think I took it on purpose? But that's absurd. Why on earth . . . ? Just because I admired it, you mean? Why, if I'd meant to keep it, would I have carried it about in my bag?" She looked sternly at her accuser. "You're very ungrateful," she said. "I've probably saved it for you. You might never have seen it again."

"Just what I was supposing," agreed Lady Bate unpleasantly.

Even Mrs. Hunter said to Caroline afterwards that a joke was a joke, but you could carry it too far.

"And say what you like, it was queer," she added shrewdly. "I don't see how even a deaf person could *not* have known what was going on."

$\mathcal{C}$HAPTER $\mathcal{S}$EVEN

IT WAS DURING the following week that Lady Bate announced her intention of going to London to see her lawyer. She didn't want Caroline to accompany her, as Roger Carlton had told her he would be going to town himself on the same day and could travel up with her.

"He tells me it's something to do with a job, as you young people call it nowadays," she continued. "I tell him not to be too precipitate, the age of fairy godmothers isn't past, and once he ties himself up he may find it difficult to get out again. Still, all you young people are alike, so headstrong, you won't listen to good advice."

Caroline's heart had given a great leap. "Roger isn't a child," she pointed out. "He's a man, he's been through the war, he must know if he wants this particular job or not."

"You're talking like a child yourself. You've always been looked after so, of course, you've no notion what it's like looking for work. You think you'd enjoy it..."

"I should," interrupted Caroline rashly.

"I wonder. Well, perhaps you'll have the opportunity sooner than you think. I'm sure I don't want to stand in your way. Roger now..."

"Aunt Bate, aren't you being a little prejudiced about him? I mean, we don't really know anything but what he's told us. I mean, I know of course you'll do whatever you have in mind, but oughtn't you to make some inquiries first?"

Lady Bate laughed disagreeably. "Piqued because he's more

attracted to an old woman than a young one? My dear, you'll never get a husband that way. Now, I've always wished I had a son. It was a great disappointment to me that I never had a child, but if I had I couldn't have cared for him more than I care for Roger. I feel he's like Barnabas, the son of consolation. And he has no one, no family. . . . It's like a pattern. You understand, Caroline?"

"Yes," said Caroline slowly "I understand. Only—does he feel like that, too?"

"I think he knows why I'm going to see Mr. Tritton today."

"You're going to alter your will."

"Yes. I'm an old woman now, though I mean to go on living a good many years if I can, and my needs are simple. Oh, don't think I shall forget you altogether, but of course you don't need money in the same way that Roger does. He's a man, he'll marry one of these days, have children. It's terrible to be very poor. I was very poor before I married Sir Charles. I'd like to save Roger that."

"How nice for Roger!" commented Caroline.

"There's no need to be flippant. In any case, I've never approved of young women having a great deal of money. It lays them open to the wiles of unscrupulous men. Besides, I think you're getting restless, and, as I've told you before, I don't wish to chain you. You've often told me you'd like to be independent, have work of your own. Well, here's your opportunity. I'm going to tell Mr. Tritton to make over a definite sum to you, on which you can have whatever training you prefer and that will give you liberty. After that, of course, you'll be able to look after yourself. Gairls didn't have all that freedom when I was young, and I was ready to take care of you, but you've made it quite clear what you want, and though, after the easy life you've led with me, you may find earning your own living more difficult than you anticipate, we all have to buy our experience."

"What it boils down to is—you're turning me out in Roger's interest."

Lady Bate flared up at once. "You're so melodramatic, Caroline. Your mother was the same. I suppose you get it from her. Naturally, I'm quite ready to give you a home so long as you

67

want it, but now you want something else and you've made it quite plain, and I'm arranging to give you that."

"But—who's going to look after you? You've always said you needed someone. . . ."

"No one's indispensable," snapped Lady Bate. "There are plenty of older women who would be glad to step into your shoes. You can't pretend I make any very great demands on your time or energies. It was different when I had my own home, but now we live in hotels and everything is done for us . . ."

"It's all right," said Caroline quickly. "I understand. I do really."

"Then that's all right. I shall be back this evening, I'm not sure what train. You'll be able to have a whole day off. Those gloves of mine want washing, but that's all. Don't go jumping to wild conclusions. I shall simply talk things over with Mr. Tritton, and get his advice."

"And will you take it?"

Lady Bate looked up sharply, suspecting insolence, but the girl's face was as simple as her speech.

"It depends what it is. I must say it will be a comfort to me to know things are settled. I hate to feel them hanging over me. We're very fortunate in being settled here, because I don't anticipate any further moves, and I shall see to it that there is accommodation available for you whenever you want to come and see me. I don't want to be a drag on you in your new life, but I'm not the sort to forget my responsibilities, and I took you for better or worse sixteen years ago, and sixteen years is a long time. Now, just put my shoes on their trees and open the window and we can go down to breakfast."

"Which train are you taking?" inquired Caroline, methodically obeying her instructions.

"The 11:02. Roger will call for me in a cab at 10:40 and he will have the tickets. If possible we shall travel back together tonight, but that depends a little on his engagements, of course. In any case, I shall be back in time for dinner, and I've invited him to join us. It's the least I can do after all the trouble he's taking for an old woman."

"Have you told Jock there'll be someone extra?" The question was purely mechanical.

Lady Bate threw up her head. "You forget, Caroline, I'm not accustomed to dealing with a servant. I shall have a word with Mrs. Anstruther before I go. They're very careful about rations here, and of course a young man with his way to make needs more hearty feeding than sedentary people like all of us. In fact," she patted her chignon and rose from the dressing-table, "I'm quite sure that a little more exercise would do Miss Twiss a great deal of good. I don't like these feminine skeletons, but she really is too plump to be healthy."

Caroline watched her sweep out of the room and deliberately go down by the private staircase. She stayed behind, ostensibly putting the room to rights, but actually because her heart was beating so furiously she could scarcely breathe, and she felt incapable of meeting Miss Twiss's cool uncurious eye and Mrs. Hunter's frankly inquisitive stare.

"She can put it whichever way she likes, but it comes to the same thing," she told herself. "She wants me to go. She never has before. I've been too useful to her. But now—I suppose I understand. She's infatuated with Roger, in a sort of maternal way, I suppose, and she wants to be first with him. She doesn't want anyone young on the premises. Her next companion will be middle-aged and probably flat-footed. It isn't that she thinks he cares two straws about me, but she isn't taking any chances."

She laughed and the sound shocked her. "Not that she need be nervous. I ought to have guessed when Roger warned me he lived on his wits what that meant. He can't afford to be sentimental about a girl without money. He's played his cards very well, though. He made me think ..." She pressed her hand to her forehead and found it burning. "Well, I'm not the first girl to be caught in that trap. I suppose everyone saw it but me. Perhaps they've been laughing. What does it matter? One day I shall laugh at it myself. When I'm married to someone decent and kind, who won't care whether I have a rich aunt or not, when I have children of my own I shall say to my husband, 'You know, when I was twenty-one I thought I was madly in love with a young man called Roger Carlton. Of course, it wasn't anything, it was just that I hadn't had the opportunity of seeing any young men. How raw and susceptible I must have been. I see now that I was likely to fall in love with anyone presentable who took any notice of me. Another girl, more sensible, with more experience, would never have taken it seriously at all. Look,' I shall say, 'I'm laughing now. But then I thought my heart was broken—I did really—I thought my heart was broken.' "

Suddenly abandoning all pretense, she sank on the bed, the tears streaming down her face.

"It's no good. I can't go down to breakfast. Aunt Bate can tell them what she likes—I've got a headache, sickening for 'flu, anything, but I can't go down and face them. I know it's true, I know one day I shall laugh, I know this happens to everyone at least once. That's how they learn wisdom. I shall know how lucky I was to find him out, because it'll mean I know the difference between the false and the true. I shall meet someone a million times better and kinder and more honest, and I shall be married and happy, and one day perhaps I shan't even remember his name, only—it's such a long way off, and in the meantime I've got to live through today and tomorrow and next week— and I don't know how to face it. I don't know how to face it."

When at last she came downstairs she was very pale and Miss Twiss thought, "A pretty girl like that shouldn't need all that powder. It makes her look positively ill, and she has such a pretty color of her own." But Mrs. Hunter told herself shrewdly, "Trouble somewhere. What is it? That young man, I suppose. The old shrew's been ticking her off or accusing her of running after him or something. No girl cries her eyes out for an old woman."

Soon after breakfast Roger arrived in a cab and collected the old lady. Caroline came stiffly down to the gate carrying an umbrella and Roger smiled and said, "Hallo, not ready?" and she returned coldly, "I'm not coming."

"Not? But ..."

"There is no need for me to drag Caroline around with me," announced Lady Bate tartly, "I am not quite senile yet, and there are some occasions when even an old woman prefers privacy. You have very kindly offered me your escort to London, and once I am there I can look after myself."

"And London too," agreed the young man. "All ready? 'Bye, Caroline. Be seeing you."

Caroline stood rigidly by the gate watching the cab out of sight, refusing to allow herself to take any comfort from the evidence of his surprise at discovering she was not to accompany them.

"That was for Aunt Bate's benefit," she told herself scornfully. She laughed, an odd hiccoughing sound that ended on a sob. "One thing—I will go and earn my own living and Aunt Bate can get one of these companions who put arsenic in your sandwiches, the kind the B.B.C. likes so much. In a year's time I probably wouldn't recognize Roger even if I met him. I wouldn't have noticed him anyway if a young man wasn't such a rarity to me."

Throwing up her head, she ran back to the house. As she had anticipated and feared, Mrs. Hunter was loitering in the hall.

"Gone off and left you behind?" she said in her sprightly voice. "Well, you could do with a rest, I should think. All the same, it's too bad when you get a whole holiday for her to take the boy-friend with her."

Caroline thought, "This is more than I can bear," and said aloud in the coolest voice she could muster, "Mr. Carlton's going back to London anyway very soon. He's been having a vacation, but he has a job waiting for him." She added lightly, "I'm thinking of getting one myself."

Mrs. Hunter's india-rubber face twisted. "I should have said you had one now. Anything you do after your auntie will be a rest-cure. What's she going to do without you, though? Not get married again?" She chuckled, like someone holding out an enormous notice—JOKE.

"Oh, I wouldn't put it past her," said Caroline recklessly. "As a matter of fact, she's going to get a professional companion, someone qualified—sewing and all that, you know."

"Well, dear, you take it from me whatever reason she's doing it for she's doing you a good turn. I tell you, it's made my heart ache to see a pretty girl like you tied to that old lady's apron-strings. You'll have much more fun when you're on your own, with friends of your own age, no one to ask where you've been if you come back late at night. You'll enjoy it. It's not natural, the life you live. Going to London?"

"I expect so. It depends on what I do. I thought of learning shorthand and typing. They say you can always get a job if you're efficient."

Mrs. Hunter nudged her familiarly in the ribs. "Go on! You won't want a job long, a pretty girl like you. But shorthand isn't a bad idea. You'll meet some people and get a chance of knowing some boys. Only don't make the mistake of going into a private house or becoming secretary to a dentist or a doctor. No fellow wants to marry a girl who knows all about his teeth or his inside. You get into a big office and don't be too careful about saving for your old age. You remember, nothing succeeds like looking successful, and it's a long time before you'll start taking the pension. Anyway, you've got a rich aunt in the background."

Caroline flinched from the good-natured vulgarity of that. "I can't count on her. She's told me so plainly. Anyhow, I want to be independent."

"That's all right, so long as you're not too independent. You bear that in mind, a man wants to marry a girl who looks as if she needs someone to look after her. You go round doing all the bossing and you'll be bossing yourself in an old maid's flat when you're forty. My sister Alice is like that. Got a good job, earns good money and what use is it to her? Takes herself out to lunch and the cinema every Sunday, and longs for Monday morning. Standing at a wash-tub may be no joke, but it's better than hanging out one pair of scanties and six handkerchiefs in a one-room apartment. That's what Alice does. Besides, a woman can't really have any fun without a man. I tell her, 'You'd do better to marry anyone than just go on the way you do.' Still, I dare say she's so bossy now no man would speak to her twice. No, you go ahead and get that job, dear, and in twelve months' time you'll be sending me a bit of wedding-cake."

Caroline muttered something incoherent and pushed past. She wasn't interested in marriage or men, she thought Alice Whatever-her-name was probably had a grand time, able to make her own arrangements without consulting someone else—and most likely she loved a meal with a book, instead of having to hear how bad things were in the city. All the same, you had to admit it didn't sound an exhilarating existence.

It was funny, when you had a whole day and nothing to do, how long it seemed. She was free to go to the town, spend what remained of her coupons, have lunch out and tea out, go to the pictures, take a long bus ride, go to the hairdresser—and really what difference was there between that and lying quietly in the tomb? She reminded herself that soon she would be in London living in a hostel with a lot of other girls, making friends, going to the pictures, achieving independence.

"But I'm out of date. I don't want independence really," she told herself despairingly. "And how can it ever be worth all the bother, just keeping house for yourself?"

Arrived in London, Roger put Lady Bate into a taxi, gave the driver the address and watched the cab drive away. The old woman had offered him a lift, but he had said no, it wasn't his direction. This would have seemed odd to her if she had realized that she was going to Bishopsgate and he to Fleet Street, but she didn't know, and he had been remarkably uncommunicative on the journey up. She had told him to think twice before pitchforking himself into a job; it was easier to get in for a man of his qualifications than to get out. He had said, "Can't eat the bread of humiliation for ever, and even this Government isn't going to keep chaps in comfort who don't want to work," to which she replied cozily if a shade mysteriously, "I don't think you need worry. I only mean don't do anything rash. It isn't as if you had no friends at court."

He hadn't asked her what she meant; it was too obvious. He thought of Caroline's face as she watched them get into the taxi. She knew something, too; her contempt had been open for all to see. He had genuinely thought she was coming to town with them, and he had been going to try to break down the barriers that had somehow been erected between them of late, explain to her about his job and the difficulties confronting a man with his

73

living to earn. However, he'd see her tonight, when perhaps she would be less unapproachable.

He went to an address in Fleet Street after parting from the old lady, and asked for Mr. Cummings. He was informed that that veteran journalist had gone out to the Black Boar with a visitor, so he followed. He found his friend drinking beer with a short, stout man in a tight brown suit, and possessed of an accent you could cut with a knife.

"Hallo, Roger," said the hard-bitten editor. "Win your bet?"

"I think so."

"Don't sound very jubilant about it. This is Mr. Crook—you know, the Criminals' Hope and the Judges' Despair."

"Have this on me," offered Crook handsomely, calling for same again. "Anything I can do for you?"

"When Crook offers to do anything for you you know you're in a spot," Cummings warned him. "He's no use for the righteous or the safe."

"You've got it wrong," expostulated Crook. "What you mean is—they've got no use for me. Now," he turned to the young man, "if you were in for a spot of bother, if the police were askin' a lot of inconvenient questions and you liked to come to me, I might be able to tell you how to answer them."

"Crook's responsible for more murderers being at large than any man living," amplified Cummings. "What's up, Roger? You haven't pushed anyone off a cliff, by any chance?"

"Not yet," agreed Roger. "No motive—up to date."

"I thought you said you'd won your bet."

"I have." He turned to Crook. "I'm a journalist. War correspondent for the past five years. Now I'm back in Civvy Street. Cummings is running a series—Why Work? You know the kind of thing."

"We did it after the last war," Cummings interpolated. "Got a chap to go round answering advertisements to show that having had a commission during a world war wasn't necessarily a passport to getting a job in the peace. A fellow called Wilson did it in 1920. We published a series of six articles, and proved that on the whole it was the chap who stayed at home who pulled down the plums. Now we're told everything's going to be different. More jobs than chaps to fill them."

"And you're runnin' the same horse in the Second Peace Derby?"

"What do you take me for? No, we thought we might show it was easy to get a living without working or risking the inside of a prison. Roger here said if we gave him a month he'd prove you could live in luxury without sweating for it, and as there are always plenty of chaps keen to know how it's done, we gave him the job. What did happen, Roger?"

Roger glanced at the watch on his wrist. "At this moment there's an old harpy closeted with her lawyer changing her will."

"Making you the heir?"

"I wouldn't be surprised."

"All done by charm," said Cummings. "Well, they say there's a mug born every minute."

But Crook, calling for his third pint, said seriously, "Now you've got to look out that she don't hand in her checks suddenly. It's a suspicious world—you may not have noticed it, bein' in the Army—but nothin' makes chaps talk more than when an old dame alters her will and then pips out almost directly afterwards."

Roger stared. "Why should she?"

"You'd be surprised how often it happens," Crook assured him in the same serious voice, "and you'd be still more surprised the way the police get around after a thing like that. Where does the dame live?"

"At the seaside."

"Spinster with a hungry heart?"

"She's a widow with no family, except a niece she's more or less adopted."

"Niece bein' one of these downright women about as comfortable to sleep with as a broomstick, I suppose."

Roger put down his tankard with more noise than seemed necessary. "Not a bit. She's a charming girl, much too charming to be tied to the old woman's apron-strings. When we have a really sane Government," he added violently, "there'll be a law against the old preying on the young."

75

"Oh well." Crook sounded tolerant. "I dare say she makes a bit on the side, too."

"She's not that sort of girl," said Roger.

Cummings was watching him cynically. "Which did you meet first, boy? Grannie—or the girl?"

"The girl. And it's aunt, not granny."

"And she introduced you to Granny, and she fell for your blue eyes?"

"Oh, shut up," said Roger, rudely. "You make me feel like a gigolo." Suddenly his expression changed. "I've just thought of something."

"Well?"

"Suppose something does happen—oh, it's a thousand-to-one chance, but they do come off sometimes. And suppose she does change her will—after all, at Lady B's age you don't come up to London for the day for fun—I shan't be needing that job."

"Just what I was pointing out," said Crook.

"But, hell, I can't take her money, not in the circumstances."

"You won't have to take much of it," Crook consoled him. "The Government's like Jonah's whale, ready to swallow anything."

"I didn't think of it turning out like this. I mean, I didn't think of her doing anything definite. I just wanted to prove that there's plenty of easy money going for chaps that live by their wits. There's another thing—Caroline."

"The girl you've diddled out of the dough?"

"I meant to explain it to her, but . . ."

"I've been in the game all my life," Cummings commented dryly, "and I know most of the tricks, but even I don't know how to explain a situation like that to a girl I've fallen in love with."

Crooks considered. "Sounds kind of mean," he acknowledged.

"I never thought of it in terms of personalities before. It's just the old confidence trick in a new guise. I didn't follow it up to its logical conclusion. . . ."

Crook clapped him on the shoulder. "You drop crime," he advised him. "That's what most newspaper work is. You get yourself a good job driving a plough or a pen or something nice and safe. Did you ever notice nobody makes a farmer or a bank clerk the villain of the piece? Not enough glamor, I suppose."

Cummings refused to be intimidated. "It'll all come out in the wash," he said. "An old girl like that, used to having her own way, will soon forget about you if you keep out of the picture. Next month she'll be coming to London to draw a new will and your name won't figure in it. Isn't that so, Crook?"

"It could be," agreed Crook cautiously, "it could be. And that bein' so all you've got to look out for is that she don't kick the bucket before she gets that new will made." He was wearing a hard brown bowler hat on the back of his head, and now he pulled it down over the red spines of his eyebrows. "And remember, if you should get in a jam, my address is 123 Bloomsbury Street, and I like cases with a lot of money about them." He nodded and stamped his way out.

"Rum cove!" said Cummings, looking after him. "I really believe he would like you better if you got yourself tied up in a murder case. But you don't have to believe the last bit. Crook's one of Nature's artists. He makes money, of course. It comes to him the way some men will attract a flea the whole length of a tube train. But if he likes a case he won't start thinking about the money till it's all over." He tipped his soft black hat over his eyes, and with an uncanny parody of Crook, considering they hadn't a single physical attribute in common, he said in a hearty, uneducated accent, "And anyway why should I sweat my guts out to support the Government, when all they want to do is make men so comfortable they won't commit any more crimes and I'll be out of a job?"

$\mathcal{C}$HAPTER $\mathcal{E}$IGHT

DURING HER AUNT's absence Caroline had spent a thoroughly unsatisfactory day. She had gone out early, determined to walk herself into such a state of exhaustion as to be beyond feeling, but a clear morning dissolved into mists of cloudy rain by noon, and she came scurrying back to The Downs to change. At lunch Mrs. Hunter came and sat beside her and suggested they might go to a cinema that afternoon.

"Too bad you should have to spend an afternoon with an old woman like me," she said, laughing cheerily. "All the same, you know what they say about half a loaf. Alfred used to say I was too like a cottage loaf ever to be mistaken for half a one, but that was just his fun."

Because anything was better than sitting in the parlor, watched by both women, and because she couldn't very well refuse and then go to the cinema alone, Caroline assented, and they spent the afternoon watching a thriller in which an engaging young man poisoned his benefactor for the sake of his money.

"Awful what money will do, isn't it?" chattered Mrs. Hunter as they came out. "Now, my dear, you're going to have tea with me. Oh yes, you are. I always thought I'd like a daughter to buy pretty things for, but Alfred and me, we never had so much as a miss, and I dare say we might have been disappointed. Anyway, as he used to tell me, nobody has everything. Let's come in here, shall we? That table in the corner. Then we can have a cozy talk."

She led the way and Caroline followed her with a sinking heart.

"Mind you," said Mrs. Hunter, who scarcely paused to draw breath, "it's easy enough for people with money to talk as if it didn't matter. The only people who know the real value of money are the people who haven't got it. You can't have any fun without a bit put by. Alfred always said that. All the same, it does show (she meant the film showed) it doesn't pay to try and get it by crooked means. That young fellow, now—oh, let's order, shall we? Tea for two and sandwiches—or would you rather have toasted scones? What? There aren't any toasted scones? That saves us the trouble of making up our minds, doesn't it? Alfred always said it was a great thing to look on the bright side. Then cakes, all the bundle." She nodded merrily to the waitress, who remained quite unimpressed. "What was I saying? Oh yes, that young fellow in the picture, he took a lot of trouble and what good did it do him? The fact is, as Alfred always said, when you're up against the police you're an amateur up against the professional, and it's sheer conceit to think you're likely to win. Besides, you never get a chance of any practice at murder, if you see what I mean. I mean, you get caught the first time. It's not like anything else. Forgers and thieves go to prison, and Alfred used to say that they learnt more there than ever they did outside. Sort of graduation course he called it. He told me he once met a man who said he wouldn't have missed his first term of imprisonment for anything, he learnt so much from the old lags. As Alfred said, what's the good of running prisons that way? I always thought myself Alfred ought to stand for Parliament, he saw things so clearly, if you know what I mean, but he said no, he preferred biscuits to blather. Ah, here comes the tea. That's one thing. They do serve you quickly here. Any sugar? Well now, isn't it lucky I always carry sugar with me? I read a book once where a fellow took his wife out to tea and he'd brought some sugar with him, the powdered kind, and he gave it to her, and what do you think? It wasn't sugar really, it was poison. She was rich, you see, and he'd met a young lady he rather fancied. . . . But of course he got caught. They always do—in books."

She didn't appear to notice that Caroline was making no reply. It was difficult to understand how Alfred could have said half the things with which she credited him. He couldn't have got a word in edgewise. But perhaps, reflected Caroline, he'd been a chatterbox himself, and they'd talked one against the other, and bits of what each had said had seeped through.

Mrs. Hunter was one of those people who make a virtue of curiosity. "Alfred always said my name ought to have been Pandora," she confided. "You know, the one that let everything out of the box, but I always say it's only people with guilty consciences that have to button up their mouths. Now, my dear, you won't mind me giving you a little advice—don't think money's the only thing that matters. You're young and there's plenty of time for young people to make money. I quite see you want to hang on to your grannie—somehow I can't think of her as your auntie—but is it worth while? I know her kind, she may go on for years, and all that time she'll be sucking you dry, and then you'll hear the will and find she's left everything to someone she hasn't known a month. You may shake your head" (though, in fact, Caroline had done nothing of the kind) "but it's always happening. There was a book I got out of the library only last month, a girl in that let her boy-friend go abroad without a ring, because her grannie had made a mess of her marriage and said all men were deceivers, and told the girl she'd do best for herself by staying with them that appreciated her, and then when the fellow had married someone else, and the girl was too old to hope for anything better than a widower with three chins, and even they can take their pick these days, the old woman died and she left all her money to some clergyman who'd made her believe her husband was in hell, and she needn't worry about ever having to meet him again."

Mrs. Hunter stopped breathlessly and dug her fork into an ersatz cream bun.

"You're quite wrong," said Caroline. "It isn't because of the money, and even if it had been it wouldn't be any more, because she's gone up to London to see her lawyer, and when people do that it always means they're going to change their wills."

Mrs. Hunter's eyes grew as round as moons. "Did she tell you?"

"She's going to get me started earning a living, and then she won't feel she need leave me anything."

Mrs. Hunter exploded. "The old so-and-so. Leading you up the path all these years. Of course, anyone can see what it is, she's fallen for that young man. Ten to one he's a fortune-hunter out for what he can get. He's very good-looking, isn't he?"

"Yes," agreed Caroline faintly.

"Alfred used to say handsome is as handsome does, and it does a good many people. Still, it's an ill-wind that blows nobody any good, and there's no cloud but has its silver lining. It'll give you a chance to get away, though I daresay you won't like it at first. Still, I should think she'd do the decent thing by you." But her tone belied the optimism of her words.

"Oh well," said Caroline, as if that were the last word on the matter, "if anyone was thinking of me as an heiress, they can change their minds now."

To Caroline's surprise, Lady Bate was back at The Downs by the time her niece and Mrs. Hunter returned. She was sitting in a simmering fury in the parlor, one foot on a hand-embroidered footstool pushed into position by a sympathetic Miss Twiss, while the wireless roared its head off. Oddly enough, for all her deafness, she could hear the wireless if it was turned full on. A matter of vibrations, she explained, to anyone who liked to listen. "Of course I can't endure music," she would add. "I don't know why it is but music on the wireless is intolerable to deaf people. It even keeps me from going to church."

"Turn that horrible noise off," shouted Lady Bate to Caroline as her niece came in. Caroline hesitated, then turned it low.

"That's all right, dear, turn it off altogether if it upsets your auntie," Miss Twiss encouraged her. "She's had a nasty fall and twisted her ankle. You mind you don't get pneumonia," she added to her outraged patient. "It's no joke at your age. My Aunt Millie . . . I've got the very thing. My shawl. It was so warm I haven't needed it today I'll just get it from outside." She

81

fussed off and Lady Bate said, "Stop that woman making a fool of herself and me. It's my belief she has a screw loose."

Miss Twiss came plunging back, flourishing the shawl, and saying, "You shouldn't take these risks, not in these days of rush and fuss. Let the young ones go by train...." She tucked up the unfortunate ankle and looked round for some other way of being helpful. Lady Bate looked past her with an expression of pure hate. Then Mrs. Hunter, who had stopped an instant in the hall to see if there was any post for her, came hurrying in, saying, "Well, well, this is a surprise. Caroline and I are only just back. How was dear old London? I dare say you'd have enjoyed yourself more with us. A very good picture we went to. Murder it was. Caroline will tell you..."

Miss Twiss, who had caught the word murder and who wished to be pleasant, said cheerfully that was quite a coincidence. There'd been a murder play at the Wednesday Matinee— *The Lady Returns,* it was called, and Sybil Thorndike had been going to play in it but at the eleventh hour she'd been prevented —so disappointing. But a good play all the same. About an old lady who was strangled by her companion...

"Ours was poisoned by a gigolo," chimed in Mrs. Hunter. And then she chuckled and turning to Lady Bate, demanded, "Doesn't it make you feel nervous, all this talk about crime?"

"Why should it?" asked Lady Bate uncompromisingly, but looking capable of double murder on the spot. "Still, if any attempts are made on my life I shall know where to look."

Miss Twiss didn't appear to have heard that, but Mrs. Hunter laughed to Caroline, and said, in tones of mock terror, "Fee-fi-fo-fum. You have been warned." Then she went upstairs to take off her things.

"Caroline," said Lady Bate imperatively, "ring for Jock. I want my tea."

Caroline looked nervous. "It's a quarter to six," she pointed out.

"Hurry up or that imbecile will start telling us about her second play this afternoon. As if I'm interested! I never heard such insolence. Expecting me to pay to hear a lot of over-accented, simpering young men tell me a lot of fandangled nonsense any sensible person knows can't be true. The fact is, they're pandering to the lazy, who want to be amused without making the smallest effort. You mark my words, in two generations half our people won't be able to read. Though," she wound up savagely, "seeing the use to which they put their reading, that may be an advantage."

Fearful of arousing her to yet greater transports of rage, Caroline nervously rang the bell, and after a moment Jock appeared.

"I should like some tea, please," said Lady Bate briskly. "Caroline, you had better take my outdoor clothes and your own upstairs. Then come down and pour out my tea, and later I shall require a cold compress putting on my ankle."

"How did it happen?" asked Caroline dutifully, taking up the dignified black hat with its curling ostrich feather and the black seal coat that seemed to their owner suitable wear for a trip to London in such weather.

"Londoners have such atrocious manners. They're all in such a hurry to get somewhere they have no consideration whatsoever for anyone else. I was deliberately pushed off the pavement, and no thanks are due to the person who pushed me that I'm not lying in a hospital. Now, Caroline, hang up my coat on the mauve satin hanger, remember, not the blue one, and bring down my loose black slippers. Not my bedroom slippers, of course, but the loose black ones. Do you understand?"

"Yes, Aunt Bate," said Caroline meekly.

The old lady turned her attention to Jock, who had crossed the room and was now making up the fire. "Did Mrs. Anstruther mention that Mr. Carlton would be dining with us tonight?"

"She did not," said Jock in forbidding tones.

"Then I will tell you. I expect him about seven." She turned back to Caroline. "I am arranging for us to have a private sitting-room for the future. It's very tiresome it can't be ready for our dinner tonight. This communal living is quite intolerable. Now, hurry upstairs, and while you're there you might brush your hair and make yourself look presentable. Really, I can't imagine how you contrive to make yourself such a spectacle."

Mrs. Hunter came in at this moment and thought the situation worthy of further remark. "You want to be careful, Lady Bate," she said. "Caroline's been getting hints on murder this afternoon. How not to do it. Alfred used to say, and I must admit I agree with him, the cinema's more responsible for crime than anyone would guess. I don't mean these silly gangster films, but all this theft and murdering husbands and wives, putting ideas into people's heads, I call it."

"In most cases there would be plenty of room," was Lady Bate's icy retort. "Now, Caroline, please be quick; no doubt you have had tea, but kindly remember I have not, and I shall be waiting for you to pour mine out. I have twisted my ankle . . ."

Mrs. Hunter never knew when to let well alone. "Still, you don't pour out tea with your foot," she observed good-naturedly. "Or, if you could, you'd make your fortune on the halls."

Seeing her aunt temporarily beyond speech, Caroline collected her discarded wraps and fled. She wondered what room Mrs. Anstruther proposed to give them for a private sitting-room, and made the surprising discovery that she was sorry to hear of the change. Mrs. Hunter might be a vulgar little nonentity, as Aunt Bate declared, but she did dilute the awfulness of *tête à tête* meals with the old lady. She only stayed upstairs long enough to hang up the coats and brush her hair into some semblance of smoothness, and came down to find a silent Jock malignantly putting a tea-tray at her ladyship's elbow.

After he had gone the irrepressible Mrs. Hunter said to the room at large, "If you ask me, that fellow could make his fortune on the films. He wouldn't have to tell you he was planning a murder; you could see it from his face."

Lady Bate ignored the observation. "I hope to goodness there's an eatable dinner tonight," she announced. "I call it outrageous the way people set up as guest-house proprietors and then keep all the best food for themselves. Yesterday I distinctly smelt chicken cooking, but when our dinner was served it was corned beef stew. I shall have to have a word with Mrs. Anstruther."

"Well, for Pete's sake!" said Mrs. Hunter, who believed in keeping abreast of the time. She got up and crossed the room

At the door she turned. "Did you want Caroline to do any tele-phoning for you or is the instrument free for *nous autres*?"

"Did you hear me ask my niece to telephone?" inquired Lady Bate in a voice that would have frozen the phœnix.

"I can't say I did."

"It must have been the only thing you didn't hear."

Caroline reddened, but Mrs. Hunter drooped an eyelid at her and marched out.

Lady Bate hardly waited for the closing of the door before she exploded, "Really, Caroline, I should have thought you could have entertained yourself for one day without becoming intimate with that common little creature."

"She asked me to go to the pictures. Did you have a successful day in London?"

"I did what I went to town to do. I saw Mr. Tritton and arranged to change my will. That's really why I want to see Rogers tonight. I do hope he hasn't made any rash decision, though in the light of what I said to him on the way up I should think that's improbable. He strikes me as being a very well-balanced young man, but sufficiently unusual to make a par-ticular appeal to employers."

She took the cup of tea Caroline passed to her and tasted it.

"Powdered milk," she said, wrinkling her face with disgust. "Mrs. Anstruther shall certainly hear about that." She set down the cup, frowned, then lifted and drained it. "No, no more. I shouldn't have drunk that if I hadn't been so thirsty. Well, what's happened to you? Have you lost your tongue? Haven't you anything to say?"

"I think you've said it all," returned Caroline. "And I expect Mr. Tritton said the rest."

"What do you mean by the rest?"

"Asked you if you were sure you weren't being hoodwinked by an unscrupulous young man. Well, it's what any lawyer would say."

"I can't say I think your predilection for cheap films or for cheap company have done you any good," returned Lady Bate furiously, and fortunately at that moment Roger was announced.

"I'm early," he said, "but you told me to come when I was

85

ready. Hallo, you've hurt your ankle. I say, that's bad luck. How did you do it?"

"I have come to the conclusion one would meet with more courtesy in the Zoo with all the animals loose than in London these days," Lady Bate assured. "You've just come in the nick of time, Roger. Caroline's warning me that you're an imposter."

"I didn't," began Caroline.

Roger laughed. "Haven't all my efforts managed to deceive you? Are you putting Lady Bate against me?"

"I never thought you were mercenary, whatever else I may have thought of your capacities," the old lady informed her niece. "In any case, I don't believe in a woman having too much money of her own. She's simply the prey of unscrupulous men. If you've only what you can earn, then you can be sure you are being married for yourself alone. Besides, I don't think you've the temperament to cut a great figure in society. You're one of the people who'll be happier living quietly looking after your house and children. Money's really wasted on people like you. It should be given to those who know how to handle it, who'll make it come back with interest."

"You ought to have gone in for commerce yourself," Roger told her. "Never mind, Caroline, don't look so down in the mouth. If Cinderella could get the Fairy Prince you ought to get the President of the United States at the very least."

Mrs. Hunter came bouncing in and greeted Roger with quite unnecessary warmth. More than ever did Lady Bate long for the privacy of the sitting-room she was blackmailing out of Mrs. Anstruther.

"What have you been doing with yourself all day?" Roger asked Caroline at last. There was a violence about Mrs. Hunter's methods that was sometimes as direct as a bruise.

"The conceit of the men," said Mrs. Hunter, before Caroline could reply. "Think we can't get on without you for twelve hours. Mind you, I don't believe those women who say they can get on without them for good. There's something queer about them, and Alfred used to say the same about bachelors. Scratch a bachelor and you'll find a rake, he'd say. Except those that are something worse."

"Mrs. Hunter and I went to the pictures," said Caroline clearly.

"Sugar-Daddy for Sue?"

"No. Poison for One. Mrs. Hunter's been giving me good advice ever since."

"I'll give you a bit more. If ever you're in a jam, Caroline, you consult my friend, Arthur Crook. He's a nailer for crime. You can murder half the community and he'll pull you out. Only I should advise you to start with one."

Later, when Caroline met Mr. Crook, contrary to all her expectations, she said, "If only one knew in advance what were going to be the important days to remember, one would notice so much more. But one evening seems just like another, and before you know where you are something frightful has happened, and you're being bombarded with questions on all sides, and how can you be sure? After a bit you could even doubt your own name."

"If it comes to that," suggested Crook resourcefully, "you've only got to produce your identity card. But you take my tip, sugar. When you're dealing with the police tell them all the truth you can, all that's safe, I mean, and after that don't tell them anything at all. Just say, 'I don't know, I don't remember, everything went blank.' Then you aren't giving them any foundation to build up a case against you, see? Most people are hanged because they don't realize that once a murder's been done the best way their mouths look is shut. Women especially don't know the policy of the closed mouth. More people get off the rope for the things they don't say than for the things they haven't done. You take your Uncle Arthur's advice. He knows. Well, I ought to, seeing I must be on better terms with more murderers than anyone in the country."

But all that came later. When Roger mentioned Crook's name that fatal evening it never occurred to Caroline that he and she would ever meet or that she might need his help. Actually, it hadn't occurred to Crook either, when he made his casual offer to Cummings' young friend. "Come to me when you're in a jam," he had said. "I'll get you out."

Thus is many a true word spoken in jest.

Chapter Nine

The happenings of the rest of that evening were the subject of so much subsequent investigation by the police, the members of the household were questioned and counter-questioned so often that the facts are probably still clear in the public mind. But at the time no one noticed anything unusual.

Dinner had not been a very comfortable meal. Miss Twiss and Mrs. Hunter sat at one table, and Lady Bate's party at another. Miss Twiss always brought a book to the table and left it lying open beside her plate, but Mrs. Hunter, of whom someone once said that she would be bound to inherit the Kingdom of Heaven, since it suffereth violence and the violent take it by force, shouted with good-natured persistence all through the meal, under the mistaken impression that Miss Twiss would feel hurt if she were ignored. That is, she would add, if she's as deaf as she makes out. If she's not, then she might be a bit companionable. She can't have it both ways.

Thanks to her persistence, she heard little of what was going on at the other table. Only during the meal she saw Caroline get up and go upstairs to return about three minutes later with a short fur jacket that she handed to her aunt.

"Couldn't you find it?" asked Lady Bate, and Caroline said, "Oh yes, but I had to get myself a fresh handkerchief, and I—I couldn't find one straight away." The girl's face looked rather red, and Mrs. Hunter smiled to herself and thought, "That woman's got no tact. The girl's got a little chill or something, that's why she didn't come down at once. You'd have thought an old woman like her ladyship would have rumbled that. Or, of course, she might want to make her look silly in front of the young man. It's obvious they've both fallen for him in a big way."

She admitted afterwards that she did notice a specially confidential attitude between the old lady and Roger Carlton, but said that, during Caroline's absence, the two had spoken together in such low tones that she hadn't caught a word. She thought Roger very assiduous in his attentions to Lady Bate, but added that his manner had not been much different from usual, and could be accounted for by the fact that Lady Bate had damaged her ankle and was, therefore, a bit of an invalid that night.

"But he always paid her a good deal of attention?" she was asked, and she grinned and said, "Well, she was a rich old party, you know."

Roger stayed and had coffee with his hostess and Caroline in the parlor, and then entertained the pair to the best of his ability with a story of a casual meeting he had had in London, though whether on that day or some time previously Mrs. Hunter couldn't be sure. But she did recollect that when Lady Bate wanted a letter that had arrived the day before, it was the young man who went up to fetch it.

Lady Bate had told her niece in her usual imperious manner that it was on her table beside her bed, but before she could move Roger had sprung up saying, "Caroline looks tired. Can't I fetch it for you?"

He went up and came down a minute or two later, and they became absorbed in the contents. Caroline broke into the conversation presently to say, "Did you get that job you went about?" and Roger instantly became evasive.

"I saw a very good chap," he said. "An editor. He got me an introduction. I fancy I'll be back soon."

"Now, don't do anything rash," Lady Bate urged him. "Remember what I've just told you."

Mrs. Hunter was drinking all this in. She was thoroughly annoyed when Miss Twiss said in her unemphatic way, "If you aren't reading, Mrs. Hunter, perhaps we could have a game of patience. I have come to the end of my colored cotton. I can't do any more of this work until I have gone down to the town and bought a fresh supply."

"I believe she was a school-marm till she became too deaf to hear if the girls were right or wrong," reflected Mrs. Hunter, saying yes, she would play patience if Miss Twiss liked. "Or, of course she may think that if she's playing patience no one will suspect her of listening. I wish Alfred were here. He'd get her measure at once. He always said being a salesman gave you a lot of insight into psychology. He'd have 'em all taped." She sighed. She did miss Alfred. He'd always been such good company, and somehow they'd always wanted to do the same things at the same time, which was an infallible recipe for success in married life.

The journey to London had tired Lady Bate more than she was prepared to admit, her ankle pained her and her temper in consequence was seriously ruffled. Roger took his leave, saying he might have to go to London again in a day or so, and apparently not treating her seriously when she told him he didn't have to worry, he had a friend at court. Caroline was also ill at ease, unsure of the young man, apprehensive about the future, fearful that by separating herself from her aunt (or being forcibly separated) she might also lose touch with Roger Carlton. Common sense told her that if he was attracted nothing would be simpler than for him to discover her whereabouts, but when he said kindly that when she came to London to seek her fortune she must be sure to let him know her address, she said he'd be far too busy to bother about her.

After he had gone and while Caroline was collecting the old lady's traps, her aunt said curtly, "You really can't expect a young man to pay you much attention if you can't even be polite to him. He's taking a great deal of trouble..."

Caroline's nerves reached breaking-point. "Isn't it worth his while?" she demanded.

"My dear, you've a very good conceit of yourself. You be careful or you'll die an old maid." Then suddenly her mood changed. "Do you think I don't know what you're hinting at, and why you're doing it? You must have thought this a very soft situation—little to do and plenty to get, and now when you think you may not be left quite so well off as you anticipated you become insolent. You don't deserve a penny from me, and what's more, I'll see to it you don't get it. And now I don't want another word from you tonight. I'm worn out and my ankle is most painful. I might have looked for a little consideration from you. It won't be your fault if I don't lie awake till morning."

Caroline, aware of Mrs. Hunter's fascinated gaze, sick with humiliation and disgust, picked up an armful of the old lady's belongings and followed her to the door. She noticed that in the extreme of rage Lady Bate had forgotten about the twisted ankle. She marched to the foot of the stairs like a grenadier. After the door had closed behind them Mrs. Hunter, who had never heard of repressions, remarked candidly to the unmoved Miss Twiss, "Well, did you ever? Mind you, I'd probably have pushed the old lady under a bus myself long before this, but all the same . . ."

"Was Miss Bate upset about something?" inquired Miss Twiss, composedly stacking the patience cards. "Perhaps she wants a dose. This weather is very trying. Senna pods and whisky was what we had when we were young."

"My, didn't you belong to an enlightened household?" exclaimed Mrs. Hunter enviously. "We had the senna pods all right, without the whisky."

"I wonder if there is anything between those two young people," continued Miss Twiss. "If so, I do hope old Lady Bate won't try and come between them. When people are as old as she is they sometimes forget how they felt when they were young."

"So that's your story, is it?" reflected the romantic Mrs. Hunter, jumping as usual to the obvious conclusion. "Oh well, if you're a spinster at fifty there has to be a young man who died of consumption or was killed in the war—the war's been very useful to spinsters—or a difficult mother. Still, there may be something in it, and it would be criminal if that pretty girl doesn't get her man because of that old dragon. Though, as Alfred would have said, you'd need to think twice before you married anyone with that tacked on to them." Grammar had never been Mrs. Hunter's strong suit. "And why bother?" she used to say. "So long as people know what you mean?" She always saw to it that they did.

Upstairs Caroline set about her usual tasks of putting things ready for the night. Lady Bate liked to have her hair brushed and plaited, her shoes polished—she didn't trust Jock's polishing, she said servants always used the same brush for all the shoes, and if you weren't in your own house it was safer not to let your shoes out of your sight; her dress had to be hung up, her underclothes shaken out and turned, her stockings rinsed through warm water, her nightgown aired at the gas fire.

"I'm sure no one could say I ask a great deal in return for all I do for you," Lady Bate liked to remark. This evening Caroline's duties seemed endless. One small job after another to be performed, and all in an atmosphere of simmering hate on one side and open contempt on the other. But then there never had been affection between them, only a sort of forced gratitude from Caroline in return for cold responsibilities coldly accepted. At last all was done, the cold compress made and applied, the nightgown aired, the bed tucked in exactly as the old lady liked it, and now she had only to mix the old lady's nightly dose of salts. These were a simple effervescing powder prepared by a local chemist, each powder put up in a separate gray paper slip. Lady Bate never touched the dose until it had stopped fizzing. She said all that gas would produce wind in any respectable stomach. Caroline carefully measured out the water, shook the powder into the glass with a trembling hand, thinking, "Almost the end, almost the end. Keep up appearances. It's such a little time now." She compelled her voice to be quiet, flattened out the resentment that burned in her, kept her eyes fixed on the glass so that she should not see that hard old face. It was queer how, when you were young, you could be shaken by spasms of pity for the autocratic old, forgiving them their cruelty and arrogance because they were so old and there was so little ahead for them. But there were times when you couldn't afford to be sorry, couldn't let your life be wrecked for a sentiment. So as she handed the glass, waited, took it back, and rinsed it out, her thoughts ran like the

92

turning wheels of a train. Not much longer—not much
longer——

"I wish you'd stop that vulgar habit of play-acting," scolded
Lady Bate. "Who do you imagine you are? Catherine de Medici
mixing the fatal draught?" She gave way to a cackle of furious
laughter. Mrs. Hunter, who had paused outside the door, not
because she was really eavesdropping, as she would have explained, but because it was a pity to miss any sort of free entertainment, and the old girl was as good as a play, was thrilled to
the bone. The jeering voice continued, "A cup of cold pizen!"

Mrs. Hunter was to remember all that next day.

"And now," went on the inexorable voice, "I'm going to take
one of my sleeping tablets. I've had an exhausting day, and I
can't say you've contributed much to my comfort. Hurry up."
She uncorked the little bottle she had taken from the drawer of
her bedside table and tipped one of the white tablets into her
palm. It looked an innocent affair—like a saccharine tablet. You
wouldn't have thought anything so small could have had any
effect. Caroline brought her the glass, and stood watching her
as the water ran down her stringy old throat.

"I hope that will do the trick," said the old lady, "but mind
you listen in the night in case I call for you. If my ankle is
troublesome it may keep me awake in spite of the tablet."

"Take two," suggested Caroline vaguely. Her head was beginning to swim; the strain was more than she could bear.

"If you're no more use than that in an office you won't keep
a job long," gibed Lady Bate. "Or perhaps you'd really like me
to commit suicide. Can't you read what it says on the bottle?
One only. However, if something happened to me tonight I dare
say that would suit your book very well. Now you can go to bed,
and if I want you I'll call. Tomorrow I ought to hear from Mr.
Tritton. I told him there was no time to waste; I don't want
Roger to do anything reckless—and then we can settle your
future."

She looked a formidable old woman sitting bolt upright with
a little gray shetland shawl round her gray hair in its short
scanty plaits. She sounded formidable, too, to the listener on the
other side of the door. Mrs. Hunter shivered with a horrid sort

93

of pleasure. She had to keep a sharp lookout in case she was seen, because people had nasty minds, and they didn't understand. Alfred had always said, "No need to listen, Winnie, that's not what a lady 'ud do, but no harm hearing anything that's going on."

"Dear me!" thought Mrs. Hunter, stealing delightedly along the corridor. "She does seem in a paddy. Mind you, I'm all for the girl. Pity that old so-and-so doesn't die in her sleep, before she has time to disinherit her, but that sort of thing only happens on the films. Oh well, it may all turn out for the best. We don't want to find ourselves with a real murder on our hands."

For a long time after she had undressed and got into bed, Caroline found it impossible to sleep. She turned this way and that, she changed her position, she thumped her pillows, she even tried to read, but she could not fix her mind on the page. Always she saw Roger smiling at Lady Bate, running assiduously round her, heard his voice saying in its charming drawl, "How do I live? By my wits. I told you that before."

At last, unable to endure this mental torment any longer, she stole out of bed and into her aunt's room. Surely, surely, even so inhuman an old lady as Charlotte Bate would not refuse her one of the sleeping tablets; she would be a wreck tomorrow unless she got some rest tonight. When she had switched on the light, however, she found that the old lady was fast asleep. There were still a number of the minute tablets in the bottle, and it seemed to her improbable that her aunt would have kept an exact tally of the number. So, trembling a little, Caroline took up the bottle, shook a tablet into her hand and stood staring at it a moment with fascinated eyes. She was not quite certain of their efficacy; one, she supposed, was harmless. She put it into her mouth, swallowed it without the aid of water, and stole back to bed.

A little later she was asleep.

CHAPTER TEN

ONE OF Lady Bate's minor triumphs over her hostess had been
that she was now brought a cup of early morning tea at seven-
thirty. There had been considerable argument over this service.
Jock had said flatly that he wasn't going to start going into
leddies' bedrooms at his time of life.

"They do it on the Continent," said Rose Anstruther, and
he looked at her with mingled amazement and scorn.

"The Continent? That's neither here nor there. It's well
known they've a power of immoral practices on the Continent.
No, if the body must have her tea, though why she canna wait
till breakfast like any ither Christian I cannot understand, then
have one of the women take it to her."

Mrs. Mack stood firmly by her rights. She was the cook and
the cook didn't wait on the bedrooms. There was a daily woman
called Mrs. Ferguson who did bedroom work, but she didn't
arrive till eight o'clock, and had to be treated like Shelley's sensi-
tive plant in any case, if Jock or Rose or both didn't want to find
themselves sweeping the boarders' carpets. The only other member of the staff was a kitchen-maid, who had recently been
engaged, and who had been intimidated into taking the tea
upstairs.

"The old cow!" she would say wrathfully, "who's she to lie
in bed and be waited on? Just wait till the Government get a
chance to put things to rights. . . ."

"That's enough of that," interposed Jock firmly. "This is a
Consairvative household, I'd have ye know. You keep all that

95

communist nonsense for these raw laddies ye go out with. Though I judge ye'll be less of one when it comes to your turn to give in your wages and such, for the common guid. Of course, ye're only a puir silly southerner, but even they stick to their siller like wax to a thread."

So, with an ill grace, Gladys carried up the tray each morning, wearing an expression that showed she considered herself above such servile employment. However, she obtained short shrift from Lady Bate.

"Good heavens, gairl, can't you even set down a tea-tray without upsetting the milk and clattering the china as though you were having a fit of hysterics?" demanded the old lady. "I don't know how far you expect to get, but I can tell you you'll never rise beyond a boarding-house if that's the best you can do. All this education they talk so much about these days doesn't seem to have taught you girls anything. When I was young you wouldn't have been kept in a good house for a week. And don't say, 'There you are!' Say, 'Good morning, Madam,' if 'Your Ladyship' is beyond you."

Even in a shawl and a high-necked nunsveiling nightdress the old woman was alarming, and Gladys found herself pulling the curtains quietly, and straightening the eiderdown. She did her best to stand up for herself by muttering that this wasn't her work, not by rights it wasn't, to which Lady Bate retorted that a gairl did what her employer bade her, and if she had any ambition . . . Gladys backed out, feeling as she used to do when she was a youngster and her father had settled a contemporary argument with a strap. One thing, she told the daily woman, that old bitch won't be here long. They'll never stand for her.

On this particular morning she came in, carrying the tray carefully, and put it down on the bedside table. As a rule, Lady Bate was awake and had got herself arranged against her pillows by 7:30. But today she didn't move. Gladys began to draw the curtains, making a little more noise with each. If the old so-and-so woke up and started fault-finding she'd say she wanted to wake her ladyship before the tea got cold. But when the last curtain had run back on its brass rings there was still no movement from the figure in the bed.

"Sleeping it orf," thought Gladys vaguely, looking round the room hopefully for an empty spirit bottle or even one not quite empty. But she saw nothing. She crossed the room and went into Caroline. She had no compunction about waking her—sleeping like the dead, she reflected enviously—and she jerked at the bed-clothes until the girl opened heavy eyes, muttering, "What is it, Aunt Bate? Oh, Gladys, it's you."

"Thought I'd just let you know I've brought up the tea. The old lady seems dead to the world. Not that I care, but I don't want her telling Mrs. A. I didn't bother to let her know the tea was there."

"I expect she's tired after her trip to town," suggested Caroline, reaching for her dressing-gown. Gladys made a sound to indicate that she didn't care if the old woman was dead, and stalked out, leaving the door open to show her independence. Caroline went into the big room and stood looking down at Lady Bate. She seemed curiously still, and there was something unfamiliar about her. As a rule, even in sleep, she gave an impression of force, if only of force at rest; today that impression no longer persisted. The first tremor of fear went through her. She stooped, said loudly, "Aunt Bate! Aunt Bate, your tea's here!"

"She won't wake for that," said Gladys in contemptuous tones. "Why, she didn't hear when I rattled the curtains ever so."

"Aunt Bate!" There was a sharper note in the girl's voice. She caught at the thin shoulder under the covering of the bed-clothes. Gladys moved languidly towards the door. "Don't go," said Caroline quickly. "I think—I wonder if she could have had a stroke. She doesn't seem..."

"Not she," said Gladys. "My Grannie had a stroke, face all went one side. Made 'er fortune in a circus, my dad said. No, she 'asn't 'ad a stroke, but..." She came nearer. "She do look queer," she conceded.

Caroline bent closer; there was something very strange here. With a premonitory shudder of foreboding, she straightened.

"Gladys, we must get a doctor, there's something wrong. I don't know—she never saw doctors. She used to say medicine was a vested interest, and she wasn't going to line the doctors' pockets. Is there someone Mrs. Anstruther knows?"

"I dare say Jock 'ud be able to tell you. D'you think she's reelly . . ."

"I don't know," said Caroline desperately. "Get Jock, please, at once. Ask him to telephone . . ."

"All right. Only if she's reelly gone there's no hurry, is there? Lucky, reelly, going off like that. You should have seen my Gran. And 'eard 'er. My mum said she could 'ave bin 'eard in Piccadilly Circus. The pain, see? She . . ."

Caroline, unable to endure any more of this, furiously rang the bell, keeping her finger on the push.

" 'Ere, there's no need to go losing your 'ead," protested Gladys. "I'm going as fast as I can. Anyway, she 'ad a good run for 'er money and saw to it everyone else should run like 'ell, too."

Caroline automatically tied her dressing-gown round her waist. She heard Gladys' slipshod steps going down the stairs, then a mutter of voices in the hall. It was Mrs. Mack.

"You weren't asked to stay and drink the tea," she scolded.

"Might as well," returned Gladys. "Seeing that old—— isn't likely to want it any more."

"Gladys, whatever are you talking about? You . . ."

" 'Appy release, I call it. Oh, *she* wants a doctor, though it's easy to see there's nothing for 'im to do."

Mrs. Mack lifted her voice and called Jock, and after a moment Jock came in. Caroline turned.

"Could you send for a doctor?" she whispered. "I think— I'm afraid . . ."

Jock came over to the bed and stood staring down at the motionless figure lying there. She seemed small and shrunken today, all her arrogant power gone, dissolved in the anonymity of death. He turned back to Caroline.

"It's no' a doctor but an undertaker you'll be wanting," he told her. "Now, miss, don't you take on. It comes to us all. Ye get yeerself into some gairments and I'll away for Dr. Kent."

By the time the doctor arrived Caroline was dressed and waiting, very pale and shaken, in her aunt's room. The doctor was

an unimpressive little man with a careful manner, and at first
he displayed little interest in the case. An old lady had died in her
sleep. Well (he agreed with Gladys) she was luckier than most.
She was not a regular patient, and could not be expected to do
him any good. The household at The Downs was known to be
standoffish, and this was the first time he had ever been called in.
Presumably, when the old men required attention, they called in
someone fashionable from Brightlingstone. He was vaguely
sorry for the girl, knowing that however old people are their
death always comes as a shock to the next-of-kin, even when it
has been anticipated, which was not the case here. He asked a
few perfunctory questions. Had she a regular medical attendant?
When had she last seen a doctor? Had she ever complained of
specific pains?

"She always boasted she was never ill," Caroline told him.
"She went up to London yesterday, that might have tired her,
though she seemed very brisk when she came back."

"What did she go to London for?"

Caroline looked startled. "She—to see a lawyer, I think."

"Sure it wasn't to consult a specialist? This is important, Miss
Bate. If she went up about her health I should have to get in
touch with the doctor in question."

"I'm sure she didn't. She went to see about her will. She told
me when she came back."

"Did she go alone?"

"She traveled up with a friend of ours. She came back alone.
She had hurt her ankle, so she came back earlier than she had
intended. That's why she took one of her sleeping tablets last
night, because she was afraid of lying awake. She only takes
them in emergencies."

"Sleeping tablets? Which are they? This bottle. H'm." He
looked at them thoughtfully. "You can't buy these in any chemist. She must have had them under prescription."

"Oh yes. She used to write when she wanted a new supply.
I could give you the name of the doctor—Davey, it was. But
she hadn't been to see him for a long time. I don't think really
she had anything wrong with her."

"People aren't found dead in bed if they've got nothing wrong

99

with them, young lady," said the doctor a little grimly. He bent over the old lady again. "How many did you say she took?"

"Only one. I saw her. Besides, it would be dangerous to take two."

"Who told you that?"

"She did. She was afraid her ankle might keep her awake in spite of the tablet, so I asked why she didn't take two, and she said that would be tantamount to committing suicide."

"H'm. You don't sleep with her?"

"No. I sleep in that little room there."

"And the tablets stayed in here?"

"Oh yes."

The doctor considered. "She might have taken another after you'd gone to bed."

"I'm sure she wouldn't. She knew it was dangerous. Besides, the first one sent her to sleep."

"How do you know that?"

"Because I came in about an hour later, I couldn't sleep myself, I knew I wasn't going to sleep, and I came to ask if I might have one of the tablets. But when I came up to the bed I saw she was fast asleep, so—so I took one without asking. I thought she wouldn't mind, she couldn't mind. I wouldn't have been any good to her today if I hadn't had my sleep."

He sent her a more penetrating glance than one would have expected from so insignificant a creature. "Bit of a tartar, I take it?"

"She liked her own way. I think her generation was accustomed to giving orders, and she was one of the ones who didn't change."

"Lucky to be able to give 'em," said the doctor grimly. "Most of us spend our lives taking 'em. Miss Bate, I'm sorry about this, but I can't give you a death certificate, not without further inquiry."

Caroline stared at him incredulously. "What do you mean?"

"I never saw the old lady alive, I know nothing about her, I can only draw conclusions from the symptoms I observe. In my opinion, this isn't a natural death."

"I thought—I thought—heart failure," stammered Caroline.

"Heart failure's a very wide term. You could put it on almost any certificate. But there's no indication that your aunt suffered from any heart disease. No, I'd be more inclined to say she died of an over-dose of sleeping draught. It'll be for a coroner's jury to say how the dose was administered."

Caroline looked like something stricken. "Are you sure?" she demanded helplessly. "I mean, I *know* she only took one. I couldn't have made a mistake, and then she went off to sleep straight away. I could hear her snores. It was partly those that infuriated me so. It's awful to lie awake while other people sleep."

The doctor looked anything but satisfied. "She didn't take any other medicine last night?"

"Only her liver salts. She had those every night."

"What are they?"

"Just powders in a box, each in a separate paper. They're made up by a local chemist. There's nothing special about them."

The doctor took up the box, unfolded one of the grayish papers, sniffed, tasted and replaced the packet.

"Nothing there to account for the condition. Miss Bate, where is the telephone?"

"There's one in the hall that we use."

"The hall?" He frowned. "Anything less public?"

"There's Mrs. Anstruther's, but the guests don't use that one."

"I'm not a guest, and in any case I'd like a word with Mrs. Anstruther."

Caroline followed him timidly from the room. "What's going to happen?" she pleaded.

"I shall have to get in touch with the coroner. Where a deceased person hasn't been receiving regular medical attention, that's the normal procedure."

"Oh!" Her relief was obvious. "I was afraid you meant the police."

"It may come to that," said the doctor sharply. "If there's any ground for my suspicion. Have you any relatives you can get in touch with? And how about hers?"

"She hasn't any, except me, and I'm so distant I'm hardly a

proper niece. There's no one to tell." She heaved a deep sigh. "It does seem sad, doesn't it, to be so old and die and nobody care."

"It's the normal lot," returned the doctor briskly. "Well, since you're next-of-kin you'd better keep on the premises in case you're wanted. There'll be an inquest, you know. You'll have to give evidence of identification, and you're sure to be asked to repeat what you've told me about the sleeping tablets. Mind you, I still think it's possible she took another—how about before she went to bed?"

"She didn't come upstairs. She'd hurt her ankle. She wasn't in her room between ten in the morning and ten at night."

"And this was her only source of supply?"

"Yes. I'm sure of that. Besides, she knew two would be dangerous, and she wasn't a bit the sort to take her own life. She'd have been horrified at the idea. Besides, she was in the middle of business. If she had been going to die she'd have seen to it she didn't die till she'd got everything tidied up. That's the sort of person she was."

"Look here," said the doctor in a gruff but not unfriendly voice, "if her visit to the lawyers had anything to do with your future . . ."

"It had. She was changing her will."

"Cutting you out?"

"Changing it. She was going to leave a good deal to a friend of ours whom she wanted to help. She didn't think women needed money . . ."

"You listen to me," said the doctor. "If the police do come into this, and I think it very likely they will, you remember that the less you tell the authorities about your personal affairs the better. Just answer their questions and leave it at that."

He marched off to make mincemeat of Jock, who stood like a lion in the way demanding to know where he was going, and Caroline reluctantly entered the guests' dining-room. The news, of course, was common property by this time, and Mrs. Hunter jumped up as the girl came in to say, "Now, my dear, don't you take on. The old lady had a hundred per cent value for her money, and she saw to it that she was paid every penny. Think

102

of the way she talked to you down here last night, and I heard her bawling you out in her room afterwards. All very well to talk about it being a happy release for her. It's a happy release for you, and I hope she's had the decency to remember all you did for her."

Caroline sat down and took the cup of tea Miss Twiss pushed towards her. "There's going to be an inquest," she told them flatly. "The doctor's telephoning now."

"An inquest?" Mrs. Hunter's eyes sparkled. "Goodness!"

"It's because she hadn't seen a doctor lately, I expect," put in Miss Twiss, who had caught the word inquest. "Nothing for you to worry about, Miss Bate. It's just a Home Office regulation. And now you must eat some breakfast. We're lucky this morning. They've given us eggs."

In the meantime, the doctor had telephoned the coroner and asked to see the Colonel. The two brothers came in together. They said in chorus that no one could see their daughter/niece. She was most upset by the news.

"Knew Lady Bate, did she?" asked the doctor ironically. The status of the guests at The Downs was well known in the neighborhood.

"They had met abroad, I believe," said the Colonel.

"She was a maddening old humbug," put in Joseph unexpectedly, "but my niece was always considerate. By the way, how long will she be here?"

"If you mean Miss Bate . . ."

"I don't. I mean the old woman."

"That will depend on the coroner. No doubt, in the circumstances, they will remove her as soon as possible. As for Miss Bate, I understand she has no friends locally and no relations to whom she can go. That being the case . . ."

The Colonel put on his most arrogant manner. "I hardly think you need concern yourself about the young lady, doctor," he said. "None of us would dream of not showing her all normal consideration in these very unfortunate circumstances. Naturally, she will remain here until she is able to make other suitable arrangements. In any case, she would have to remain for the funeral."

"She won't want to listen to gossip all day," continued the doctor, undaunted, but just as Joseph opened his mouth to say, "My dear sir, you can hardly expect us to restrain the conversation of our boarders," there was a faint rustle of skirts and a new, gentle voice said, "Dr. Kent? Jock has told me what has happened. I am very sorry indeed for Miss Bate, poor girl. Naturally she must stay here for the time being, and you may be sure we shall give her any help we can. She must have relatives..."

"Apparently not," said the doctor. "And no friends either. The old lady seems to have kept her claws on the girl."

Joseph disgraced his kin by saying abruptly. "There's some young chap in the neighborhood she goes about with. I've seen 'em in the town. Nice-looking boy. Might get in touch with him. He was here last night, Jock tells me."

"If he saw her last night the authorities may want to get in touch with him," said the doctor. "Yes, contact him by all means."

"The jargon these fellows use," said the Colonel disgustedly to his brother when the doctor had gone. "Contact. Sheer commercial slang."

"It's damned irritating of that old witch to die on our premises," observed Joseph. "I hope it don't make trouble."

There was a tap on the door and Jock came in. "I told you it was a mistake keeping yon leddy," said he. "There's such a hum in the boarders' parlor they can't even see you. Madam said the young leddy might bide here awhile."

The Colonel, with real kindliness, pushed past him and held out his hand to Caroline.

"Very sorry to hear your news, Miss Bate. Must have been a great shock. Anything we can do to help.... Had your breakfast?"

"Yes, thank you. Colonel Anstruther, do you think I ought to get in touch with Roger? He did travel up to town with my aunt yesterday and he was here last night. He might have noticed if she seemed strange, or perhaps she told him something she didn't tell me...."

"She was never a very easy customer, I take it," said Joseph.

"Now, if your aunt had a lawyer you should let him know. He'll take a great many burdens off your shoulders."

"Oh yes. Of course." She glanced at her watch. "He won't be at his office yet, though."

"No hurry. Only if there's going to be an inquest it's as well to have him down in good time. Some of these coroners don't know their job any more than some of the motorists that are on the roads at present. Skid about all over the place."

"In any case, Miss Bate will want her lawyer to arrange about the funeral and so on," suggested Rose. "She certainly shouldn't have to be worried over that."

Caroline, almost overwhelmed by so much consideration and wanting nothing so much as to escape from it all and find Roger, sat down and accepted a cup of coffee from Mrs. Anstruther's silver pot.

"Do you know if your aunt left any special instructions?" inquired Joseph.

"She always said she must be buried with her husband. He's in Manchester."

"Shocking city," growled the Colonel. "Don't know how the inhabitants stand it."

"My aunt used to say she was never going back there except in a coffin."

She looked at the three solemn faces that hemmed her in. It was irrational, it was ungrateful, but oh! how she longed for the warm humanity of Mrs. Hunter, garrulous though she was, or the cool indifference of Miss Twiss.

"I shouldn't take it too much to heart," said Joseph. "Old people are bound to die some time. All got to come to it. And I wouldn't be surprised to hear she suffered from high blood pressure. If you have that you've only got to get in a paddy, like she did last night. . . ."

Caroline looked up, startled. "She wasn't—she didn't," she began, but Joseph told her gruffly that it was no good telling fairy tales at this stage. "I dare say she broke a blood-vessel. Very natural if she did, I'm sure. That and the journey and her accident—you can't monkey about with your health at her age," said Joseph, who was seventy-nine and looked considerably younger.

"I—the trouble is— I'm terribly sorry because it's bound to be very upsetting—but the doctor seemed to think she'd taken too much sleeping-draught."

Instant concern was registered on the faces of all her listeners. Joseph recovered first. "Well, she wasn't any chicken and I dare say she didn't realize what she was doing."

"You don't understand," said Caroline desperately. "I saw her take the sleeping-draught—and I know it wasn't too much."

CHAPTER ELEVEN

IT WAS the indefatigable Mrs. Hunter who insisted on ringing up Roger. She had heard him mention the address where he was staying, and commandeering the telephone, she sat grimly with the receiver at her ear, refusing to be intimidated by rudeness, impatience or blank ignorance, until she obtained her connection. When she did she said in an excited conspiratorial whisper, "This is Mrs. Hunter speaking from The Downs. You'd better come at once. Something's happened. The old lady's dead and they think there's something fishy. They won't say as much but I know."

"I wouldn't put it past Jock to put arsenic in her coffee," said Roger coolly. "Is it arsenic poisoning she's supposed to have died of?"

"No one knows, but there's going to be an inquest, and they're all going round with faces as long as fiddles. One thing, once this is over, Caroline can start living her own life."

"How's Caroline taken it?"

"Like something in a tale—turned to stone. The Anstruthers have got hold of her. I don't trust that gang. And that Miss Twiss just sits in her chair looking like—who's that woman with the smile?"

"Mona Lisa?"

"That's the one. Might mean anything and probably hasn't got an ounce of brain behind it. But it's annoying just the same. You come along and cheer Caroline up."

"Is she frightfully depressed? I mean ..."

"Now, don't you go playing the innocent with me," Mrs. Hunter adjured him. "You know as well as me what nasty minds people have, and there's no denying the old lady had played her a very nasty trick. If ever a girl earned her money . . ." She broke off abruptly. She had heard a door close, and looked up to see Miss Twiss unhurriedly mounting the stairs. "Well, come anyhow," she said, "and come soon or you'll find they'll already have started saying Caroline poisoned her auntie for what was in it for her."

As she hung up she had a second shock. Jock appeared apparently from thin air and, taking up the telephone, asked for the number of a local tradesman. "Mrs. Anstruther is very anxious there shouldn't be any fulish talk about Lady Bate," he observed sternly. "There's enough in the world making trouble as it is." And before the outraged Mrs. Hunter could think of any reply, he had got his connection and was asking for information about fish prospects.

Roger arrived shortly afterwards. Cummings, he reflected, would find a story like this pure jam. Poor young ex-serviceman makes up to rich lady, persuades her to alter her will in his favor—that would be the press version—and dies as soon as she's seen her lawyer. The great point now—and one he'd got to ascertain as early as possible—was: Had Lady Bate signed the will? Knowing her tempestuous temperament, he thought it probable she'd made a clean sweep of the job when she was in town, and from what she had told him last night he believed this was so. After all, it only required a codicil, he reflected hazily. Then, the next point was: How much had Lady Bate confided to Caroline? If it blew up for dirty weather, and it looked uncommonly as though this would happen—a good deal might depend on whether she knew the exact position with regard to the old witch's money.

Caroline, questioned, said, "Oh, no, I'm sure she hadn't signed it. She said she was expecting to hear from Mr. Tritton."

"Did she in so many words say it wasn't signed?" Roger demanded, looking pale. "I certainly got the impression . . ."

"I can't be sure. I'm sorry, Roger, but so much has happened."

"The best thing you can do is come for a walk with me.

There's nothing to be done here at present. As for your lawyer chap, you can ring him up from a post office somewhere. It's much too early to hope to get him at present. And the last thing you want to do is sit round and listen to people gossiping...."

"An excellent suggestion," observed Joseph, appearing as if by magic. "Fresh air is the very best thing for the young lady. By the way, I take it you will be back in time to see any authorities who may wish to interview you?"

"Of course," said Roger, a little testily, "and we shall telephone Mr. Tritton from some local post office. But you may be sure we shall be back before his arrival."

He fetched Caroline's coat and the pair went out. "Now look here, Caroline," he implored her, "don't take this too much to heart. And don't listen to everything that well-meaning nincompoop, Mrs. Hunter, says. She's the kind that could find melodrama in a B.B.C. broadcast."

"You don't understand, Roger." Under her surface calm Caroline was desperate. "It couldn't have been suicide, and it wasn't natural death. And I don't see how it could have been accident."

"Foul play?" Roger whistled. "Mrs. Hunter said something over the phone but I didn't take it at its face value. It doesn't seem possible—though I have to admit if anyone on the premises was likely to be pushed over a cliff I'd have plumped for your aunt. She was a woman of striking character, no doubt, but she did manage to make the fur fly. How does the doctor think ... ?"

"An over-dose of sleeping-draught."

"Who could have got at that?"

"Anyone. It was kept in a drawer by her bed."

"She didn't keep the drawer locked?"

"No."

He considered that. "Who would be likely to know that she had it?"

"I'm not sure. She never minded talking about the things she took. I've heard her tell Mrs. Hunter that if everyone had the sense to take a dose of salts at night doctors would start lining

109

up for outdoor relief. She might have said something about the sleeping-draught, too."

"You never actually heard her?"

"No."

Roger considered. "That room was left more or less unprotected yesterday. You were out with Mrs. Hunter, Lady Bate and myself were in town—that leaves the Anstruthers, Miss Twiss and the servants.

"Oh, it's not as simple as that," cried Caroline. "I went up as soon as I came in, and again later when she sent me for her fur jacket. You remember?"

"I remember." He remembered, too, that she had been a very long time fetching it. He wondered who else would recall that when the inquiry began. "Of course," he went on, "there's motive..."

"The will," said Caroline. "What's the third thing?"

"Means, motive and opportunity."

There was a little pause. "I had them all, hadn't I?"

"The police will have to put up a lot better case than that. Now, don't get alarmed, Caroline. No one who knew you would dream of suggesting you were implicated."

"The police don't know me," said Caroline in a small voice.

"Still, these managing old women contrive to make a good many enemies."

"You don't go round poisoning people just because you don't like them."

"That's true. Why can't these old souls realize that no one likes to have his or her life arranged over his head? That was the root of her trouble. She was too infernally managing."

"She was trying to arrange your life for you, wasn't she?"

"Yes. Not that it would have worked. I happen to dislike interference, even where it's well-intended."

Caroline spoke in a tone of light bitterness. "You didn't seem to mind so much at the time."

"I think," said Roger awkwardly, "I'd better explain the position." Somehow he found Cummings was right, it wasn't easy to put the situation into words.

"I think I understand," said Caroline at last, "but it's a good thing Aunt Bate didn't know. She'd probably have died of apoplexy."

"I couldn't know that it was going to turn out this way," Roger protested. "That I was going to fall in love with you, I mean."

She looked at him steadily. "You never said that before."

"Even a howling cad of a journalist hesitates before proposing to an heiress-presumptive."

"Oh, Roger!" Caroline sounded contrite. "I've been thinking the beastliest things about you."

"I dare say you were justified."

"It was really because I couldn't bear to think badly of you, and I was so miserable. . . . Roger, if I really had put the stuff into the glass I'd have laid some evidence pointing to someone else, wouldn't I?"

"They might argue it showed great intelligence to do nothing of the kind. I believe that's one of Crook's contentions, that the successful criminals are those who commit their crimes and clear out. No false alibis, no false clues. Leaves all the work to the police, you see."

"Yes. As a matter of fact, there was some mystery about Aunt Bate and Mrs. Anstruther. I don't know what it was, but she certainly did practically what she liked. Why, she was talking of having a private sitting-room, which meant invading the Anstruthers' part of the house."

"What's Mrs. Anstruther like? I don't think I've ever seen her. A femme fatale?"

"I should think she must have been lovely when she was young. Do you think Sir Charles, Aunt Bate's husband, could have had an affair with her or something?"

"Hardly an inducement to live under the same roof, I should have thought," said Roger candidly. "Perhaps she was a gambler and was caught cheating at the tables. People seem to think that's much worse than murder."

"There's something anyhow. The two old gentlemen never let her go out alone, and Jock protects her from everyone—Aunt Bate's the only person who's ever got through to her at all—it does sound rather sinister."

111

"Perhaps she's dotty—or has homicidal tendencies. It'll all come out at the inquest, I suppose. Caroline, when does your doctor think the overdraught was taken? When she went to bed?"

"It couldn't have been then. I tell you, I saw her take the tablet. Could it have been in the coffee?"

"Shouldn't think so," murmured Roger dubiously. "It came in in a pot and she poured it out and we all had it, and neither of us is suffering from ill-effects. Besides, you took a tablet yourself last night, and you'd had the coffee, and still you weren't affected. Anyway, Lady Bate drinks her coffee black. If it had been mixed in anything, being a white powder it would probably be in the milk."

"That's it," exclaimed Caroline. "The milk she had with her tea. She insisted on tea at six o'clock, and when it came she said the milk was powdered, and she was going to complain about it."

Roger considered that suggestion, too, but regretfully discarded it. "Won't hold water," he decided. "If the powder was in the milk you couldn't leave it obviously floating on the top, and she wouldn't have more than two cups anyway. You couldn't be sure she'd take enough. Besides, that was six o'clock and she was as lively as a cricket at ten, and asking for sleeping-tablets because she was afraid of staying awake."

"You mean, she'd have been asleep long before? Yes, you must be right. Then how?"

"She didn't have a hot drink sent up to her room?"

"No. She said she was brought up in an age when women didn't pamper themselves, and anyway you had to consider the servants. That was a bit queer, coming from her."

"You're sure she had nothing after going to bed?"

"Only her salts. You don't think...Roger! But no, it couldn't be that. I mixed them for her myself."

Roger looked very grave. "What are the salts like, Caroline?"

"An ordinary white powder—like any other liver salts you see advertised so much on the hoardings."

"And the sleeping-tablets would crush into a white powder, I suppose."

112

"Y-yes. Yes, of course they would."

"Then if they were mixed with the salts . . ."

"But, Roger, I didn't, I swear I didn't."

"My darling Caroline, no one ever thought you did. But—that room stood empty most of the day. You admit that people knew about her taking the salts regularly."

"Oh yes. I remember Mrs. Hunter remarking that it was amazing how the old lady thought her intestines were more interesting than what you read in the newspapers."

"That opens a fresh avenue. Anybody could have got into the room during the day and taken possession of the tablets and added them to the salts. Are they in a bottle?"

"No. A cardboard box, each dose separately wrapped."

"Then you'd simply have to open one of the papers, add the fatal powder, probably not more than a pinch even if two or three tablets were crushed, and you'd be sitting pretty. Any way of knowing if the servants or the members of the household would know about the salts?"

"The box is on the table by her bed, with her name on it, and an instruction, one to be taken each night, just before retiring. Even if she did miss a dose one night she'd be sure to take it the next."

"Bit of a chance," said Roger. "Suppose *you* took one, and it was the fatal dose?"

"I suppose you always have to run a certain amount of risk when you're planning a murder," suggested Caroline gravely. "Roger, do you think Joseph Anstruther could have anything to do with it? He's a great crime fan, and he's always explaining how he'd bamboozle the police, if he were the criminal."

"Motive?" murmured Roger.

"I don't know—yet. But he's the one most likely to appreciate the fact that, if anything did happen to Aunt Bate, I should be the obvious suspect. We've gone into all that—and we did have a sort of a row last night, and when Aunt Bate was in a rage you could hear her a mile away. I'm sure Mrs. Hunter would be able to repeat our conversation word for word. You know, Roger, if you just read this case in the paper, your first idea would be that I had a hand in it."

113

"Not once I'd seen you. And anyway, Caroline, you don't have to start getting in a sweat till you've been accused of the crime. Do you suppose that hulking lawyer of yours will be at his office yet? We might as well try from the next telephone we can find."

A path to the left led to Bellington, where they obtained their connection at the local post office. Bellington is famous for the little gray church tourists come miles to see. It was a squat gray structure, insignificant enough from without, but once, long ago, the sea had flowed up the High Street and into the church, and the ancient pillars still bore fossilized imprints of the fish that had come pouring through the door. Roger went inside while Caroline telephoned. There was an old gallery at the west end, and the tomb of a crusader in the northern aisle. It made present troubles seem remote until he came back into the sunlight and found Caroline in the porch.

"He's coming down at once," she told him. "Oh, ¸there's no doubt about it, he's absolutely horrified. He kept saying, 'But she was so well yesterday, Miss Bate. It's—it's incomprehensible. I suppose it was heart failure, but . . .' and of course I had to tell him it was an overdose, and he said, 'But she was the most careful of women, and she was waiting to sign her will. She would never have allowed herself to make such a tragic mistake at such a time.' I laughed there, and he was more shocked than ever. But I couldn't help it, Roger, I couldn't help it."

"All right," said Roger, "hold on. It's quite natural for him to be surprised, you know. I bet wherever she is, Lady Bate's surprised, too."

"Oh, Roger, don't. I said there was going to be a post-mortem, and that means an inquest. Shall I have to give evidence?"

"Sure to, I should think. Anyone who saw her last night will probably be called in, and certainly the person who claimed to be the last to see her alive. All the same, if the police really think it's foul play, they'll play canny. Probably only ask for evidence of identification so that funeral can take place, and then get the inquest deferred while they make further inquiries. Of course, if they don't suspect any particular person they may leave it to the coroner's jury, assuming he sits with one, to come to a decision. However, Tritton's the best chap to give you advice. What's he like, by the way?"

Caroline looked dubious. "I've only seen him once. A neat little man with a buttoned-up mouth. He said he was coming down at once. We ought to be back before he arrives."

"Quite so. Where the body is there are the vultures gathered together. All the same, you don't want to hang about the premises a target for those two harpies." (He meant Mrs. Hunter and Miss Twiss.)

"He said one rather odd thing. I'd been explaining the position and asked him if he thought the police would be called in, and he said—he said if they were I should be quite in order to refuse to answer any questions until I'd seen my lawyer. That sounded rather sinister to me."

"These legal chaps are all the same," said Roger, with an ease he was far from feeling. "All the same, it's amazing what the police can make out of next to nothing. The Minister of Food ought to call 'em in when his department's in difficulties."

"He made it sound very menacing."

"It isn't he who's made it menacing," said Roger soberly. "It is menacing, and there's no getting away from it."

CHAPTER TWELVE

ROGER WAS NOT the only person to take this point of view. When the young couple reappeared at The Downs they found Mrs. Hunter in the hall, capering about like a flea in a gale of wind. The instant she saw Caroline she swooped down upon her.

"Have you seen anyone except that young man?" she demanded.

"No. We've been on the Downs. There wasn't anything else to do."

"Quite right. Now, my dear, I'm going to give you a bit of good advice. Don't answer any questions until you've seen your lawyers."

Caroline looked more startled than ever. "That's what he said when I rang him up. I told him I didn't know anything."

"My dear Caroline, you've no idea how much you know until you see it written down in black and white by a policeman. Besides, they're like the men who make up the crossword puzzles. That's what Alfred used to say. Out to catch you out if they can. I'm sure it's not your fault if your auntie lost her head. We all know she was in a tantrum last night. I heard her bawling you out when I came past your door."

"Whichever way you look at it it doesn't make sense," said poor Caroline.

"You leave it to the police. They're like the White Queen who could believe six impossible things before breakfast."

Mrs. Anstruther sent a message to say that if Caroline preferred she could have lunch with the family, but Caroline refused.

If there really had been a murder committed she didn't want to find herself with members of the household. A policy of complete silence was surely the best for anyone connected with this miserable affair. She didn't even suggest to Roger that he should stay, because lawyers are notoriously suspicious, and Mrs. Hunter would have no scruples about putting questions to him as to his impression of the case. So off Roger went, saying that Mr. Tritton knew where to find him, if necessary, and in any case they'd meet at the inquest. Lunch was just being served when Mr. Tritton arrived by car, and since he made it clear that he couldn't be asked to lunch with the boarders a small table was put into a sitting-room in the other part of the house, and he and Caroline lunched *à deux*. It was obvious that he was very much put out. When he heard what Caroline had to tell him, in detail, he was more disturbed than ever.

"A coroner's jury—and I don't see how we're to avoid that— won't like this at all, Miss Bate," he warned her. "I admit that suicide isn't a pleasant thing to happen in a family, but it's a great deal better than foul play."

"I was talking to Roger Carlton this morning," said Caroline, "and he says he doesn't see what alternative verdict there is."

The offended Mr. Tritton made it understood that he couldn't be expected to take a layman's opinion seriously. He didn't like the position and he said so frankly; when he added up the sum total of Caroline's answers he felt positively ill.

"You must appreciate that if the jury bring in a verdict of murder—no sense balking the word, Miss Bate—it's going to be most unpleasant sifting the evidence. The only people who had access to the tablets and the powders were the people responsible for this establishment, their employees and presumably your fellow-guests. Now as to motive . . ."

Caroline stifled her impatience. She had been thoroughly over this ground with Roger, but common sense assured her that it was unwise to antagonize your legal adviser, so she patiently answered questions about her last conversation with her aunt, and was rewarded by seeing Mr. Tritton look more gloomy than ever.

"Did anyone overhear any of this—disagreement?" he inquired.

"I think—probably Mrs. Hunter—anyway, part of it."

"Is she likely to be called as a witness? I gather from what you have told me that she is a fellow-guest here."

"Yes. I don't know if she'll be called or not. I'm sure she wouldn't want to do me any harm. She always has seemed very friendly—and sympathetic."

"In my experience, Miss Bate, more harm is done by well-meaning witnesses than by any other kind. What precisely do you mean when you say she has been sympathetic?"

"About my aunt, I mean."

"About her poor health, do you mean?" Mr. Tritton looked puzzled.

"I don't think she ever thought of her as having poor health. No, about her being rather—difficult sometimes."

"You mean—as affects you?"

"Yes."

Mr. Tritton frowned. "I hope she will have the good sense to keep that to herself if she should be called. Now, Miss Bate, I cannot disguise from you the fact that this is a most unfortunate situation. I can only counsel you to be as brief as possible in answering any questions that may be put to you by the authorities, either at the inquest or subsequently, and I do urge you not to put forward any suggestions of your own."

After lunch he got into touch with Dr. Kent, who told him tersely that he had informed the coroner of his suspicions and that a post-mortem was being performed. When the result of this was known the inquest would be arranged. The long afternoon dragged on. Mr. Tritton, aware that no action was likely for the remainder of the day, booked a room at the Down Hotel a short distance from the house, and spent a considerable time telephoning to London, all of which charges would, of course, go down on Caroline's bill. There would be some difficulty about arranging for the funeral in Manchester, and he recalled that Lady Bate had expressed herself very strongly on the subject of cremation. If, as seemed probable, this developed into a Crown case, there was bound to be a good deal of highly undesirable publicity, and

he considered whether he should not arrange for a London firm
to send a hearse and make the necessary arrangements. However, transport difficulties were still pretty acute, and eventually
he went into Brightlingstone and explained the position to the
head of an undertaking firm there. He had actually known of a
case where a coroner had given instructions to a local firm to
make burial arrangements, and he had no intention of being
over-ridden. The manager he interviewed seemed what Mr.
Tritton described as a sensible, gentlemanly sort of fellow, who
clearly thought that if the post-mortem should reveal traces of
an overdose the responsibility would be the old lady's. He
queried whether it would be possible to take the coffin by road,
but assured Mr. Tritton of his very best services, and promised
that, if this suggestion was "not feasible," a representative of the
firm would see the coffin off at the station and travel on the same
train to Manchester.

Mr. Tritton returned later in the day to The Downs to find
an atmosphere of acute tension. Caroline and he had tea together, and as she passed him the sugar she said, "It's extraordinary, isn't it, one's always reading of things like this, but they
never seem to register? I mean, they happen to other people,
never to oneself. I was thinking . . ." She laughed a little.

"My dear Miss Bate, it is of paramount importance that you
should keep control of your feelings," Mr. Tritton told her.
"This tragic event . . ."

"I was thinking," explained Caroline, "that sugar looks so
innocent, her salts looked so innocent last night . . ."

"Salts? What are you saying?" He looked round apprehen-
sively as if he expected the walls to part and reveal a listening
ear. "We don't know yet that your aunt did actually die of an
overdose, and even if the post-mortem proves that she did, we
don't know that the fatal draught was given in the salts."

"I can't see how else it was given," protested Caroline.

"My dear young lady, that will be a problem for the authorities. Once again, I do urge discretion. Your observation about
the sugar, for instance . . ." He eyed the bowl with distaste.
People shouldn't put ideas of that sort into your mind. Anyway,

119

he had been meaning to adjure sugar for a bit. He was getting altogether too plump. He pushed the bowl aside.

"No, no sugar," he said quickly.

"You see," said Caroline. "You're beginning to feel it, too, a sense of insecurity, I mean. I've had it ever since I heard about Aunt Bate. Suppose it was foul play—oh, it's all right, there's no one else here—and suppose whoever it is wants everyone to think it's me, as of course they must? Well, if I were out of the way, how that would simplify matters."

"I do sincerely hope you won't say this sort of thing to anyone else," exclaimed Mr. Tritton in great distress. "It would certainly prejudice your position. After all, innocent people have nothing to fear."

("D'you mean to tell me he said that and didn't drop dead on the spot?" demanded a scandalized Mr. Crook at a later stage of the proceedings. "You know, there are times when I'm tempted to wonder if there's any justice left on earth.")

Later still information was received that the inquest would be opened on the following day. They weren't losing any time, reflected Roger grimly. Going it hammer and tongs to get the result through the same day. The girl Gladys and Jock had been subpoenaed to attend the inquest alone of the household side of the menage, but Joseph Anstruther turned up among the spectators. Caroline, Roger, Mrs. Hunter—they were all there.

After evidence of identification the inquest was deferred till the result of the post-mortem was known. And after that, it having been established that death was not due to natural causes, the police came on the scene, making inquiries. They took away the bottle of tablets and the box of powders and went through all their routine experiments. The box gave them no results, but the bottle showed fingerprints of the dead woman and Caroline, but no one else. These prints were recent and clear. They interviewed various members of the household as well as Roger Carlton, in short, to use a colloquialism, they left no stone unturned. Their search exasperated the Colonel, who had to be calmed down by his brother.

"They're only doing their job," he said. "They've got to be satisfied how the old woman died."

Mrs. Hunter was the only person who took no exception to their presence. She had the exuberant personality that Crook was later to recognize, and everything that happened possessed for her its own peculiar value.

"They're like that woman in the Bible who lost a piece of silver," she confided to Caroline. "Turned the whole place upside down and gave a party when she found it. Humph! I always knew she wasn't Scotch. The party must have cost twice as much as the value of the silver. What do you suppose they're really looking for? Do they imagine we all have poison bottles hidden under our mattresses?"

The police, sensibly enough, were taking no chances. It was reasonable to assume that the old lady had died of an overdose of her own sleeping-draught, but there was a 100 to 1 chance that there were other agencies on the premises. And it was their experience that it doesn't do to rely solely on reason. In point of fact, their search produced no satisfactory alternative. Gladys and Miss Twiss had aspirins, Mrs. Anstruther produced a harmless sleeping mixture, not much stronger than a bromide and certainly not capable of causing Lady Bate's death, and—this was the most promising of their discoveries—there was a supply of morphia concealed in Colonel Anstruther's bedroom.

The Colonel was furious at what he called their damned interfering ways, nor would he be apologetic when questioned as to his silence on the point.

"Tell you? Of course I didn't tell you. Why should I? The stuff had nothing to do with Lady Bate's death."

He admitted under pressure that he was suffering from an incurable disease, which was progressively serious, and his doctor had recently given him a supply of morphia for emergencies.

"He knows I'm safe, shan't be likely to overdo it," the old man added.

"Do you give yourself the injections?" asked the police.

The Colonel looked as if he could hardly credit such insolence. "Mostly," he said at last.

"Who else . . . ?"

"My brother knows about it and so does my daughter. The doctor considered it wise for me to take them into my confidence.

Both could give me an injection in an emergency, but I'm not helpless yet, thank God."

And after all, it was proved that this drug could have played no part in the tragedy. When the adjourned inquest was resumed the medical evidence showed that the old lady had died of an overdose of her own sleeping-draught, and a wooden-looking local jury brought in a verdict of wilful murder against Caroline Bate. They seemed impressed by the fact that her aunt had had enough poison to kill three people, arguing from this that it had been administered by an amateur.

"Well, there aren't any professional murderers on the premises," said Mrs. Hunter sensibly.

This verdict was what most people had anticipated. A composite picture had been built up of a pretty pampered girl finding herself about to be disinherited and flung on a not particularly sympathetic world where training and experience were all. Even if she had contrived to keep her head above water it would have been a scanty existence for one accustomed to Lady Bate's standards. Mrs. Hunter had unwittingly blackened the picture by describing the scene she had overheard on her way to bed, and the girl, Gladys, said sullenly that the old woman was a terror, led her niece a dog's life, and any girl would be glad of a chance to get out. Also she had lost a ring a week or two previously and had made some very nasty insinuations. True, the ring had turned up within twenty-four hours, but that didn't alter the position. Mrs. Hunter had added that the old lady had been trying to come between Caroline and her boy-friend and altogether no one could blame the jury for their verdict.

The family gave the briefest evidence conceivable, their main reply being, "I'm afraid I can't help you. I have no information on that point." They never went into the guests' part of the house, they explained, and the old gentlemen didn't so much as know which was Lady Bate's room. Mrs. Anstruther admitted that she had met the dead woman some years before at an hotel abroad, but their acquaintance had been of the slightest, and she could offer no practical assistance.

Only, in the instant of silence that followed the jury's verdict, Caroline, incredulous, white-faced, swaying where she stood, faced them all crying desperately, "But no, no. I didn't do it. You can't say that. I didn't do it. I—didn't—do—it."

It was all horribly painful and Mr. Tritton felt the need of a strong double whisky. It was typical of post-war Britain, he felt, that it should be out of hours.

$\mathcal{C}$HAPTER $\mathcal{T}$HIRTEEN

IT WAS nine o'clock in the morning and Mr. Crook had already been at work for more than an hour. Mr. Tritton would have been highly indignant had he known. Ruining the market for respectable solicitors, he'd have said. But then he would have considered Mr. Crook a disgrace to his profession in any case.

Criminals, Crook remarked to Bill Parsons, seemed to have picked up a lot during the war; they'd had advantages—travel broadens the mind, he quoted—that hadn't come the way of the police, stuck in their home town for six years. Foreign manners were impinging on the natural enterprise of the Briton, and at that moment Crook claimed that there were six unsolved murders in the London area alone.

"And four of 'em domestic," he added juicily. "Husbands and wives—well, it's the most natural form of murder. If X is a born murderer the person with most opportunity for putting him out of the way is going to be X's husband (or wife); and if he's just an unpleasant feller, then his wife's goin' to suffer more from his unpleasantness than anyone else because she sees more of him. It's all this new education," he went on chattily. "In the old days the peeler went round his beat like a dormouse round a wheel—round and round and round. And if anything queer was happening he saw it. Now we have a gent with a 'varsity voice sitting in a flying squad car at the corner readin' philosophy and waitin' for a call. . . ." He shook out his morning paper, glanced at the ravishing headlines and announced, "Blimy, they've done it again."

124

"Murder?" asked Bill with no particular interest. He regarded crime as bank clerks learn to regard bank-notes, just part of the day's work.

"This Bate case. They've arrested the girl."

"Obvious thing to do," suggested Bill.

"And trust the Home Office to do the obvious thing. One thing, there ain't many Government Departments that can say as much."

About twenty minutes later someone came barging into the office and said to Crook, "I dare say you don't remember me, Mr. Crook, but . . ."

"Chap called Carlton. Met you with Cummings at the Blue Boar." His interest sharpened suddenly. "Don't tell me this is your old dame. Well, you can't say I didn't warn you."

"You told me if ever I was in a jam to come to you."

"And are you?" asked Crook with interest.

"The fools have taken Caroline Bate."

"And don't you agree with them?"

"It's ridiculous. She wasn't that sort of girl."

Crook shook his head. "It don't do to generalize—not about murder. There's no knowing who may fall by the way."

"But—there's no sense in it."

"Old lady left a packet, didn't she? And she hadn't signed the new will."

"Then Caroline must have known that if anything should happen she'd be the obvious suspect."

"That's the trouble with amateurs. They're so infernally conceited. They don't think anything will go wrong. Besides, try and see the police point of view. Who else might have had a hand?"

"Anyone in the house," suggested Roger recklessly.

"You mean motive?"

"And opportunity."

"I grant you opportunity, but motive's a bit more difficult, ain't it?"

"Come to that, I might have done it myself," said Roger. "I was up in the room that night."

125

"Doin' what?"

"She asked me to fetch her a letter. At least, she asked Caroline and I volunteered." He looked hard at his companion. "That strike you as sinister?"

"Don't seem to have impressed the police. How long were you up there and who noticed you go?"

"As a matter of fact I just grabbed the letter and fled, but . . ."

"Nothing doing." Crook shook his great red head. "You were in London all day. You didn't come down till after she did. You didn't go upstairs till after dinner. You just went into the room and came out again. We had the perfect witness on the premises—Mrs. Hunter. I always say a nosey witness is worth the twelve apostles lumped together. She noticed the girl took a long time fetching the old dame's coat, didn't she?"

"You'd have to be blind and deaf not to have noticed, the way old Lady B. pitched into her when she came back."

"All the same, the odds are Mrs. H. would have noticed if you'd been a long time, if only by way of contrast."

"That means, does it, that *you* think Caroline's guilty?" Roger's voice was a blend of incredulity and scorn.

Crook shrugged his broad shoulders. "That don't enter into it. You tell me to show she didn't, and I'm your man. Remember what Mark Twain used to say? Git the facts and then arrange them how you please. Some—the police—like one pattern. You and me like another. You pays your money and you takes your choice. Every time a blood-orange or a good see-gar."

"You mean, you don't really care if your clients are innocent or guilty?"

"My clients are always innocent. Otherwise, they wouldn't be my clients. Now, come down to brass tacks. Wasn't this young lady represented at the inquest?"

"A piece of limp elastic called Tritton was there, but he was old Lady B.'s lawyer, and anyhow he was like those females who claim to oblige and spend most of their time assuring you they never had to soil their hands before they came to you, but . . ."

"I know. Anyway, I can see he's no good or you wouldn't

be here. He'd have been up and doin' already. The fact is, Carlton, it don't do to be a gentleman in our line of business. It's
the essence of gentility to play safe, not, as you said just now,
to get your hands soiled. Now mine have been down in the muck
so often they know the feel of it. What horse are you backin' in
this run of the Murder Stakes?"

"I wouldn't like to put a name to it right now," returned
Roger cautiously, "but there's something odd about the whole
business. Old Lady B. was a terror, no doubt about that, she'd
been shot out of so many hotels she had cauliflower ears. But
she told Caroline she was settled at The Downs for life. Don't
tell me that was because she was popular. If you'd seen the looks
that fellow, Jock, used to give her, you'd wonder she didn't
shrivel, till you remembered she was made of granite. The fact
is, she had some hold over Mrs. Anstruther . . ."

"Fairy tales?" asked Crook, lighting a cigar and offering his
visitor a cigarette. "This ain't Fleet Street now, you know."

"It was obvious," Roger insisted. "She used to give orders
all over the place. She wanted this and that, a separate table, she
was asking for a separate sitting-room. And she let on to Caroline that she'd known Mrs. Anstruther years ago—met in the
same hotel, I gather—when her name wasn't Mrs. Anstruther."

"You may have got something there," acknowledged Crook.
"On the other hand, seein' they were acquainted . . ."

"It wasn't an acquaintance Mrs. Anstruther was anxious to
acknowledge. Not to put too fine a point on it, it was blackmail.
Come to think of it, it isn't likely Mrs. Anstruther would marry
a man of her own name, and of course that sort of household
always get gossiped about locally. Apparently she went away to
get married years ago, and one morning she turned up as cool as
ice-cream and settled down with her father. The secret of Lady
B.'s hold over her must lie in those years when she was Mrs.
Someone Else."

"Somethin' pretty drastic if Lady B. could retain a hold after
all that time."

"That's how it struck me. Another thing. She never has
visitors, never goes away, hardly goes out. Jock does the shop-

ping and when she takes the car the whole family go. It's one thing to tackle a lone widow, but quite another when she's got those two old battle-axes for a bodyguard, to say nothing of Jock. He's a tough customer if you like. Cut your throat with a razor and then curse you for blunting the blade."

"If you've got your facts right," suggested Crook, "anyone of 'em might have done it. I wonder if she'd taken the men into her confidence."

"They all had an opportunity. The room was open. Caroline and Mrs. Hunter were out the greater part of the day, the servants would be downstairs after, say, eleven-thirty. The tweeny had an afternoon off, Mrs. Mack was so fat she never went upstairs at all, even slept on the ground floor. There's another thing. The coroner pointed out that the only fingerprints found on the bottle of sleeping-tablets were the old lady's and Caroline's, and they were both very clearly defined. He used that to show that no one else had touched the bottle, but—supposing X had wiped it clean after abstracting the necessary tablets, as he would if he knew anything about police procedure . . ."

"And Joseph has a crime library and murder is his hobby—oh, yes, I get you."

"I mean, if it hadn't been touched for weeks, as Caroline said, and if it stood about on that little table, surely the hussy who cleans the room would have moved it . . ."

"Half a shake," said Crook, "you've got that wrong, haven't you? As far as I remember, the tablets were kept in a drawer."

"H'm." Roger considered that. "Still, I don't think it makes much difference really. The drawer wasn't locked and a girl of that type would be pretty certain to examine anything she could lay hands on. The point I'm trying to make is that it isn't natural for those fingerprints to be so clear. The glass itself was pretty clear, too, whereas if it had been lying about in a drawer it would have been smeary."

"I wonder why the heck you called me in," said Crook, a little huffed, "seeing you have it all so pat."

"I've given you all I've got," Roger told him. "The rest is yours. Though how the deuce you're going to prove anything if the rest of the household stick together, as I'm pretty damn sure they will, is beyond me. But, as you've just been kind enough to point out, I'm only the amateur."

"If that's the case it's going to be a whale of a job bringing it home to one of them," said Crook unpromisingly. "And just stirring up enough suspicion to get your girl acquitted on a not proven verdict ain't good enough. They're just regarded as the lucky ones that got away with it, not the unfortunates that were wrongly accused. If, as you say, the others are all goin' to cover up for each other, it's goin' to be a deuce of a job catchin' 'em out, but once they know Arthur Crook's on the warpath the odds are they'll start trying to lay a false scent and that'll be my chance."

"They weren't born yesterday," Roger warned him. "Old Joe Anstruther has his head screwed on all right, and I'd be surprised if the Colonel was in on this. But Jock and Joseph and the lady—and there's an old body called Twiss no one, not even Winnie Hunter, who could get truth out of a Government Department, has been able to place."

"You leave it to me," said Crook, "and when I say leave it I mean leave it. You get back to your writin' or whatever it is you do and I'll go ahead on the detectin'. Then we'll both be earnin' our bread and jam."

Crook, who liked his jokes to be very simple, was fond of saying that his favorite pub was the Fountain Head. He said you might get a bit of something useful at the Rumor and Gossip, but the Fountain Head was your safest bet. And if he was going to make anything of this case against Caroline Bate he must see her and find out if she had anything more to tell him about the mysterious link between the dead woman and Rose Anstruther. But first of all, as a matter of etiquette, he went to call on Mr. Tritton. Roger had prepared him for a blank-wall mentality, and when he met his fellow-practitioner he thought rudely, "Another little Strube-like figure linin' up in the queue."

Mr. Tritton had heard of Mr. Crook. Probably the lawyer didn't exist who hadn't; but he couldn't for the life of him think what that breezy (though admittedly efficient) vulgarian wanted in his refined office.

"Representing Roger Carlton," explained Mr. Crook. "This Bate case, you know. If Caroline Bate don't swing the bloods 'ull be out for someone to stand in her shoes."

"And you think their choice might fall on Mr. Carlton? Really, Mr. Crook, I find that rather far-fetched."

"Ever backed an outsider?" asked Crook. "They do sometimes come home, bringin' the bacon. By the way, you actin' for the girl?"

Mr. Tritton became very fussy and discreet. "That is hardly possible. Naturally, she will require adequate defense, but in the circumstances it would hardly be suitable for me—you see, I acted for her aunt for many years, and if I were to accept such a—accept Miss Bate as a client—it might seem as though I were—er—betraying my trust."

"You mean, you think it's your job to bring Lady Bate's murderer to justice?"

"No, no, Mr. Crook." Mr. Tritton looked shocked. "That is for the police. But I could not feel—er—happy attempting to achieve an acquittal for a dependent who has been accused of her death."

"Meaning you think she did have a hand in it?"

"I must admit that I found myself in agreement with the coroner and the jury. It is a classic case, a girl who never had to do a hand's turn for herself . . ."

"Only because the old lady saw to it that she spent every blessed minute turnin' hands for her benefit," interrupted Crook rudely.

Mr. Tritton looked offended now as well as shocked. "Naturally, as a rich woman she expected some return for her money . . ."

"Ah well," said Crook, getting up to indicate that he had no more time to waste, "she's got more than she bargained for."

"And in any case," wound up Mr. Tritton, also rising, both looking and sounding uneasy, "no one else had motive. Murder's a serious crime."

"You're telling me," said Crook, clapping his loud brown bowler over his aggressive red-brown eyebrows. "As for motive, what you really mean is that so far the police haven't bothered to look beyond Miss Bate. They're like the chap who set out to propose marriage, met a rabbit on the way, got to thinking about large families, and went home and died a bachelor. Mind you, I don't say he wasn't right; but it just shows you what can happen when a fellow lets the first thing in the road pull him up short. The police didn't think of anyone else, because they found one person who seemed to fit the bill, so what the hell? Now, I'm bein' paid to show that if they'd gone a bit further they might have found something that would surprise 'em. No, don't ask me what it is, because I don't know, and if I did I wouldn't tell you."

Striding out, he made his way to Victoria and caught the next train to Brightlingstone, where Caroline was incarcerated in the local jail. The prison here is commonly held to be a model of its kind, and the inhabitants of the town point to it proudly, almost as if you might expect people to look forward to being taken there. In fact, one of the Hot Gospellers who paraded the sands at Brightlingstone on Bank Holidays, went so far as to censure the authorities for housing sin so comfortably. To those within the walls, however, the cheerful blue paint of the sanitary fittings and the vases of seasonal flowers placed in the entrance hall had very little effect. Prison was prison, and if you were waiting to be tried for your life all the amenities of Buckingham Palace would have made little difference. There is a theory that those facing some appalling catastrophe automatically develop the courage to meet it, the iron front, the steady gaze, the stiff upper lip. But if this is true, then Caroline was a lamentable exception to the rule. It would, indeed, have been difficult to recognize in this haggard, white-faced girl the happy young creature who ran out in all weathers to meet Roger Carlton. Crook's name obviously meant nothing to her. She had been informed she would have legal advice and adequate counsel (what these chaps want is a dictionary, said Crook. Adequate my Aunt Fanny's fat cat) when the trial actually came on, and she supposed that Mr. Crook, whose appearance at first glance aroused in her no sense of confidence whatsoever, was the State's notion of adequate legal defence. She was intensely frightened, and quite unable to conceal the fact. She came towards him, accompanied by the wardress, shocked, appalled, full of terror and mistrust.

"Your friend, Roger Carlton, sent me to see what I could do to help you," Crook told her heartily, offering a huge freckled hand like a ham, "and when I say help that's just what I mean. I've seen that worm, Tritton, and put that right, in case you think I'm abusin' professional privilege," he added encouragingly.

"Mr. Tritton thinks I'm guilty." The words were as colorless as her face.

"Well, there's no denying he has his doubts," Crook agreed. "But isn't that a bit of luck for you?"

The unexpectedness of his words aroused in her the first sign of energy she had shown since her arrest.

"Luck?"

"Yeah. If he'd wanted to fight the case for you you couldn't have refused. Old family lawyer and all that sort of thing, and then wouldn't you have been sunk? Not that his firm ever touch this sort of thing. Pitch and all that, you know. Besides, it don't do an attorney any good to get mixed up in a murder if he don't get his client off, and Tritton wouldn't convince a moron. So that leaves the field open for me, and believe me, sugar, by the time we're through you're goin' to be down on your marrowbones thankin' the Almighty He lets fools survive. Now, there's one thing you've got to get into your head right away, and that is—we're partners, and me, I've never gone bankrupt yet. Got me?"

"Do you mean you think I—I have a chance?" She was dazed at the bare suggestion. It was like watching the flicker of a newly-kindled candle. First the flame wavers, burns so low it is almost extinguished, then feebly straightens itself.

"A chance?" said Crook in good-humored contempt. "It's a certainy if you help me. I tell you, my clients are always innocent. Only, mind, you've got to do your share. You know the layout of the house and I don't. You can't blame the jury for picking you for the job. It was anybody's choice. They couldn't see anyone else who'd benefit. But you and me we know there was someone else because . . ."

He paused encouragingly. "Yes?" breathed Caroline. It was like watching blood flow into an erstwhile paralyzed limb, seeing the hope come back into that hopeless, terrified face.

"Well, obviously somebody killed her and it wasn't you. Now, your young man's got a story about your auntie knowing this Mrs. Anstruther a long time ago, and knowing something about her that gave Lady B. the whiphand. Right?"

"I'm sure it's true. Only I don't know what it was. It was a very long time ago."

"About twenty years," agreed Crook. "So your boy-friend says. But what's twenty years?"

Caroline looked doubtful. "It wasn't quite as long as that, I don't think, about sixteen or seventeen. Anyway, Mrs. Anstruther won't tell you anything, I'm sure."

"Be your age," said Crook kindly. "Would you? If it was going to land you in the little covered shed?"

Caroline looked startled. "Oh, I don't say she . . ."

"That's all right. You don't have to say. That's what I'm here for. Trouble with amateurs is they always have too much to say. Now, you lived with the old lady most of your life, and she told you she'd met Mrs. A. before. She never dropped a hint as to what her hold might be?"

"Only that when she met her before she wasn't calling herself Mrs. Anstruther."

"Inference bein' that X wasn't all to the cream-puffs, she preferred to forget all about him and go back to her own name."

"And she said that Sir Charles—that was Lady Bate's husband—had admired her very much. And one day when I came back from a walk Aunt Bate and Mrs. Anstruther were talking in the hall and Aunt Bate said something about a husband and Mrs. Anstruther said 'You'll never forgive me for that,' and Aunt Bate said she was sure she—Mrs. Anstruther—was wise to come back and live quietly here, because even the English read newspapers, though most of them seemed incapable of reading anything else."

"Now that's a help," said Crook approvingly. "Your young man didn't mention that."

"I may not have told him," returned Caroline, instinctively defensive.

"The important thing is for you to tell me. You see where that gets us? There was something in the papers, and what was in the press once is there for ever. And of course, newspapers only print the truth." He winked at her. "You ask my friend, Cummings."

"The truth as they see it," amended Caroline, and he agreed carelessly well maybe she was right, only such a lot of them seemed to be squint-eyed.

"Where was this place? Riviera? Wonder how much damage has been done down there, if we could get hold of any records. Might get Bill to go over. He talks their lingo. Don't much care about all this getting around myself. I know what they tell you about travel broadening the mind, but my mind's broad enough for most people and that's a fact."

He seemed so pleased with himself that he infused a little of his enthusiasm into Caroline's despair. She spoke suddenly.

"You can't think what it was like," she said. "To know you hadn't done a thing, that you'd never even thought of it, and yet to be told you were guilty—and you can't prove you're not. You can't prove it. That's the terrible thing. You couldn't understand if it hadn't happened to you."

Crook gave her a paternal pat. "You trust your Uncle Arthur and stop havin' bad dreams," he advised her. "I believe in you and so does your young man, and surely that's enough to be goin' on with."

"I've just remembered something," said Caroline.

"That's the girl," approved Crook. "Let's have it, sugar."

Caroline began to tell him about her aunt's cuttings book. "She called it the history of her married life," she explained. "There might be something. He was a very distinguished person. Sat on boards and things."

"No wonder she was nicely padded. What was his line?"

"Flour. She said it was the safest of all investments, because you might have prohibition, and there would always be vegetarians, but even people who didn't eat bread ate biscuits, so you could never go out of business."

"I like the sound of that chap. Same like me. You can have the most perfect Government in the world—though, mind you, honey, I'm not saying that's what we've got at this minute— but even in Utopia you'll get crime, just to liven things up a bit, so the bad men'll always want lawyers. But you were saying?"

"Do you remember what I told you just now, about a husband? Well, suppose Lady Bate meant her own husband, there might be something in the book. And I remember something else. The first time she came back from seeing Mrs. Anstruther, and finding she was someone she had known before under another name, she got the cuttings book down and unlocked it. It has a sort of brass lock and she kept the key on a bracelet she always wore."

"The hidden places of the heart. Honey, you're fine. Who'll have the book now? What's happened to all your auntie's stuff?"

"I suppose Mr. Tritton will be looking after it. Mrs. Anstruther will want the rooms back for someone else."

"She won't have to advertise long. Put an advertisement in the window and they'll come in their queues; can't get in fast enough till they know I'm on the job, and then they won't be able to get out quick enough."

Caroline looked her perplexity.

"Y'see, sugar, I've got what you might call a reputation. And once they know I'm franking you, then they'll know whoever put the old lady underground it wasn't you, and if it wasn't you then it was someone in the house, and—would you choose to live in a place with a murderer on the premises? He—or she— might take a dislike to the next lodgers just the same way. And even if they don't think of that for themselves, you can bet Winsome Winnie will tell them. Now, let's go over a few points again—no sense leavin' any stone unturned and its' funny, the housin' shortage bein' what it is, what lives under stones these days—and then I'll beetle down to Sunbridge and see about that Big Business Bible you were speakin' of."

After he had taken himself off, as self-important and conspicuous as the Scourge, his unspeakable little red car, Caroline

135

said in wondering tones to the wardress, "He makes it sound as though it might be all right, after all. And I had begun to lose all hope."

"No sense in that," said the wardress. "Of course if you didn't do it you'll be all right. I've told you so from the start."

CHAPTER FOURTEEN

CROOK CAME roaring up to the door of The Downs like a fore-runner of the atom bomb, and pressed the bell as though he wanted to push it flush with the wall.

A furious Jock opened the door and said at once that Mrs. Anstruther was seeing no one.

"She's seein' me," Crook assured him blithely. "You can't refuse the police, y'know."

"You didn't say you were the police."

"My strength is as the strength of ten because my heart is pure," chanted Crook. "Not to deceive you, Mrs. 'Arris, I am not the police. But I am their antidote. Naturally Mrs. Anstruther don't want an innocent girl to hang, and I'm here to see she don't."

He refused to be put off with Jock's offer of himself as a substitute, but he didn't see Mrs. Anstruther. It was Joseph who came to meet him, and who exclaimed at sight of him, "Why, damme, I've met you at the Bull and Bush."

"Well, isn't that a coincidence?" exclaimed Crook. "Meet the Man Who Can Commit Murder and Get Away With It."

Joseph's eyes narrowed; his face hardened. "Joke, Crook?" he snapped.

"It's what you told me. And here we are with a murder on the premises, and the police, poor fish, barking up the wrong tree."

"Fish don't bark up trees," Joseph suggested, but Crook only replied, "You'd be surprised what the police can do when they get on the track, even when it's the wrong track."

"What can we do to help you?" Joseph inquired, his voice still very stiff. "You'll understand my niece has been just prostrated by what has happened. That girl, too. Mind you, I'm not saying she did it. She seemed a nice girl, what I saw of her. My brother's taken it hard, too."

"There's others besides the girl stand to gain a bit by the old lady's fadin' out," Crook assured him. "Mind you, I don't think there's any great harm, having the girl where you know she's safe. I often tell my clients to go and have a nice rest in a nursin' home and refuse to see anyone till the case is closed. But you know how people are about takin' good advice."

Joseph looked puzzled. "You mean, you think it's a good thing they arrested Miss Bate?"

"Now, don't you go pulling my leg, Major. You're a student of crime, you know that murder's like those snakes. You kill one and the mate comes up to join it, and you've either got to whack him over the head, too, or take the rap yourself. Once you start runnin' amok and puttin' your enemies out of the way, you'll find it don't often stop with one. I should know."

"So—you anticipate a second murder?"

"I'm always ready for it. You'd be surprised how many chaps ' have tried to put Arthur Crook out. Well, makes sense, don't it? Supposing you put out someone's light, and the police take the wrong chap, and then I come along to wipe the police's eye for them, what would you do, chum?"

"Send you to follow my first victim."

"Makin' it look like an accident. Right first time. Well, that's what we think X will do."

"You mean, you expect someone to make an attempt on your life?"

"Could be," said Crook. "Could be. Now see here, Major, I want to range among the old lady's things. Might be something that 'ud give me a line."

Joseph looked hesitant. "I'm not sure what's happened to them. That fellow, Tritton . . ."

"All I want to know is—are they here or have they been shifted?"

"Her room hasn't been touched. Tritton said he was busy, he'd come down when he could. He took the jewelry, I understand, but the clothes and so forth—well, you know what lawyers are. All burning to qualify for the Civil Service."

"Lead me to the telephone," said Crook simply. He made Joseph stand beside him while he obtained his connection, and later shoved the receiver up against his ear so as to hear Tritton say coldly that he had no objection to Mr. Crook making any necessary examination, though he, Tritton, would expect to be kept informed of any articles Crook might wish to remove.

Crook hung up the receiver and trotted towards the staircase. If he'd followed his first hunch and gone to see Tritton in town, the odds were the little man would have telephoned to The Downs to announce Crook's coming, and the information would have filtered through, with the result that X would have had time and to spare to remove anything of a damaging nature. As it was, he had, in his own vulgar parlance, caught 'em on the hop, and now he went bouncing up the stairs in the direction of the visitors' apartments.

"Which was her room?" he inquired, and Joseph had to admit that he didn't know. He and his brother never came into this part of the house, and the only time they caught sight of their guests was when they chanced to see them from the long upper corridor.

"Matter of fact, the police went through everything with a tooth-comb," Joseph warned Crook.

"Maybe they're like the poor goof who found a diamond and thought it was a bit of glass."

Joseph looked at him suspiciously. "What is it you're looking for?"

"Matter of fact, there's a diary ..."

Joseph looked perplexed now. "You think she made a note of some suspicion? If so the police would have been on to it like winking."

"It could be that winking isn't the police's strong suit."

Joseph looked a little sulky. "I don't know anything about a

139

diary," he said, "but if it was here when she died, then it's here still. We've touched nothing."

They came out into the hall, where they were unexpectedly joined by the Colonel. He looked questioningly at Crook, who was instantly explained by Joseph.

"I'll ask my daughter if anything has been removed from Lady Bate's room," said the Colonel with polite and obvious dislike. He opened the drawing-room door. "My dear, there is a lawyer from town with permission from Tritton to examine some of Lady Bate's possessions."

Rose came into the hall. She'd been a looker once, thought Crook, though not his cup of tea, but she looked haggard enough now, and who could blame her?

"If we can help you . . ." she began. She had an odd air as of being one removed from life. What he could see of the room behind her was the same, remote, subtle-flowers, books and curtains, all stuff that would fetch a packet in the Black Market.

"I expect you've told the police all you know," suggested Crook resourcefully. "From all accounts, the old lady didn't go out of her way to make things easy, but some folk are born like that, putting their beetle-crushers on other chaps' necks, and I suppose by the time they're old it's become a habit."

"I didn't really know her well," said Mrs. Anstruther in a voice as remote as her appearance. "I met her many years ago in a hotel in the South of France, when we were both spending a holiday there with our husbands."

"That's right," encouraged Crook. "The girl told me her auntie had told her about you rooming together in the pipin' days of peace."

The Colonel looked a bit sick. No wonder the world was in a mess when chaps calling themselves lawyers went about talking this sort of jargon.

"Yes. As far as I remember she stayed about three weeks and then her husband had to go back to London. He was a business man. . . ."

"Let's hope he managed his business better than he managed her," remarked Crook in his painfully outspoken fashion.

"Oh, I think he knew how to get his own way. He was an

extremely successful man or so I've always understood. But Lady Bate was not a popular person, I don't think she wanted to be. . . ."

"I know," nodded Crook. "I'm not rude, I'm rich. Was she stayin' here permanently?"

"She seemed very satisfied with her conditions. I'm afraid it's unquestionably true that she did tend to irritate the other guests, but both Miss Twiss and Mrs. Hunter are good-natured people, I understand, and no actual complaints were ever made. I had a certain amount of sympathy for the old lady. She had grown up in such a different age, she was accustomed to deference and service, and she found it almost impossible to acclimatize herself to modern conditions."

"Lucky to find anyone so sympathetic," was Crook's blunt retort. "Still, it all goes to show, don't it? She was exertin' all she knew to stay, and if only she could have seen round the corner she'd have realized she was safer in any other house in England than this one."

All three of her hearers were perceptibly startled by this example of plain speaking.

"May I ask, sir, what you intend to convey by that?" demanded the Colonel in his barrack-square voice. Crook, however, had been accustomed to sergeant-majors in World War No. 1, and it took a lot more than a colonel to intimidate him.

"Obvious, ain't it?" He even looked surprised. "I mean to say, here she died, and though I dare say she was a tough nut you've got to be right up against it before people start puttin' out your light."

"I can't believe that girl did it," said Joseph, "so young, so pretty," but Crook rounded on him at once, saying, "I'm surprised at you, Major. You should know it don't do to go by appearances. Look at criminal history, girls like angels looking as if butter wouldn't melt in their mouths, and the things they do 'ud bring a blush of envy to a butcher's cheek. If you'd said you couldn't believe she did it because Arthur Crook was frankin' her I'd see your point all right."

"Perhaps," suggested Rose with that gentle finality of which she was mistress, "we had better go up."

141

She led the way and the three men followed her. But as she paused outside the room Lady Bate had occupied, turning slightly to say, "I'm afraid this affair has rather demoralized the household; I can't answer for the condition of the room," the Colonel exclaimed in slightly testy tones, "My dear, I'm afraid we're all a little demoralized. This isn't the right room."

Rose's hand fell from the door-knob. "What are you saying, Father? Of course it is." She looked at him in perplexity. "I didn't know you knew which rooms the guests occupied," she added.

"If you're sure you're right, then I've been suppressing evidence all this time," was the Colonel's grim retort. "Naturally it never occurred to me it had any significance—in fact, I'd forgotten all about the incident until this moment."

"Stop talkin' like one of these missin' clue crosswords," Crook begged him. "Why do you think this is the wrong room?"

"I'll tell you. On the afternoon that Lady Bate was up in town I was playing chess with you, Joseph, as usual, when I had an attack of nose-bleeding. It was sufficiently severe for me to go to the bathroom to get some cold water."

"If you'd let me put a key down the back of your neck as I wanted we need never have stopped the game," was Joseph's spirited reply.

"I don't hold with superstition," returned his brother.

Crook said heartily, "Neither do I. I don't know what surprise you're goin' to spring on me, Colonel, but if it helps to clear my client, then I'll swear off superstition for life."

"As I say," continued the Colonel, in a manner that said that in India a man would be hanged for less than this cavalier treatment of a superior officer, "I went upstairs to the bathroom, and then I went into my own room for a clean handkerchief. I remember that as I was coming away the grandfather clock began to strike four. You know what a sudden chime it is, startling even to those who're accustomed to it, and positively alarming to strangers or comparative strangers."

"Hardly alarming," demurred Joseph.

"It was alarming to this lady all right. But I must explain. Now I remember thinking we should just have time to finish

142

the game, which I was on the point of winning, before tea at 4:15, when my attention was caught by the sight of an elderly figure creeping along the passage and pausing in front of this door. As my daughter has just told you, I never meet any of the guests and shouldn't have recognized any one of them face to face, but this lady was noticeable because she wore a large grayish-blue shawl right over her head. You remember, Rose," he turned courteously to his daughter, "that small picture in a French gallery that we both liked so much many years ago. I think it was called 'The Shawled Figure,' and I immediately recalled it when I saw this lady open the door of this room in front of which we are now standing and enter, closing it carefully behind her."

Crook pricked up his large intelligent ears. "Didn't think of mentioning this to the police, Colonel?"

"I thought I had explained that. Good heavens, man, I had no reason to suppose there was anything unorthodox about the whole proceeding. This isn't a girls' school or a penitentiary. Our guests have the run of their part of the house for twenty-four hours of the day, and certainly it would never have occurred to me that there was anything peculiar about a lady visiting her own room at about tea-time. As I say, I haven't given the matter a thought till this moment."

All three listeners were impressd by his obvious sincerity, and it was only Rose who said, in a rather timid voice, "You couldn't possibly have been mistaken about the room?"

"I'd take my oath on it, and that's a thing I wouldn't do lightly, as you know."

"Damned odd," agreed Crook. "Did she stay there long?"

"Really, sir, I am not accustomed to hanging about outside ladies' bedrooms." The Colonel sounded outraged.

"Does you credit," said Crook heartily, and only Joseph was quick enough in the uptake to get his meaning. Hurriedly he smoothed over what might be an awkward situation.

"Careful, James. Mr. Crook will think your middle name's Lothario. Well, begum, this throws a bit of fresh light on things."

Crook stroked his aggressive chin with a huge freckled paw.

143

"No chance of you bein' mistaken? No, all right, all right. No offense. So it was Miss Twiss you saw?"

"I shouldn't have known that much—one of these ladies looks much the same as another to me—but of course when the police started making inquiries we were all questioned, and—yes, it was Miss Twiss."

"Know anything about the lady?"

"I? Certainly not."

Crook looked at Rose.

"I'm afraid this must strike Mr. Crook as a very unusual situation, but the fact is Jock interviewed all our prospective guests."

"Begin as you mean to go on," said the Colonel. "Give these folk half an inch and they'll take a mile. I only agreed to my daughter's scheme of letting rooms in the first place on the understanding that she wasn't to be plagued with the visitors."

"Jock said she seemed a decent body and not likely to make trouble, which were our main considerations."

"And that's all you know about her?"

"She looks a half-wit to me," said Joseph, who could be as direct as Crook.

"As I say, the clock struck four at that moment, and I don't mind admitting it gave me a bit of a start, though I'm used to it. But as for that woman—well, she nearly jumped out of her shoes at the sound. I didn't think anything of it, but now it looks to me like evidence of guilt. No reason why she should appear so startled if she was where she had a right to be."

"H'm. No friction between her and her ladyship that you ever heard of?"

"I gathered they scarcely spoke."

"Probably the old dame had collared the best chair or something like that. No, don't look that way. The Major here will agree with me that there's no reason too small for murder. I remember a girl once strangled her mistress when she was ill in bed because she wouldn't lend her a string of blue beads to wear to a dance. Besides," he added charitably, "these elderly ladies are often a bit bozo. Not their fault, poor girls, but that's the way it is, and p'raps she resented the old lady's attitude towards her niece. Reminded her of her own childhood or something."

"And she thought she would save the girl from a similar tyranny? Isn't that rather far-fetched, Mr. Crook?"

"So far you wouldn't catch me trying to lure it into court. But what was the old dame doing in someone else's room anyway?"

"I believe I can supply the motive," said Rose slowly. "At least, it's possible. Lady Bate used to wear very handsome rings and brooches," she added, turning to Crook, "and Jock told me once it was as good as a play to see Miss Twiss watching her. About a week ago Lady Bate complained that a ring she had left on her dressing-table had disappeared. It was exceedingly uncomfortable. She came to me in person. I asked her whom she suspected, and she said, as she naturally would, the servant. I asked for proof, and the whole matter was intensely disagreeable. The girl was questioned, and she flared up and asked if I thought she was a thief."

"Probably had it in her apron-pocket all the time," said the imperturbable Mr. Crook. "Ever noticed it's only guilty folk who get in a paddy when they're accused? The innocent ones are so certain of their virtue it don't seem to occur to them anyone will disbelieve their yarn."

"Oh no, you're quite mistaken, Mr. Crook. It was Miss Twiss who had it."

"Kleptomania?" Crook winked. "When it's a lady it's always kleptomania."

"She said she had found it in the bathroom."

"Maybe she did."

"Lady Bate was very angry because she kept it all day without returning it. Miss Twiss said she had forgotten she had it."

"It could be," acknowledged Crook in the tone of a man who wouldn't refuse to believe that pigs could fly.

"Jock tells me that precious stones are a sort of mania with her. I'm not suggesting there was any thought of dishonesty in her mind, of course, but I do wonder if she kept it deliberately for a few hours just for the pleasure of feeling she owned it just for that short time."

"Chaps have got a couple of years for less," was Crook's unsympathetic comment. "What are you drivin' at, Mrs. Anstruther? Thinkin' the lady may have been pickin' her chance and makin' another raid?"

"It did go through my mind," acknowledged Rose. "That would account for her being so jumpy, as father says she was."

"Wouldn't account for her murdering the old lady, though. Not unless she stood to gain something."

"Perhaps she did," said Joseph. "I wonder if anything is missing from Lady Bate's things. Would the girl know?"

"That lawyer chap ought to. He must have a list of her stuff for probate. All the same, I dunno how you'd ever prove that old Miss T. had anything that might be missing. She couldn't be such a half-wit as to hang on to the stuff once she realized the fat was in the fire."

"And of course Lady Bate did tell me she intended to keep everything under lock and key for the future."

They had been standing just inside the doorway while this conversation was in progress, and now they entered the room. It had a bleak clean look as of a place whence a body had just been removed. The bedclothes had been folded up and were covered with a cotton quilt, the dressing-board was bare, everything had been swept into a square cardboard box. Normally, of course, Caroline would have sorted the things by now, but Caroline was no longer available.

"Where did she keep her papers?" wondered Crook.

"There were some things in a drawer in the bedside table. The drawer was unlocked, which seems to show there was nothing particularly valuable in it."

"I understand there was a diary. I don't know whether that would help at all."

"There was," put in the Colonel. "The police examined it. But I understood from them it was simply a record of the late Sir Charles. He seems to have been an important chap in his own way—but the last records dealt with his funeral, the better part of twenty years ago."

"Old sins have long shadows," said Crook in his cheerfully

146

platitudinous way. "I'm always ready to put a couple of bob on an outsider."

He pulled open the drawer. The diary referred to was inside. Obviously the police hadn't thought it important enough to remove, and anyway at the time the last entry was pasted in Caroline hadn't even been a member of the household. It was a handsome morocco-bound volume with Diary stamped in gold letters on the cover. Mrs. Anstruther said something about the key, but Crook, tucking the book under his arm, said that 'ud be Bill's headache. He offered to leave a receipt for Mr. Tritton's benefit, but there were no takers.

"Do you really think that's going to provide you with a clue?" inquired Joseph, wishing he could establish a firmer relationship with this odd personality.

"I'm like the starving millions, no crumb's too small to be overlooked. Well, hang it for all, for the sake of my reputation I've got to put someone in the girl's shoes."

"There's the question of proof," suggested Joseph dryly, but Crook had no time for that sort of thing.

"Before I'm through I'll have got enough proof to hang an archbishop, even if it don't come out of this 'ere," he slapped the book under his arm. "Well, be seeing you."

And he stamped out like a whole regiment of Guards.

CHAPTER FIFTEEN

AFTER HE had gone with the Colonel to see him safely off the premises, Rose and her uncle looked at one another.

"I don't like it," said Rose. "That man suspects one of the household."

"My dear girl, don't lose your head. All he means is that he intends to get that girl off, and, as he explained to me, that involves finding another culprit."

"Do you remember the proverb he quoted? Old Sins Have Long Shadows? I knew the instant I set eyes on that woman she spelled trouble."

"I told you not to keep her."

"If I'd asked her to go she wouldn't have gone. Or not until she had ruined my reputation."

"Look here, my dear, I don't want to pry, but surely you can tell me what it is."

She turned to him with tragic intensity, the more remarkable and painful because she so seldom showed signs of deep feeling.

"Uncle Joseph, try and realize my position. That woman's connected with a part of my life I do my best to forget; sometimes I think I've succeeded and then, like a snake creeping out of the brushwood, the past steals up to me again, and I know I'm not safe, that I'll never be safe . . ."

"You mean your life with your husband, I suppose. But you couldn't help the feller being a rotter."

"It's not that. It's all the circumstances of his death."

"All the same, m'dear—I suppose being his wife makes you

148

see things twice as large as life—but he's not the first chap by a long chalk to shoot himself because he's come to grief at the casino. They're doing it all the time, or were up to the war, and they will again as soon as they get the chance. And, hang it all, it's a devil of a time ago."

"But, you see," said Rose, paying no attention to the last words, "Gerald didn't shoot himself. I shot him—and Lady Bate knew it."

There was an instant of appalled silence. Rose looked at the old face opposite hers and was smitten with a pang of self-hatred, and self-mistrust mingled with fear. She had kept the secret so long, she had played her cards so well that even the police authorities had never tried to find an alternative verdict. That Lady Bate would have ruined her at the time had that been possible she was well aware, but when she left the Riviera and returned to the tranquillity of The Downs she had allowed herself to believe that the past was indeed dead. There were so many million people in the world and so few, so infinitely few, ever came near that household, that surely it was beyond the bounds of probability for the one woman who knew the truth to track her down. Yet, Crook's influence being still with her and his habit of quoting cliches still coloring the atmosphere, she remembered—the mills of God grind slowly but they grind exceeding small. Of all the women who might have come for accommodation to this remote house, it had to be this dangerous woman from her past who broke through and resurrected the ghosts of that dreadful time. The police, the other guests at the Hotel Girofleur, her father, all had believed the story she had told. Gerald Fleming had been dead in his dishonored grave for so long he was now no more than a handful of brittle bone indistinguishable, except to the eye of the criminal expert, from any peasant or fisherman. Yet here he was returning to menace her as he had menaced her through the six wretched years of her married life.

She was recalled from her thoughts by the appalled voice of the old man.

"You know what you're saying, Rose?"

"Yes, Uncle Joseph."

"Then it's true?"

"Yes."

"Your father? Does he know?"

"I'd kill myself before I told him."

"That 'ud only be a form of indirect murder." Joseph's voice was grim. "You'd better tell me. How did this woman find out?"

"The first part of the story I told when I came back was quite true. Gerald was a desperate gambler. He took everything; he had no conscience, no remorse. But—I don't know if I can make you understand—he had charm, he could be irresistible. When he first told me he was in difficulties and didn't know where to turn, it seemed so simple to say, 'Take this ring, take this chain ...' I used to urge him to give up gambling but he said it was in his blood, he had the perfect system, one day he would justify it. I knew in my heart he was undependable, had no sense of money, no feeling of responsibility, but—I loved him, Uncle Joseph."

"You must have thought the world of him to have left your father the way you did," agreed Joseph gruffly.

"Yes. At the time it seemed the obvious thing to do. Nothing else, nobody else, mattered. Now I seem as if I must have been crazy, yet, given time over again, I dare say I should do the same thing. Even when my jewels went, when I knew that Gerald spent the money he got for them on drink and having a good time, I couldn't stop feeling that way about him."

"Never did understand women," growled Joseph.

"Though you may find it hard to believe me, other women envied me. Even those who realized what he was envied me. He was such a splendid figure of a man, he could be the most marvelous company, he made a woman feel as though she were queen of the universe. There aren't many men who can do that. He furnished a room by coming into it. I used to see people watching him wherever he went. When we were together they nudged each other—I hadn't lost my looks then—oh, I suppose I was besotted about him."

"You must have been," agreed her uncle in the same heavy voice. "All counter trimming, though."

"Yes. But I thought I could put up with his reckless extravagance, his unreliability, my own knowledge that he would never really amount to much—his army career had been meteoric, and he left because it was the only course open to him—so long as he was faithful to me. I gave him my jewels, I even gave him back my diamond engagement ring. Since then I've thought I probably paid for it anyway. All the money I could handle I passed over to him. Then he reached even his limits, exceeded them. He was losing on a lunatic scale. People began to whisper. I heard someone say once, 'He'll end like all the rest, over Suicide's Point.' That didn't frighten me—I was sure he wouldn't do that. It was the chink in his armor. He was desperately afraid of death, not just in love with life, though he was that, too, but afraid to die. I did begin to wonder, though, what would be the end of it all."

"What did you suppose would happen?"

"I thought when he had exhausted all our resources and there was no room for him in Monte Carlo any longer, when the Casino was virtually closed to him, then he'd bow to the inevitable and come back to England to live on the small income I inherited from my mother, whose capital was tied up in such a way that I couldn't touch it—but I expect you know all that. Of course, I understand now he would never have considered such a plan. It would have been a sort of living death to him. You know, Uncle Joseph, I was a comparatively rich woman. My godmother's money was all mine, and I could touch all the capital of that. And did. Then we ran through my convertible property, chiefly jewelry, and after that, when he'd had everything I could lay hands on, Gerald behaved as though I'd treated him badly, deceived him about the inheritance from my mother. He insisted we could get round the provisions somehow, that people—gamblers of another sort, I suppose—would be prepared to lend us money on it. The interest would be high, of course. . . . I said I wouldn't consider it, and I wouldn't. It was the only time I ever stood out against anything Gerald wanted. You see, by that time I knew only too well the sort of man I'd married. Once that money was gone we were sunk. There would be nothing. He had nothing, of course, he couldn't work—what do they

151

call those men who go round in the East doing nothing, living on the population?"

"Beach-combers."

"That's what Gerald was at heart. He not only couldn't work, he really felt he had a grievance against society in general and of course me in particular, when money stopped falling into his lap. He began to show me that he realized I was, in his phrase, letting him down. He didn't always keep appointments with me, would be engaged when I wanted him to fall in with some plan of mine, like entertaining our neighbors. There are so many ways in which a man can pay back a woman who has annoyed him. Then he told me that he had a commission to write a book on gambling, he never went into much detail, but he said he had been lent a villa by a friend and he was working down there. I offered to help but he said it wouldn't be interesting to anyone who didn't care about gambling. I didn't press him; I thought probably he was mixed up in some private gambling hell, and by that time I was afraid of something desperate."

"Meaning?"

"If I opposed him too much he might go off. I couldn't bear the thought of that. I was still fond of him, still felt responsible for him. Then came the crisis. He lost not only everything we had, but more money than we could repay. He told me about it quite proudly. You see, he thought that now I'd have to fall in with his suggestion of raising capital on my inheritance. He said if I failed him this time he'd be drummed out of Monte Carlo in disgrace."

"Best thing that could happen," growled Joseph.

"I said much the same. He told me then I'd never understood him, asked me why I'd married him. Oh, it was horrible. But that part of it doesn't matter. He told me that if I still refused to help I'd probably seen the last of him. But I didn't believe it. He was charming and good-looking, though he'd begun to get a little flabby, but you can't live entirely on charm and good looks even in Monte Carlo."

"Fellow sounds no better than a gigolo," muttered Joseph.

"I knew he'd never stick to anyone once the money came to an end, and he knew I still had money, that so long as he stayed with me he wouldn't starve. He flung out in a rather dramatic way saying I needn't expect to see him again; one or two people overheard him say that, but I suppose they'd heard it so often. Anyway, I wasn't afraid of him doing himself any mischief. When dinner-time came and he wasn't back I did begin to get a little anxious. It wasn't like him to miss his meals. There were only two alternatives in my mind. Either he had found someone else to provide him with dinner, or he had had a last fling at the Casino and had been suddenly lucky and was hoping to win back his credit. As soon as dinner was over I went up to the casino, but he wasn't there. Hadn't been there all the evening, they said. They looked at me in an odd way. I'd seen them look like that at other people. They weren't really interested. It was such an old story to them. There was only one other place where I could look for him, and that was the villa. I knew if he was there he would never forgive me for following him, but by that time I was desperate, too. It seemed to me I'd nothing to lose by taking this last chance."

"You didn't expect to find him dead?"

"No. And I didn't." She laughed suddenly, a terrible sound to come from that lovely throat. "When I got there there was a little red and cream-colored car in front of it. There are so many cars in Monte Carlo, you don't notice them specially, unless they're very ostentatious indeed; but this one looked new, and I thought perhaps Gerald really was going to make a bolt for it."

"How about luggage?"

"I hadn't looked in his room. For all I knew, he'd taken a bag, or had one sent down. The French windows were wide open and there didn't seem to be anyone about. I walked through the French windows and listened. It was a very hot night, and very still, too still. If he wasn't here, then for the first time I began to wonder if he had done what he had threatened, if perhaps the notion of life separation from gambling had been more than he could face. Then I heard a door upstairs open, and for a fraction of a second I wondered how I was going to explain my presence there. But before I could speak a woman's voice called, 'Gerry!' I froze where I stood. I suppose I must sound a fool to you,

153

Uncle Joseph, but this was the one thing I had never thought of."

Joseph made a sound that was meant to be sympathetic, but in his heart he wondered why women were sometimes so daft. Why, as soon as he heard about the villa he had connected it with a woman.

"I understood then that there had been no book. Oh, I don't think I'd really believed in the book from the beginning. Why hadn't he ever shown me a contract or a publisher's letter, anything to back up his story? But he'd seemed so affectionate until just lately, and even in Monte Carlo, where everyone gossips, I'd never heard anyone linking up his name with another woman's. Before I could pull myself together the woman had spoken again. 'Don't give up hope, darling,' she said. 'She may come round even now.' And my husband replied, 'Not she. I know Rose's type. They've a spinsterish miserliness, they'll never let anything go.' And then in an aggrieved voice, 'How was I to know the bulk of her money was tied up? She really cheated me into marrying her.' "

"My dear Rose!" Joseph Anstruther put his hand on his niece's shoulder. "Is all this necessary? You're tormenting yourself...."

"Yes. I must make you understand why I did—what I did. It was like hours and days of experience passing in the minute I stood there. Then I heard him coming towards the head of the stairs and I vanished. I couldn't be found there. But equally I couldn't go back to the hotel. For the first time in my life I felt absolutely lost. I didn't seem to belong anywhere. I slipped back through the French windows behind some bushes; it was one of those moony nights when the moon is suddenly obscured by cloud and then sails out again. It gave me a chance to slip for cover. Presently they came into the room together. They were laughing. Uncle Joseph, I had never known hate before. But at that moment I hated them both. I would have killed them where they stood. He offered her a drink, but she said not now, too hot, and then something that made it only too obvious what their relationship was. Since then I've often wondered if everyone in

Monte Carlo except me knew about it, if they'd been laughing in their sleeves."

"Not likely," said Joseph, saying whatever he thought would comfort her most. "You'd have heard, bound to."

"They say wives don't. They're conceited or confident, which comes to the same thing. They stayed there talking, joking with the sort of intimacy husbands and wives achieve. I waited where I was. I burned with furious impatience. I wanted to get up and shout, 'Go, go. Can't you see that you're not wanted? That I'm here—his wife?' I couldn't have moved, not if the ground under my feet had burst into flame. And at last—at last—she went."

She drew a long breath. She was shaking from head to foot. Joseph was looking at her, nearly as shaken as she. Now he would believe anything she told him. A woman like this was like fire, shriveling anything she touched. He'd prided himself that he understood the murderer's mind, now he knew that it is only when he is, in fact, out of his mind that a man is prepared to slay. There seemed little connection between the quiet Rose Anstruther they all knew and this tigress of a woman at his side.

She went on: "At last she went, and her last words were, 'Don't forget your letter,' and she laughed and he called back, 'Not I. I don't care about writing letters as a rule, but I'll enjoy writing that one. She'll get it after I've gone.' The car drove off, and Gerald came back into the room. I thought he was going to have a drink, and I think he did hesitate, then perhaps he thought it best to get rid of the letter first, for he came to the writing-table and took a pen out of his pocket and began to write. I waited for a minute or so—he'd written about three lines—and then I could wait no longer. I came out from behind the bushes, appeared in the window. I suppose my shadow fell across the paper or he heard me or something, because he said before he looked, 'Back already, darling? Give a fellow a chance. This is going to be my swan song.' And I said in a voice I would never have known as mine, 'Yes. Your swan song.' He did look up then, and when he saw me he began to shout furiously, 'What are you doing here, following me? Don't you know there's nothing alienates a man so much as being spied on?' I was mad, too. We were all mad that night. I've always loathed viragoes, those vulgarians who bring shame on their sex, but I could have taken my place with any of them then. I taunted him, said I wasn't surprised he spent so much time on his book or that he hadn't wanted my help. I asked him if he was sure there was enough money in this new venture to make it worth his while, that he might even now be letting the substance go for the shadow. And he laughed and said, 'Oh, I know where I'd always get a welcome. Don't forget to leave me your address.' He hadn't been drinking while I was there, but he must have been drinking before. Though, come to that, anyone might have been justified in believing I'd been drinking too. I've always thought women with a decent tradition hold their tongues when things go wrong, when they're humiliated and cheated. It isn't true. Kipling was right when he said the Colonel's lady and Judy O'Grady are sisters under their skins. My own maid couldn't have behaved any differently. But if I was angry, so was Gerald, partly because he felt a fool, partly, I think, because he knew he was in the wrong. And even then, Uncle Joseph, there was one instant when I could still have forgiven him, one minute like the leaping of a candle-flame before it goes out for ever. But it went out. He put it out with those last words. I said, 'I knew you were worthless, unreliable, a gambler. I knew you'd take the clothes off my back if they'd buy you a ticket for the casino, but I didn't think you'd betray me with another woman.' "

"Poor Rose!" whispered Joseph inadequately. "Poor Rose!"

"Uncle Joseph, there's a moment in every situation when a decision is made. People talk as though violent crimes are planned detail by detail and sometimes perhaps they are. But the instant when Gerald laughed and said, 'D'you mean to say you never guessed there'd been other women?' and even told me their names—one of them a maid I'd had to dismiss because she was in trouble—in that moment he really killed himself."

"This is an awful story," said Joseph soberly. "If that fellow, Crook, unearths it—still, go on. No sense meeting trouble half-way, and if there had been even a vestige of proof against you we were bound to hear. What happened then?"

"I lost control of myself utterly, and yet at the same time I was planning, in a flash, but quite, quite cold-bloodedly. I knew what I was going to do. You remember that rhyme, 'Between the saddle and the ground, He mercy sought and mercy found,' to show that gigantic resolutions and changes can take place in the space of two or three seconds—I made up my mind without any sense of haste, but my decision was irrevocable. The weakness of murderers, as you've probably discovered, is that they can't look beyond the immediate present. I couldn't look as far as the next morning when they found him, as eventually someone was bound to do, I couldn't stop to wonder if I'd been seen, if I'd left any traces of my visit, I couldn't begin, then, to think of the questions that might be put to me, that I might be asked to provide an alibi—every scrap of energy, imagination and purpose was absorbed by that instantaneous, immovable resolution. I came right into the room. 'You're planning to go away,' I said. It was a statement, not a question. I didn't even speak very loudly. No one in the next room, if there had been anyone else on the premises, could have heard me. He laughed, not quite so confidently now, though I don't think—I'm quite sure he had no notion of what I was going to do. 'I was writing to you,' he said, and he stepped aside a pace for me to see what he had written. He had put my name on the sheet, and then, 'I am getting out. The situation is hopeless. We had all that out this afternoon. There is nothing now to be done. I am a ruined man and you will probably be congratulated when the news is known. You'll be better off without me. You can go back to England—that is what you have always wanted and now you will be free.'

"You see how an ordinary person would interpret that letter, Uncle Joseph. He had been going to write more, but I'd interrupted him at the psychological moment. It was a complete alibi for suicide and I saw that, too, as I stood beside him. There's a state of mind called schizophrenia; you're two people co-existing in one body, yet apparently acting irrespective of each other. That was my state then. I could watch myself, first thinking and then carrying out the consequence of my thought. I said, 'I could kill you for what you've done to me tonight,' and he laughed and pulled open a drawer and took out his revolver. 'There you are,' he said. 'Now's your chance. No one knows you're here. It's perfectly safe. Everyone will think it's suicide.' "

157

"But—didn't he realize your state of mind?" asked Joseph.

"He couldn't have believed I would really turn against him. He thought even at that stage I would plead with him to give up this other woman, to come back to England with me. He may even have thought I would offer to raise money somehow on my inheritance. In any case, everyone knew I was terrified of firearms. That was my safeguard."

"You talk as though you thought all this out in a split second, but . . ."

"Uncle Joseph, that's what I'm trying to make you understand. I did. Or rather, it was as if time had stopped. Those instants when one took action are Now, and when it's done they become Then. But you couldn't mark them on a clock. Even as I put out my hand towards the revolver Gerald didn't believe my purpose. He even picked it up and handed it to me. 'You've got a very obliging husband, my dear,' he said. He'd always told people that if I wanted to get rid of him I'd use poison. 'I don't believe my wife knows which end of a gun the bullet comes out of,' he used to say."

Joseph had a horrible mental picture of the pair of them, the man mocking and unafraid, a scoundrel to his bones but still a living human being about to be put summarily out of existence, and that frenzied woman in whom love had curdled into hate.

"I hadn't a doubt in my own mind of what I was going to do. All my force went into that physical act of raising the gun and pressing the trigger. It was just before my finger moved that he knew at last I wasn't bluffing. I saw the change in his face; he was—terrified. He half-lifted his hand, made a queer sound like an animal. It was only a second, but it was time for him to appreciate that he was going to die—and he was desperately afraid of death. I saw his eyes change; he knew there was no hope, crying out wouldn't help him, nothing he did or said could help him. He died at once, he didn't suffer any bodily pain, but I've sometimes thought that instant's torment before the bullet struck him must have seemed as long as a lifetime."

She paused, apparently oblivious to her audience, living over again after so many years that moment of horror, of fierce and bitter triumph, of a ruthlessness that shocked the old man, who had never been known for his tender feelings.

"Best thing I ever did," he said jerkily, "was stay a bachelor. God, Rose, how could you?"

"It seemed the only thing to do. Even when I saw him crumple up, saw the blood welling, knew he was nothing now, I couldn't be sorry. He didn't seem to be anything to do with me. I certainly wasn't afraid. I remembered what I'd heard and rubbed my fingerprints off the gun, and dropped it on the ground beside him, and walked out of the villa through the windows. I felt empty, but curiously at peace. All my rage had gone. I wasn't even tired. I walked like a girl, I came in without anyone seeing me, and I went up to my room. We had two rooms, communicating, because Gerald would gamble half the night, and he always woke me up when he came in. Once in my room I was suddenly desperately tired, so tired I could hardly pull off my clothes. I had sent my maid out for the evening—she had some local acquaintance—and somehow I managed to get into bed, and I went to sleep at once. I lay like a log. Even when I realized hazily what I'd done I wasn't afraid. I was too tired to feel anything at all.

"But since then? My poor Rose, all the years being afraid!"

"Why do you say that? No, Uncle Joseph, I wasn't. It probably will be hard for you to believe, but for months on end I forget, and even when I remember it's as if it was something that happened to another woman. Then—then Lady Bate came, and everything flashed back into perspective. That first day, after I realized who she was and that she remembered me, as of course she would, that was when the nightmare began. But before then—when I woke the next morning at the hotel, the morning after I had killed my husband, I mean, I had a sense of oppression. For the first minute I couldn't remember what had happened to make me feel like that. Then it all came back to me—that woman, Gerald, my hand reaching to take the revolver he contemptuously offered me. I began to wonder if they had found him, but if they had they would have wakened me before. I didn't know how often people visited the villa, if there was any sort of *bonne* who went in by the day. It was my husband, but I didn't know anything. And I couldn't ask questions. It wouldn't be safe. I lay there waiting. Every time a footstep came near I nerved myself for the inevitable. They would tell me and I must look amazed, shocked, horrified. I must play a part but I mustn't overplay it.

"The girl came up with my *petit déjeuner*. She didn't say anything, didn't look at me in a particular way, so I knew they still didn't know. I asked her what sort of a day it was. She threw open the window and said, Madame, it is good to be alive. I nearly betrayed myself then. I had heard Gerald say that so often. By Jove, it's good to be alive. I think that was the first minute when I believed that he was dead. I'd known it before, just as you know there is a figure called the Statue of Liberty, or the Venus de Milo, but when you see it for the first time, then you believe it. I pulled myself together.

" 'Have you taken in Monsieur's *déjeuner* yet?' I said.

"She looked at me oddly. She told me Monsieur was not in his room, his bed was unslept in. I knew what that look meant. Not suspicion of the truth. No one, except Lady Bate, ever had that, but—she had heard the rumors. She wouldn't be shocked or surprised to hear that Gerald was dead. What was there left for him to live for, she would say. They get used to his kind so easily, you see. There are always suicides, every season. I pushed my tray aside. 'Are you sure?' I said. She nodded. She must have seen something in my face, because she said swiftly, 'Perhaps monsieur went to the Casino and his luck turned and he did not wish to break it.' I said, 'No, he didn't go to the Casino last night. I went up to ask. I wanted him...' And then, because I was afraid of giving myself away, I added, 'Are you keeping anything from me? Tell me the truth at once.' She said, 'No, Madame, there is nothing, nothing... But it was hot last night, too hot to sleep.' I said, 'Perhaps he went to the villa to work,' and she said, yes, no doubt that was it, he would be back in a moment and how he would laugh to see me so pale. I thought she'd never go, but at length she did, and I found myself praying that they'd find him quickly before the suspense broke my nerve."

"And—go on, Rose, go on."

"The police came about an hour later. I was finishing dressing and they waited for me. Then I knew I was in danger, I'd been careless the night before, perhaps I'd dropped a handkerchief, a letter. But I told myself that even if I had it wasn't important. I might have to admit I had been at the villa, that Gerald had confessed he was finished, done with, and then after I had left him he had taken the only way out. Even if the police were suspicious, I argued, they'd no evidence. Besides, everyone knew I was devoted to Gerald and terrified of firearms. But I did begin to understand then why a criminal so often returns to the scene of his crime; he has to make sure he's not overlooked something, he wants to know exactly what the police have discovered, what line they're taking. . . ."

She drew a deep breath. "I'm making a long story of this," she said. "It was Juliette who called me. She looked very white herself now, and she said the police were downstairs, there had been an accident. I said, 'Monsieur?' and she said, 'An accident,' so I went down. The police were very polite, not very interested, not in the least moved. It was such a commonplace to them; another poor fool of a gambler who had lost everything and threw away his life as well. I had the sense to keep my mouth shut, to ask as little as possible. I was afraid of seeming to know too much. They told me simply that they had found him, that there was a letter. They showed it to me, and I said, yes, it was his writing. And then I said, 'But I can't believe he would have done it. I never thought he would do that.' They got me to admit that he had threatened suicide, as indeed he had, but I repeated, 'I never believed it would happen.' They told me gently that it couldn't have been a thief, nothing had been touched, not his money or watch or his gold pencil. The gun was beside him on the floor, there was no sign of a struggle. I didn't say much; I didn't quite know what a woman in my position should say, and as it happened silence served me very well. Everyone took it for granted that it was suicide, the people in the hotel found me more interesting than they had ever done, though not, of course," she added with a twisted smile, "nearly so interesting as they would have found the truth. A few of the women came up and spoke to me. Some of them had been half in love with

Gerald themselves. Oh, I suppose I was lucky. No one ever suggested it might have been murder."

Joseph was frowning. "These continental chaps seem pretty slack," he commented. "Didn't they test the barrel for finger-prints?"

"I don't know. Anyway they'd much prefer a British suicide to a British murder."

"And no one ever questioned it? What about the woman who was with him that night?"

"She couldn't speak. It would have been ruin for her. She had a position, too, and how could she come forward and say, 'He was my lover and I know he had no intention of taking his own life'?"

"But if your husband was going to elope with her . . ."

"It wouldn't do her any good to have her name associated with a suicide. Anyway, the dead can't do anyone any good."

"I see your point," Joseph conceded grudgingly. "And where does Lady Bate come in?"

"She found—something—that, if it didn't prove I shot Gerald, did prove that I'd been at the villa or very near it that night. As you've probably noticed, Uncle Joseph, I'm a very neat person. I hate things to be out of order. I don't lose things or spoil them, but I had been so exhausted the night before, drunk with exhaustion, that I failed to realize I had lost an earring some time between dinner and getting back to the hotel. They were very noticeable earrings, too. Not very valuable, I sold all my real things to help Gerald, but these were specially made for me by a man in Paris, a tiny flower set in diamanté. Several people had noticed them, complimented me on them, wanted to know where I bought them. I didn't tell them, of course."

"And you were wearing those ear-rings that night?"

"Yes. I dare say a dozen people in the hotel would have corroborated that fact if they'd been asked. Next day I was in the lounge when Lady Bate came in. Of course I knew she hated me."

"My dear Rose!"

"Oh, it's quite true. She was a very possessive woman. You could tell that the way she behaved to her niece and to that young

162

man. Oh yes, I noticed a good deal about her. You might say she forced herself on my attention. And her husband had made it obvious that he—that he admired me very much. He was one of those Englishmen who are never really at home on the continent. He only came because she thought it was chic. And after all, his life with her can't have been paradise. There were no children so all his energy went into his work. He couldn't speak French and he was much too shrewd to gamble. He explained to me once that he had a dead certainty for his money. . . ."

"Flour," said Joseph in disgust.

"He said you couldn't lose on a universal commodity like that, not if you knew how to handle markets, and I suppose he did. Well, he'd never learned to play and I didn't care about it, so when his wife and my husband were enjoying whatever it was they had come to Monte Carlo for, he and I entertained one another. He used to talk about his early life. He became a wage-earner very young, and he didn't mind who knew it. He had a strong North Country accent, and for some reason that usually strikes English folk abroad as comic. Lady Bate, of course, had conveniently forgotten that he began life as little Charlie Bate in Manchester. I don't think she considered he existed before he married her. We were talking that afternoon, and he was saying that probably I'd want to get back home to my own people as soon as I could, and he'd be going back within a few days for an important board meeting, and if he could be of any service . . . It was pure kindness of heart on his part. He was afraid I'd be stared at, pointed out, and he wanted to offer me his protection. Then Lady Bate came in and saw us together. She came straight over to us and she put an earring down on the table. 'I believe that is yours, Mrs. Fleming,' she said. I knew at once that she knew, or at all events guessed, and that it wouldn't cost her an hour's sleep to ruin me. She went on, 'I found it near the Villa Mimosa this morning, and I recognized it at once.' I had put out my hand to take it, but when she said that I drew back. 'I didn't know there was another pair like it in Monte Carlo,' I said, 'but if that's where you found it it can't be mine. I was wearing mine last night, and I wasn't near the Villa.' 'How very strange,' she said. 'I thought this was an original design.' 'It was,' I told her,

163

'but even original designs can be copied, and there are a great many very clever merchants in this part of the world.' She picked it up and held it in her hand. 'I wonder how I can find out who it belongs to,' she said. By this time, of course, she had attracted quite a lot of attention, which was what she intended. People were staring. You know how quickly suspicion is sown, and if it isn't scotched at once the damage is gone. 'Perhaps you went by the Villa without remembering it,' she said. It was Sir Charles who saved me. He took the earring out of her hand and said, 'Surely this is the bauble we picked up near the Casino this morning. We haven't been near the Villa. Not likely in all the circumstances.'

" 'If it was the Casino,' I said, 'then, of course, it's mine.'

"He put it into my hand as though it was something quite unimportant. 'I'm glad we could restore your property to you,' he said. If ever I saw a woman look murder, Lady Bate looked it then. There was nothing she could do, you see, and the people listening thought she had been trying to pay off some old score. She couldn't protest that she had been down to the Villa like Peeping Tom, though that was what she must have been, and she hadn't an iota of proof. On the contrary, her husband had publicly stated that they found it near the Casino."

"Quite a number of women might have stuck a knife into their husbands for that," suggested Joseph ungrammatically. "What did the old boy really think?"

"Sir Charles? Oh, I don't think he was deceived. Probably he knew she hadn't been near the Casino that day, and as it happened I noticed they didn't go out together. Later, he came up to me when there wasn't any likelihood of our being over-heard and said, 'Mrs. Fleming, m'dear, I'm old enough to be y'r father, and I'd like to give ye a bit of advice. The wife and I are going back even earlier than I guessed—tomorrow, as a matter of fact...' "

"She'd hardly want to stay on in the circumstances," Joseph agreed.

" 'We'll be going to Manchester,' he went on. 'I dare say you don't visit a lot at Manchester.' I knew what he meant, of course; that we shouldn't meet again, and it was a good thing. 'Now as soon as the funeral and all that's over,' he went on, 'ye'll be going back to your own people.' I'd spoken of father, you see. He knew I had people to go back to. 'And I dare say you'll be glad to stay quietly at home for a while.' Oh, I saw what he meant. Stay in the shadow, stay away from places where you might meet any of this set again. I felt then I never wanted to stir from The Downs. I'd had all the excitement I should ever want."

"He was quite right. Some of these women have tongues as long as their mothers' hair used to be."

"I knew I was safe with him. He might agree with his wife, but he'd never give me away. I said, 'You're very kind,' and he said emphatically, 'I'm a plain man and right's right, but I've always believed Britons should hold together, particularly when they're in outlandish parts.' I never saw him again."

She lay back, as though utterly worn out by her recital.

"And you didn't meet Lady Bate again till she came here?"

"I'd almost forgotten she existed. When Jock said, 'There's an auld body called Bate with a pretty niece ready to take the rooms,' it never occurred to me to connect her with my Lady Bate."

"Did she come deliberately?"

"I'm sure she didn't. I don't suppose she even connected the name of Anstruther with the death of Captain Fleming. But naturally, the instant she set eyes on me, she realized the tremendous pull she had. She'd only to drop a hint, and a woman like Mrs. Hunter would have a three-volume novel ready for publication next morning. The entire game was in her hands and she knew it."

"She'd no proof," objected Joseph.

"She couldn't have got me arrested for Gerald's death, if that's what you mean, but if she had begun to talk—Uncle Joseph, it all fitted together too well. My coming back here and living like a recluse, never seeing anyone I had known during the years of my married life, changing my name. It would have been intolerable. Bad enough for her simply to remember me as a woman whose husband killed himself, but this was worse, far, far worse. She might even say I had somehow compelled her husband to falsify evidence, fascinated him, anything, though perhaps her pride would have forbidden that. Don't you see, it isn't the truth that matters so much as what you can make people believe?"

Crook at least would have agreed with her there.

"All the same," her uncle urged, "though this story you've just told me may have given you a motive for wanting Lady Bate where she couldn't do any harm, it doesn't provide a shred of evidence against you so far as her death is concerned. I think, my dear, you're letting your very painful recollections cloud your judgment. I admit you must have been living under a most terrible strain, but . . ."

"It's that man, Mr. Crook. He's ruthlessness personified. All that matters to him is to find a substitute for that girl. He said as much. If he finds out this story—and why did Lady Bate keep all those cuttings? Oh yes, she did. She told me as much. That's what is in the diary he took away."

"Still, even if that's so, and it may not be true, I gather there was no suggestion of anything except suicide even in the local press."

"Who can say what she may have added by way of comment? I know it's not proof in law, but it's quite enough to set that man on the trail."

"But, look here, Rose," expostulated Joseph, "I don't quite get the hang of this. You're talking as if you'd had a hand in the old lady's death. If you had I quite see you might feel apprehensive, but you hadn't, so you've nothing to be afraid of."

"Oh, Uncle Joseph!" Her voice was soft with amazement. "I'm encircled by fear. It's like living next-door to an unexploded bomb. At any moment it may go off, and wreck you and everything you have. Besides, have you thought of the reaction my story would have on father? He's not like us, he lives in his own particular world. He wouldn't think in any circumstances one could shoot one's husband. To watch you while I told the story, one might almost think you'd heard it a dozen times before, but I couldn't endure him to know."

Joseph passed a sinewy old man's hand over his clean-shaved

jaw. "It's a mess, Rose, and that's the truth. Still, that fellow's a lawyer, for all he looks like a bookie's tout. He'll know you can't drag out a story twenty years old in support of a theory. Question is, if he does tumble to the facts, what pattern is he likely to make of them?"

*C*HAPTER *S*IXTEEN

UP IN LONDON Crook was busily putting two and two together. The diary appeared to be a record of the married life of the Bates, with particular emphasis on the exploits of Sir Charles. From one of the paragraphs it appeared that he had sprung from lowly beginnings to an eminence any man might have envied. The first mention of Lady Bate was an announcement of the engagement, from the date of which Crook deduced that she had been no chicken when she married. Shortly before the announcement of the wedding Mr. Charles Bate received his title. Crook wondered if her ladyship had postponed the wedding on purpose, feeling Mrs. Bate too proletarian for one of her exalted outlook. After that there were columns and columns of speeches, reports of meetings, important engagements, directors' boards, the star turn on each occasion being apparently Sir Charles' contribution to the day's entertainment. Sir Charles evidently believed with Crook in the essential simplicity of the average man. "You can't bate Bate's flour," was one of his slogans. "Bake with Bate," was another. "De-bate everything except your bread."

"It's a wonder to me how a chap with his gift of the gab ever escaped getting into Parliament," was Crook's characteristic comment, as he flicked over the pages. "But perhaps he was wisecracking so hard he walked past without noticing."

It was near the end of the diary that he came to the story of Gerald Fleming's death.

RIVIERA TRAGEDY

ENGLISHMAN FOUND SHOT

That was how it began.

"Funny lot, these foreigners," observed Crook to Bill Parsons in indulgent tones. "Don't seem to have worried over the fellow not signing his last letter to his wife. If a chap's goin' to put out his own light you'd expect him to leave all the ends tied up. Besides, how about the two glasses? Someone was expected at the villa that night, and it wasn't Mrs. Captain Fleming."

"No," agreed Bill.

"Well, hell, didn't they care who?"

"Why should they?" asked Bill, who appeared to share the opinion of at least half his countrymen that a slander at the expense of a foreign nation isn't slander at all. "What does it cost to have a murder trial? About five thousand here before the war, and I dare say it's gone up like everything else since then. Besides, the Frenchies don't like having an Englishman murdered on their soil any more than we like our victims to be foreigners."

"Suit me if they were all foreigners," said Crook in his sweeping fashion. "Besides, why wasn't he sitting down if he shot himself?"

"English gentleman always dies on his feet," returned Bill solemnly. "And it was his own revolver, you note."

Crook turned over the next page. There was an interview with the widow.

" 'My husband told me we were ruined, that he could not meet his obligations. I had done everything possible to help him, but I was at the end of my resources. I told him that if we returned to England we could settle on a small property I had.'

" 'And he refused?'

" 'He seemed distrait. He said that unless a miracle happened he would shoot himself.'

" 'And you were not alarmed?'

" 'I never thought he would do it. He was—afraid of death. I had heard him speak of it so often.'

" 'Speak of it—in connection with himself?'

169

" 'Oh no. When he heard of other men committing suicide. He said even prison would be better than that.'

" 'So when he didn't return that night you thought nothing of it?'

" 'I thought he might have gone to have a final fling at the Casino, and then perhaps stayed out at a café. He was so often late, and it was agreed that I should not wait up for him.'

" 'You—were not occupying the same room, madame?'

" 'Communicating rooms. But I often didn't hear him come in.'

" 'And when did you realize he had not slept in his room?'

" 'When Juliette—the chambermaid—told me.' "

"Nice, accommodating wife," suggested Bill, as Crook paused for an instant.

"It could be," said Crook. "Or on the other hand, it could be she guessed he was at the villa."

"Alone?"

"I ask you, Bill, does even an Englishman take a villa to be alone in? No, I'll tell you how it might be, that she went down to the villa—just an idea of mine, but I don't see why women should have all the intuition on the board—and found he wasn't alone and . . ."

"Plugged him?" asked Bill, as Crook paused again.

"If she hadn't guessed there was another dame—don't forget the two glasses—and then she found there was—well, she might have got a bit annoyed. Women do, you know."

Bill's eyebrows arched. "You have to be quite a lot annoyed before you start shooting your husband," he suggested.

"Maybe Vesuvius was her middle name. It has happened before. Quiet for twenty years and then shoots the moon. Anyhow, Bill, there was something. Something that explains why she lives like a lady nun now, with only those two ancient walking oak-trees for company. It ain't natural. Women want someone to take their back hair down with. Why don't she ever see her guests or go visitin'? And how is it Jock runs that establishment? What's in it for him and what does he know? You take it from me, she's got her reasons. Women always have, even if they ain't reasonable. Y'know, I wouldn't be surprised if Lady B. mightn't have told us what those reasons were." He turned another page. "Hallo! Here's a bit in her ladyship's own writing. About as sympathetic as a U-boat, our Lady Bate."

Under the printed columns, in a harsh pointed hand, were the words, "But she doesn't say how her earring got to the Villa Mimosa that night. She was wearing them at dinner, and she wasn't wearing them next morning. Whatever Charles may say to save that hussy's face, I found that earring near the Villa, not by the Casino." And then, as though spleen had got the upper hand, she had added in dashing, infuriated characters, the one word, "Murderess!"

"One thing, having Lady B. about you'd never need to go to the Zoo," was Crook's characteristic comment. "Like havin' a private snake-house on the premises. Y'know, Bill, I'm beginnin' to come out of the tunnel. She and Sir Charles went for a walk by the Villa, I suppose the story had started to circulate by then, and they found the earring, and put two and two together. Why didn't Lady B. go to the police? She had a witness—her husband."

"If he had any sense he wouldn't want to get mixed up in a foreign crime," Bill returned. "Besides, he may have admired the lady."

"The things you think of!" said Crook. "You could be right at that. I wonder what Mrs. A. did find when she reached the Villa. It wouldn't surprise me to know there was someone else, besides the Bateses, who knew the gallant Captain didn't die by his own hand."

"Anonyma?" inquired Bill languidly.

"Keep that for your toney friends," Crook implored him. "Just plain English is good enough for me."

Bill considered. "Couldn't have been Lady B. herself, of course?"

"Be your age," Crook advised him scornfully. "A chap like Gerald Fleming would as soon have thought of taking a rattlesnake to bed. Besides, in that case, she wouldn't have any hold over Mrs. A. The other way round, in fact. Because Mrs. A. had only to swear she was en route to the Villa, and bein' a lady born and bred hustled round and pretended not to have noticed

171

a thing, and Bate's flour wouldn't be in it with Bate's wife. No, no, Sir Charles is the crux of this situation. Probably he'd cottoned to the lady. Maybe he thought it 'ud be nice to have something a bit softer than that old battle-axe to go around with. There was a line I found a bit earlier." He turned the pages back. "A note of the people at the hotel and what she thought of them. Here's Mrs. A.'s epitaph: 'One of those red-haired women who can never be trusted. But Charles seems impressed. He appears to keep his sense for his business affairs.' Well, we're buildin' up the case, ain't we?"

"You ought to have been one of the Children of Israel," Bill congratulated him. "Talk of making bricks without straw."

"All the same, it does add up. Lady B. couldn't go to the police with the earring if her husband didn't back her up. It would be just one woman's word against another, and they might even ask questions about what her ladyship was doing near the Villa. But she knows there has been some funny business. Because if Mrs. A. ain't mixed up in the affair and yet she did go to the Villa, either she saw her husband alive, in which case why deny it, unless she shot him, of course, or else she found him dead, in which case why keep your mouth buttoned up about it? She'd have called in the police right away. No, Mrs. A. knows a whole lot more about her husband's death than she ever told, and Lady B. knew more than was convenient."

"She couldn't have done much about it after all these years," pointed out Bill sensibly.

"She couldn't have got her swung, if that's what you mean, but she could have made life here damned uncomfortable for her. Can't you imagine it? See that woman, that's Mrs. Anstruther. Her husband was found shot in a villa in the Riviera. It was all hushed up, but Mrs. Anstruther came back and lives in seclusion, and she's changed her name. Oh yes, it was Fleming really. You wouldn't like it, Bill, and no more would I. As for the two old gentlemen, it would probably kill them."

"Meaning they don't know?"

"Well, I put it to you. Would you come waltzing back and say, 'Oh, Dad and Uncle Joe, I've just put my husband under the daisies, and I'm open to accept an offer as housekeeper.'

Why, even Madeleine Smith had to go abroad to get away from the scandal. I wonder where that chap, Jock, comes in."

"Think he may have poisoned the old lady?"

"I wouldn't put it past him, but, though I don't often see eye to eye with the police, I do admit that when it's murder you do want some proof."

He continued to turn the pages of the record. "Here's a reference to it or I'm a Dutchman," he announced presently. "This is Sir Charles speakin' at Liverpool just after it all happened. 'It has always been my rule never to interfere in other people's concerns unless some good could come of it. I stand, as you all know, for private enterprise, and it is the essence of private enterprise that snooping is barred.' Wonder if he put that in for Lady B.'s benefit? Come to think of it, Bill, it wouldn't do the great Sir Charles Bate any good to be mixed up in a murder case. The only people murder does good to is counsel and the chap who uncovers the clue. But if he'd let Lady B. push ahead, he'd have found himself subpoenaed and kept hanging about—you know what French trials are—and if there had been another dame mixed up in it there'd have been a lot of yap about crime passionnel, and all true Frenchies would have spat at the old boy for lettin' a lady down. No, he knew his onions all right when he told his old Dutch to keep her nose where the Almighty put it, which was on her own face. Point is, where do we go from here?"

"No suspicions?" suggested Bill. "Ah, but you will have."

"Remember that little chap, Barton, the police pulled in for murdering his wife ten years earlier, the Dear Dead Woman Case, it came to be called? I promised myself then I wouldn't take on another case that involved delving into the past long after any clues could be left. It's no concern of mine who shot Captain Fleming, but if his wife did it, then she's one step nearer poisoning the old lady than anyone else in the house. It always comes more natural the second time."

"And—evidence?"

"Give me a chance. There must be a loop-hole somewhere to enable me to get a verdict for my girl. Of course if, when I've gone through things with a tooth-comb, I still can't see any

173

light, I shall have to get out me little acetylene blowlamp and make a hole myself. Now, let's get down to work."

"*Against Mrs. Anstruther.* She had a guilty secret and Lady Bate knew it. Lady B. was presuming on her knowledge and she intended to go on doing so till the end of her natural. Lady Bate was out all day and her room was unlocked. The niece went out in the afternoon, likewise Mrs. Sleuth-Hound Hunter; the old men never came into that part of the house. Mrs. Mack never came upstairs. The girl, Gladys, was out. That gives her a clear field."

"Jock?" suggested Bill.

"Not likely he'd be in that part of the house, specially at that hour, but even if he was he'd lie himself black in the face for her. Easy to see that. That gives her motive and opportunity."

"And means."

"Question is, did she know about the sleeping-tablets? Mind you, I don't say Lady B. died of one of her own tablets, only we haven't traced similar tablets to anyone else in the house, and it's always easier when you're makin' a pattern to use the bricks that are lyin' about."

"The old lady seems to have talked pretty freely."

"Question is, did she talk to Mrs. A.?"

"Wonderful the way things get round. Well, there's Case A. Wash out the old men—don't know whether it's safe to wash out Mrs. Hunter, but I'd be inclined to say yes. That leaves Jock, the other servants—that girl's worth watching—and our Miss Twiss."

"I wondered when you were coming to her," said Bill.

Crook looked dignified. "I'm like that chap in the hymn— one step enough for me. I dare say when I know what she was doin' in Lady Bate's room I'll have solved the puzzle, always assumin' the old boy really did see her."

"Think he suffers from D.T.?" asked Bill with interest. "At four in the afternoon?"

"I don't think he suffers from D.T. But if he has any sense he'll know a lot of awkward questions are goin' to be asked, most of them directed towards his darlin' daughter. You know British law, Bill. You can't suddenly dig up something some time after the crime and bring it out as evidence. He can say he never thought it was important, but—why didn't he happen to mention that he saw the lady roamin' round the corridors that afternoon? He must know he can't prove it. If she says she wasn't there, as of course she will, who's to say she was? No, the police can't move a step on that, and nor can Arthur Crook. Anyway, we'd have to show motive. As you've observed, you dislike a lady quite a piece before you start puttin' out her light."

"The Mystery of Arabella Twiss. She might have gone sneaking up looking for another ring, you know. These women with a mania for precious stones go to all lengths."

"You should know," agreed Crook. Bill had been one of the kings of the jewelry underworld in his time, before an inconsiderate police bullet, catching him in the heel, had put an end to his career. You can disguise a lot, he and Crook agreed, but you can't disguise a limp. "Still—murder!" demurred Bill.

"I know. Still, I ain't the police and I don't like the obvious. Y'see, if this is an amateur's crime there won't be anything obvious about it. Amateur murderers are like bad writers—they don't use one syllable if they can use six, and the more tangled they can make a case the more likely they think they are to get away with it."

"Seems to have been premeditated," reflected Bill. "I suppose everyone knew about the old lady going to town."

"They knew after she'd gone." Crook stopped suddenly. "Bill, I believe you've got it. All this while we've been assuming it was a premeditated crime. But—suppose it wasn't anything of the sort? Suppose it was one of these spur-of-the-minute crimes? She went in to get something she wanted—never mind what, for the minute—and she came across the sleepin' tablets, and she thought, well, why not? As you said, women haven't any sense of proportion. If they want a thing, that seems to them a good enough reason for havin' it, never mind about consequences. And why should anyone ever know? These solitary dames are generally a bit bats, at that," he added, with that sweeping air of his Bill knew so well. "And it might so easily come off. I'm inclined to believe the Colonel's story, after all, Bill. It's all beginnin' to fit."

"Glad of that," said Bill politely. "Now tell me the rest. She was an amateur so of course she made a mistake. I'm just waiting to hear what it was."

"It wasn't even a mistake," said Crook in sober tones. "It was somethin' she couldn't foresee. Mind you, she hoped it 'ud pass as natural death, but in any case she couldn't guess she was goin' to be seen, and she had that crazy one-track mind all murderers have, male and female, can't see the crime as it affects anybody but themselves. So far as I can see, she had nothing against the girl and she must know, if there were suspicions, it was Caroline Bate who'd foot the bill, but it didn't matter to her. Nothin' mattered but gettin' the old woman out of the way."

"And the mistake?" urged Bill.

"You mean the thing she couldn't foresee? She couldn't guess that presently she was goin' to find herself up against Arthur Crook, the Criminals' Hope and the Judges' Despair, and that, my boy, is goin' to be her undoin'."

CHAPTER SEVENTEEN

CROOK, NO FOOL, realized that the greatest optimist could not hope to prove or even to bring a case against a suspect without any hint of motive, and so far as his present knowledge went there was no reason why Miss Twiss should take the tremendous risk of putting old Lady Bate out of the way. But that some such reason would eventually emerge, he was convinced. Convinced, too, that he was going to need all the help he could get, he took the Scourge back to The Downs and appeared on the doorstep with all the aplomb of Lucifer, son of the morning.

"Bad penny," he announced rapidly to Jock, who opened the door and surveyed him with undisguised disapproval. "A word with Madam?"

Jock looked doubtful but said he would inquire. Cautiously admitting the visitor to the main hall, with instructions to come no further, he advanced to Mrs. Anstruther's room. After a moment he returned.

"Madam has a few minutes if it's important," he said.

Crook came marching in. "If you want information, come to the fountain head," he announced. He didn't miss an almost imperceptible sign between Mrs. Anstruther and Jock, and instantly interpreted it in his own way.

"Sure, let him stop," he announced. "Matter of fact, he might be able to help more than anyone." He turned cheerfully to the rigid figure of the servant. "Soften up, sourpuss," he advised him. "Look, you passed the time of day with Miss Twiss when she first came?"

"Aye."

"What did she tell you about herself?"

"I wasna much consairned. I asked where she had been, for reference, ye ken, and she told me a big hotel but they were putting up the prices. Very open in her speech, she was, and said she kenned it was playing the radio, and would we object to that? She played it a wee thing loud, on account of one of her ears not bein' all it once was. We'd but Mrs. Hunter here at the time, and a couple we'd be glad to be quit of anyway, them not living up to their reference, so we took up hers and it seemed right enough, and she moved in the next week."

"And no trouble till Lady B. came? She was a—what's the word?—an agitator by nature as well as choice, that dame."

"She said the wireless was enough to send a body daft, and Miss Twiss promised only to play it loud when she was alone or when Mrs. Hunter was there. No noise could upset that one. No, I wouldna say there was trouble. . . ."

"I'm not talking about the wireless," said Crook bluntly. "I mean the ring. Did Lady B. threaten to prosecute?"

"I've always believed it was a genuine case of absence of mind," put in Mrs. Anstruther quickly.

Crook slowly drooped an eyelid. "You ought to be on the bench," he told her. "You'd have 'em all clamoring to come up in front of you."

"You mean, you think it was deliberate?" Her voice sharpened.

"I don't think a lady that doesn't own anything better than a necklace of glass beads picks up a diamond ring and puts it in her bag and forgets all about it. Well, she'd open her bag during the day, wouldn't she?"

"There was no sense in her keeping it, Mr. Crook. She couldn't wear it. Lady Bate would have noticed it at once, and she made no attempt to dispose of it."

"Lady Bate ain't with her twenty-four hours of the day. Besides, they've got a screw loose, these dames with a yen for jewels. You ask Bill. That's Bill Parsons, my partner. Used to be in the jewel trade himself once. He could tell you that women'll sell 'emselves any hour of the day—if that's their make-up, mark you—to get their hands on a few colored stones you can't eat and half the time they couldn't wear, husbands bein' unreasonable and askin' funny questions if a wife turns up with a ruby bangle he knows he couldn't pay for in a hundred years. It's more as if they just wanted to own 'em, Pete knows why."

"But—we never had any trouble previously."

"How long had Miss Twiss been here?"

"Oh, not quite a year."

"And Mrs. Hunter buys all her stuff at Woolworths. How about the others? Or weren't there any others?"

"We had two elderly maiden ladies after the Duncans went," said Rose, and Jock cut in grimly, "Very religious they were. Believed in the ornament of a meek and quiet spirit. For ever talking about pomps and vanities. Why, they only wore bone buttons to their dresses and whiles not even enough of them."

"There you are then. No temptation. She didn't come into your half of the house and nobody her side wore anythin' worth pinchin'. It was only when Lady B. started lookin' like the Burma Gem Company at breakfast that the trouble began. No use blaming her, though that's just what the police will do. Might as well blame a dip, for puttin' his nose inside a pot. Or an epileptic for havin' fits. No, when Lady B. arrived, somethin' like a wheel started goin' round in our Miss Twiss's maiden breast. Why, didn't you say she offered to put down the wireless just to please her ladyship? Did she make any sort of offer to the Misses Button?"

"It's a thocht," agreed Jock reflectively.

"You're telling me. Well, she kept her eyes open and presently she saw her chance. The ring. I don't say she found it in the bathroom. I wouldn't know. You could search my bathroom all day and you wouldn't find anything more valuable than a broken stud—not unless you chanced in while I was havin' my matutinal. But I do know that the amount of stuff ladies leave about in washrooms makes you wonder how the other sex ever came to give 'em the vote."

"And you really think we have a thief on the premises?" Rose Anstruther looked incredulous.

"A klep," amended the charitable Mr. Crook. "Y'know, I'll

179

be frank with you. I wasn't sure at first if y'r dad had really seen the lady goin' into Lady Bate's room, but now I'm inclined to think he did. I mean, such an opportunity—and this time she'd be cleverer."

"But if anything was missing she would be the first suspect," argued Mrs. Anstruther. "Besides, Lady Bate told me she would leave everything locked up."

"Ah, but did she tell Miss Twiss that? And if she did, did the old girl cotton?" He nodded sagely. "Mind you, I don't say you haven't got something there. You don't usually take to pinchin' rings in middle life, not if it's a yen with you the way it is with Miss T. I wonder why she really got the boot from her last place?"

"If there was anything suspeecious they were wrong not to gi'e us a warning," exclaimed Jock indignantly.

Crook looked at him with indulgent red-brown eyes. "Ever heard of the law of slander—or libel? Besides, if you run a pub you don't want to go gettin' mixed up with the police. Anyway, when it's a lady they can always get one of the Harley Street boys to say it's glands," he continued, with a sublime disregard for his own strictures anent the law of slander.

"But—you really think this may have happened before?"

"It could be, lady, it could be."

"And—Lady Bate knew it?"

"Well, now, that's something we can't ask her, but it wouldn't surprise me."

Mrs. Anstruther had clearly been hesitating for an instant, but now she spoke. "You have reminded me of something," she said slowly. "I don't know whether it is of any assistance or if it's too trivial. . . ."

"Not too little, not too much," quoted the ebullient Mr. Crook. "Let's have it, lady."

"She came to complain to me, as you know, when the incident of the ring took place. She was disposed to make trouble, but I urged her to do nothing. After all, there was no proof that Miss Twiss had any criminal intent."

"Whole place was buzzin' like a hive of bees, I understand, with her ladyship for queen."

180

"Ah, but she was deaf, and she had the peculiar immobility of the deaf. She would sit reading or sewing, I am told, quite untouched by what was going on round her. I noticed that when the news of Lady Bate's death became public, she seemed—untouched—by it. Even my father, who had disliked Lady Bate, and my uncle, were more distressed. I suppose it is a fact that the deaf live to a very large extent in a world of their own. They've lost a dimension. . . ."

"Oh, very toney, she was," said Crook, recounting the interview to Bill Parsons, "but there's a story by G. K. C.—I forget the name—about a chap who set up to be a prophet and murdered an old lady by lettin' her fall down a lift shaft, and then when the shimozzle started he was out on the balcony communin' with the infinite, and nothin' disturbed him. All the disciples said how spiritual, but Father Brown drew the obvious conclusion that he wasn't stricken with surprise for the simple reason he wasn't surprised. It could be the same with our Arabella."

But that was later. Now, continuing the conversation, Mrs. Anstruther went on, "Lady Bate said, 'I consider the woman a menace. I shall make inquiries.' Now, suppose she had, suppose she had found out anything."

"If it was in writin' the police would have come across it when they tooth-combed her papers," Crook reminded her. "She wouldn't be fool enough to get the information and then burn it. Mind you, X. (he was very punctilious and wouldn't refer to any suspect as a criminal until he had his proof, if necessary home-manufactured) may only have gone in to snoop, to see if these inquiries were actually bein' made. My notion," he added earnestly, "is that the lady didn't mean to put the old girl out. If she had, the odds are she'd have provided her own weapon—after all, it's asking rather a lot of a murderee to give you the means—and then when she got there, maybe she pulled open the drawer and saw the stuff. . . ."

Rose Anstruther looked at him in amazement. "But, Mr. Crook, how could you hope to prove. . . ?"

"I don't. The lady'll have to give herself away. By the way, is our Miss Twiss anywhere around? I'd like a word with her—

181

on the strict q.t., you understand? And say, don't spill any beans, will you? It's never a good idea to put suspects on their guard."

Miss Twiss was in the guests' sitting-room. Mrs. Hunter, not realizing what she was missing, had gone down to the town for her usual elevenses, yet another café, The Golden Kettle, having opened. She intended to sample it and see whether she could give it her patronage, and so Crook had his interview in complete privacy. A little thing like deafness didn't defeat him. He had a voice that could have borne comparison with a deep-sea fisherman, and he roared out his welcome with such zest that Miss Twiss heard even above the sound of the wireless. She switched off the set—the programme dealt, as far as Crook could understand, with increases in the birth rate and coy references to Mr. Stork, a subject which surely, he thought, for all the combined miracles of nature and science, could hardly be of much interest to Miss Twiss.

"Weren't you here yesterday?" she asked him composedly, picking up her sewing.

"So I was. Observant of you. Friend of Caroline Bate," roared Crook.

"Such a pretty girl," said Miss Twiss. "Such a pity—but I dare say a great temptation."

"Now don't you start putting the comether on me," Crook warned her. "I'm on her side. I say she didn't do it."

"Oh really!" Miss Twiss looked interested. "Who did?"

"That's what I'm here to find out. I wondered if you could help me. You knew Lady Bate, y'see."

"I saw her every day," amended MissTwiss. "I would hardly care to say I knew her. I'm afraid there wasn't a great deal of sympathy between us. We should all be as considerate to one another as we can, and when I realized she disliked the radio I used to turn it down, but I must say she seldom seemed to consider the position from my point of view. With my affliction it was a little dull for me if even that pleasure was removed. So few people employ a tone of voice that I can hear. You are most exceptional." (So's a fog-horn, thought Crook, tactfully keeping the notion to himself.) "But if I have the radio at a certain pitch—a specialist once told me it is a matter of vibrations—I can hear voices. Not music. For some reason music is torment—I believe that is the case with numbers of deaf people—but I confess that I do enjoy the talks and plays, and even if I miss a word or two I can generally fill in the gap."

"I didn't mean that," shouted the mendacious Mr. Crook. "But—didn't you both come from Manchester?"

"Manchester?" She looked at him in amazement. "Oh, no. I hail from Liverpool."

"Liverpool? My mistake. Don't know how I got the idea into my head. But you've lived south for a long while, haven't you?"

"Since I was quite a girl. My mother married again when I was ten years old, a jeweler, quite an expert—that's how I knew at once that Lady Bate's jewels were, as they say, the genuine article."

"It's nice to meet someone who appreciates the real thing," was Crook's hearty response. "You ought to meet my pal, Bill Parsons. But if you're so interested in stones, Miss Twiss, I wonder you didn't stay in the business."

Miss Twiss folded her hands. "Forty years ago it wasn't very usual for a daughter to be taken into a family business. Besides, I was only a stepdaughter, and my stepfather had sons of his own after his marriage. And then, of course, it was generally supposed I should marry. But for years I had the care of my Aunt Millie. . . . I wouldn't like you to think I wasn't devoted to her—after all, she made a home for me for years—but I do think there is such a thing as becoming too attentive. After all, even the most charming aunts don't live for ever. . . ."

"You keep your pecker up," bawled Crook. "One of these days Mr. Right'll come bowling round the corner, with apologies for bein' a bit late. . . ."

"That," continued Miss Twiss, as though he had not spoken, "was why I felt a little anxious about that girl. She was so very much at the old lady's beck and call. And meanwhile there was that delightful young man. . . . You see, I didn't want history to repeat itself."

"Cuckoo!" decided a resigned Mr Crook. "Completely cuckoo.

After all, you don't go round poisoning tiresome old ladies because they've pretty nieces you're sorry for. I wonder what more there is to this story."

"I can tell you one thing," he went on aloud, "you can stop worrying about the young lady. She ain't going to swing, as sure as my name's Arthur Crook. I'm on the track of the real whodunit, so you can put your bet on Wedding Bells for first place."

As he was going he was met in the hall by Jock, who said he would be glad of a word.

"No extra charge," said the genial Mr. Crook.

Jock drew him into some private sanctum, and said, "It's to do with Mrs. Anstruther. In a sense, she's in my care, ye ken. Oh, I'm aware she has a father and an uncle, but ye'll have seen for yeerself that they're auld gentlemen and then they don't know everything. What I'm wondering is, if it's quite the thing for Madam to stay on the premises with that Miss Twiss. If it was her did for the old lady...."

"Oh, I haven't said that." Crook looked shocked. "No proof, man."

"Still, there was a suggestion..." Jock sounded obstinate. "If it should be true, she might take another chance..."

"And put out Mrs. Anstruther's light? Not so long as she don't know she's suspected. Besides, she never comes your side of the house, does she?"

"I'd be easier in my mind if she was off the premises," muttered Jock.

"I dare say she will be quite soon. Me and the Scourge are goin' back to London to make a few inquiries, and I dare say what we learn will surprise us all. Meantime," he laid a thick finger on his big pugnacious jaw, "mum's the word."

Jock followed him as far as the little red car. "It would be simple for Madam to take a rest cure for a while," he proposed.

"Much better have her under your eye," Crook advised him. "Anyone can go visitin' in a nursin' home. Here you can play Angel Gabriel with the flamin' sword. You trust Arthur Crook. He won't let you down."

The last thing he wanted, he reflected, as he bounced back to town, was a break-up of the household. He expected fresh developments pretty soon, and he wanted everyone on the premises when the next break occurred.

CHAPTER EIGHTEEN

THE NEXT STEP was to discover whether he had any ground for his suspicions regarding Miss Twiss's past, and he put a man on to search the registers at Somerset House for notices of a marriage occurring approximately forty-five years before—she was ten years old at the time, according to our Arabella, and she should know, Crook told Bill, and she must be an easy fifty-five now—between a Mrs. Twiss, widow, and an unknown gentleman in the jewelry trade. It took his man a little while to trace the connection, but eventually it was discovered that in July, 1899, Margaret Emily Twiss, widow, married John Henry Elthorp, bachelor, of Liverpool. The bachelor's profession was given as jeweler.

"That's our man and our woman," said Crook jubilantly. "Now, Bill, you handle the next bit of the case. If I bounce in and announced I'm a lawyer they'll think there's something screwy. They always do. Funny thing," he added ruminatively, "the nobs may not like me, but they do accept me. But these other chaps—they know I'm dirt and they make sure I know they know it. Now you, Bill, you go along looking like Savile Row, and they'll tell you anything."

Bill, delving into his past, said casually, "Oh, I know Elthorps. Sound respectable business house, the type that co-operates with the police when there's trouble, and would be prepared to have their books opened on the Last Day without a qualm. Surprising if you learn anything fishy from that source."

He went up to Liverpool, however, and stopped at the Swan

for a quick one, realized he was wasting his time as the young lady behind the counter was young enough to be Miss Twiss's non-existent daughter, went on to the King's Head and struck oil. He learned here that old Mr. Elthorp (John Henry) had died just before the war, and the eldest son had obtained exemption from service to keep the business going. He was a man in the middle forties, a family man with the sized family that must delight the heart of the Minister of Health, provided he wasn't responsible for housing them, and had successfully kept the business going for his two brothers, one of whom had served with distinction in the Army, while the other had been drafted into the Civil Service for special (unspecified duties). The Army one was now home with an artificial foot, the Civil Service one still couldn't be spared, but there was a son also back from the forces, helping to keep the flag flying, and the Civil Service one was badgering the life out of his M.P. to get his release.

"Quite a family affair," commented Bill. "No daughters?"

"I believe Mrs. Elthorp had a daughter by her first marriage, but she didn't get on or something. Anyhow, she went down to live with her mother's sister when she was quite young."

"Trouble with stepfather?" suggested Bill.

The sturdy man behind the bar—he must have been about twenty at the time Mrs. Twiss presented her daughter with a new papa—shook his head. "Don't rightly know. There were some as said Mrs. Twiss thought she'd married beneath her, going into trade, her father having been a minister of the Established Church, and she wanted her girl to have a good chance in life, so she sent her south to her unmarried sister, who was a school teacher. But she never came back, which is queer if you come to think of it."

"Married?" asked Bill.

The man shook his head. "I never heard of it, and she never visited her own folk. But then families don't always get on. The mother died when the boys were at school, and Mr. Elthorp got a sister to come and keep house."

"You'd have thought he'd send for his stepdaughter," mused Bill.

"Well, she might have her own family. Anyhow, Mr. Elthorp

may have felt she wasn't anything to do with him. What's your interest in them?"

"I'm trying to trace the daughter," explained Bill. "I thought the family might be able to help."

"She can't be any chicken now. Philip Elthorp's a man of forty-six or thereabouts and she'd be a good ten years older than him."

It all seemed to hang together very well, and Bill, having had one for the road and invited the landlord to join him, wandered out of the pub and turned into the main street where Elthorp had his premises. Elthorps was typical of the dignified prosperity that jewelers' establishments always contrive to maintain. The windows were plate-glass and perfectly polished, the wares they exhibited were solid and in good taste, without being priceless. In peace-time the shop probably made an excellent annual turnover. Bill noted that, to help tide over the difficulties of the hour, it had opened a second-hand department with some really good examples of silver and silver-gilt.

"Not a second Cartier but quite a nice haul for any snatch-and-grab raider," was how he put it to Crook on his return.

Even after six years of war the place breathed money in a discreet fashion. A lady was looking at an engine-turned cigarette-case when Bill came in; she looked pretty engine-turned herself. Someone else was examining rings. A middle-aged man came forward to attend to the new customer and Bill asked to see Philip Elthorp. "I represent a legal firm in London," he explained. "A personal matter." He thought he detected a gleam of apprehension in the other man's face, but if so it vanished the next instant. He was taken into a handsome room as discreetly comfortable as the rest of the premises, containing a leather-topped desk, saddlebag chairs, a certificate of merit of some sort on the wall. A striking clock ornamented the mantelpiece. Philip Elthorp was a quiet man in the mid-forties, a solid respectable citizen with a reliable appearance, probably an excellent business man and an example in the home.

He introduced himself and Bill's guide as his brother, Albert, and Bill promptly got down to brass tacks. "I'm calling in connection with a lady who is, I believe, your half-sister, a Miss

Twiss, at present living in Sussex." This time he was certain he detected apprehension in the faces of both men, a lightning glance flashing between them before each resumed his impassive expression.

"Oh yes," said Philip. "I'm afraid there is very little communication between us. She was our mother's daughter by a previous marriage, but she left Liverpool while she was still a girl and she has never been home."

Bill drew a bow at a venture. "I believe I'm not the first person to inquire about her recently. When I was in Sussex I understood . . ."

This time the glance between the brothers was obvious and unmistakable.

"I think we understand one another," said Philip. "You say you represent a firm of solicitors?"

"Yes. This is quite in confidence, of course, but there was an unpleasant affair about a missing ring. . . ."

"Subsequently restored?"

"Well, yes, but . . ."

"It's no use burking the issues," said Albert, the younger of the two brothers, who walked so well you'd never have guessed he had an artificial foot. "We know what Bella is." He turned to Bill. "I take it she's been at it again. I told you years ago, Philip, we should have had her shut up. She's dangerous."

"My dear fellow." It was clear from the elder brother's voice that this matter had been constantly under debate. "She's not certifiable. Besides, the disgrace and the expense."

"The expense we can stand. It would be far more of a disgrace to have her in prison." He turned to the politely-attentive Bill. "If this gentleman will be kind enough to tell us exactly what the position is. . . ."

"I guess it's pretty well the same every time," Bill suggested. "Something disappears, there's trouble and talk about the police, and it turns out that whatever it is is in your sister's handbag."

"Our half-sister," said Albert. "Actually, not even that."

Bill didn't argue the point with him. In any case, brothers aren't responsible in law for their sisters. It was a good thing that reputation still mattered to some people. "In this case," he added, "Miss Twiss claimed that she found the ring in the bath-room and took it, meaning to give it back to the owner . . ."

"And forgot about it. I know. Other times she's found it on the stairs or out in the street. What's the owner's attitude?"

"Ugly," said Bill. "A regular old battle-axe."

"Naturally we should prefer to settle the matter out of court."

"I suppose that's the way it's generally done," Bill agreed. "As a matter of fact, the owner won't take action, but you can't keep a thing like that quiet when the whole household knows what's happened, and of course the other guests are a bit put out. Does this happen at regular intervals or just as the mood takes her?"

"I—it's difficult to say. We had heard nothing for the better part of a year, and we hoped that perhaps . . ."

"It was never much of a hope," said Albert curtly. "We may as well be frank with Mr. . . ."

"Parsons is the name."

"It's like a disease, you never know when she'll have another attack. This has been going on forty years, you see."

"I wondered why she went south," Bill acknowledged.

"Yes. It was an ugly affair—a pendant. And we had an apprentice who was suspected. Case looked very black against him, and—in point of fact, it was Bella's mother who found out. She was terribly distressed. It had never happened before, and . . ."

"Well, I dare say she hadn't had the opportunity before," said Bill, reasonably. "Living quietly with a widow, and she a little girl, jewels wouldn't mean much to her. Then she's brought here and put in the middle of them—one's seen it happen again and again."

"It's what I've always said," intervened Philip. "It's a sort of phobia, like drugs or . . ."

"It's too bad the police don't always agree," Bill murmured. "Do you get the stuff back?"

"Oh yes," said Philip. "That's the curious part. Miss Twiss doesn't take things for what she can obtain for them—as to that, she has no need to be concerned for her livelihood, she has an income from her mother and if that were insufficient, naturally we should acknowledge our obligations. But she has what I once heard described rather unpleasantly as a lust for precious stones for their own sake. It's quite different from the case, which all men in our profession encounter from time to time, of people who are regular thieves and sell their stuff to a fence. The police can deal with them, though not so effectually as we could wish, particularly since the war, when weakened morale and cheap money have caused the situation to deteriorate very considerably."

"This chap must be a lay preacher in his spare time," Bill reflected.

"And so Miss Twiss left Liverpool and went south," he observed. "I suppose her aunt knew of the situation."

"We felt it only fair to warn her. The trouble in the first place had been that no one had suspected or had had any reason to suspect this—taint—in Miss Twiss. Naturally, afterwards, we couldn't run the risk of keeping her here. Things were quite unpleasant enough as it was. My father had already dismissed the apprentice, and when he learned the truth he went round to see the lad's parents and arranged for compensation. Obviously we wanted to keep the matter out of the courts."

"And from our neighbors," cut in Albert.

"Fortunately there wasn't very much gossip. Probably it didn't seem very odd that my father shouldn't be particularly anxious to keep a stepdaughter in his house—that is to say, it occasioned considerably less comment than if she had been his own child."

"You mean, you decided on the strength of a single incident that Miss Twiss had got this—propensity." Bill could use long words too if he liked.

The brothers looked awkward, then Philip said, "As a matter of fact, my father yielded to my mother's pleading to give Bella a second chance. I think she was afraid that if a similar incident occurred in other surroundings it might develop into a police-court case. She promised to keep a close eye on her daughter, and see that she had no access to the showroom. But Bella was very cunning. I still don't understand how she eluded her mother's vigilance" (Oh, damn it, thought Bill, this must be the Civil Service one, after all.), "but the fact remains that a

191

little later a ring was missing. My father instantly asked Bella if she had had anything to do with its disappearance, and threatened to thrash her within an inch of her life if she didn't produce the missing article. She said she knew nothing about it, whereupon our mother said, 'In that case, we must send for the police at once, and this time, Henry, you must prosecute.' That upset the apple-cart all right. Bella admitted she had taken it, and after that my father put his foot down. Bella must leave the house and the town. Her aunt, Millie, living in Sussex, was prepared to take her—it was naturally made worth her while—and she went a few days later, and has never been back."

"But the trouble went on?" Bill suggested.

"For two years we heard nothing, and we began to hope it had been merely a matter of opportunity and a young woman's vanity. Then Bella became engaged and there was a question of what to send her for a wedding present. Normally we should have selected some piece of jewelry from our own stocks, but my father was afraid that might start up the old trouble. Before the date of the wedding was fixed, however, we received a visit from her fiancé in a great state of distress. Bella had been at it again. He had taken her to a fashionable jeweler's to choose a ring, and—well, they left the shop with more rings than they had paid for. The jeweler had discovered his loss, and Bella's aunt had to admit that there had been previous incidents. The young fellow was very bitter that he hadn't been warned."

"Can't blame him," murmured Bill, reasonably.

"My mother said that there had been no trouble for the better part of three years, and it would be wicked to brand a girl for what we all hoped was a passing phase. However, the upshot was that the engagement was broken off, and there was another period of peace."

"Not for Aunt Millie," suggested Bill.

"It was really more a question of keeping Bella out of temptation's way. Her aunt lived in quite a small town and entertained on a very modest scale. It's probable that Bella never saw anything to distract her. We had no further trouble until Miss Wayne died, and then the question arose as to what to do about Bella. She was, of course, of age, in fact she was in her mid-thirties, and unless we were prepared to make the whole thing public we had no authority over her. She had her own income, she was, in every other respect, perfectly normal, and once again we hoped that her experiences would be a lesson to her and history wouldn't repeat itself."

"But it has?"

Philip Elthorp nodded. "Every now and again, say an average of two years or so, the trouble breaks. Bella invariably returns the goods when it's obvious that she has no choice, and on a number of occasions we have paid damages. Whether there have been any occasions when she has been unsuspected we have no means of knowing."

"Restless life for you," suggested Bill.

"So much so that my wife and I have discussed having her up here under our eyes, but we have always decided against it. She would have more opportunity here than in most places and the attendant publicity would be so much greater. It would affect not only us, but our children." (There were, Bill subsequently discovered, seven of these.) "My brother had proposed having her certified, but I doubt if this would be possible. And if we raised the question and the medical profession were non-co-operative, then we might find ourselves involved with the police. It's a great problem."

"Must be," agreed Bill. "You hadn't thought of getting her a—well, sort of guardian angel?"

"We made that experiment once but it didn't work. Naturally, the job wasn't one to appeal to the majority, and then our half-sister is very self-willed."

"So you just chance your arm?" He thought they had probably done the best thing. He knew that, provided the goods were returned, the average person prefers to keep out of court.

"I think," continued Philip Elthorp painfully, "you said your client does not intend to prosecute?"

"Oh no. That is, she died pretty suddenly shortly afterwards, so she's out of the picture. . . ."

Elthorp rose in horror from his leather-seated arm-chair. "Died? You are not, Mr Parsons, suggesting that . . . ."

"Speaking as a lawyer," said Bill, which, strictly speaking,

193

he was not, "I never suggest anything. Besides, the police have got someone for the murder. But this story of the missing ring has upset the household—this was one of the occasions where things couldn't be kept quiet—and I didn't know . . ."

"You mean, they wish her to make other arrangements? You can hardly blame them, but really I'm at my wits' end. I had thought of a doctor's household, but that again presents difficulties. Besides, if she refuses our suggestions, we can't withhold her income without establishing mental instability, and, as I say, I doubt whether we have a case. Her normal health is excellent, except that she complains nowadays of deafness."

"Difficult," agreed Bill, ready to depart now he had learned what Crook wanted to know.

"And in point of fact, Bella is not a fool. For instance, in the present case, could you be sure of a conviction even if the matter were taken to court?"

Bill considered. "No," he agreed after an instant, "we couldn't. That's British justice for you. She has to be proved guilty on facts, not appearances, and if she repeated her yarn of finding the ring in the bathroom and intending to return it, but forgetting she'd got it . . . She made no attempt to sell it. . . ."

"Sounds thin," objected the comparatively silent Albert.

"It is thin, but thick enough to keep her out of quod. She didn't try and dispose of it, she didn't refuse to hand it back, and she told a story that could be true."

"With the whole place humming with the loss?"

"She's deaf, remember. She could get by on that. Well, I'm very much obliged to you." He got up to go.

"But we can't leave matters in this inconclusive state," protested Philip Elthorp. "What precisely is the position? Is it possible for her to remain where she is any longer?"

"I'd leave it for the minute," said Bill. "Her story's been accepted, and now the old battle-axe is out of the way I doubt if she'll have any temptation for a while. You needn't be afraid you won't be informed if they do want to get rid of her; and they'll come to you before they approach the police, I can promise you that. It doesn't do a guest-house any good to get mixed up with the authorities. In any case, if trouble should develop we'll keep in touch."

Walking back to the station, Bill reflected that they weren't really much further on. Miss Twiss had never displayed homicidal tendencies, but then, he reminded himself, probably she'd never had a chance hitherto. As for the mysterious inquirer who had preceded him, that would probably be a private investigator put on the track by the deceased and certainly unlamented Lady Bate. Now, suppose Miss Twiss knew that these inquiries were being made, would that be sufficient incentive for murder? He wondered if that was the line Crook was taking, but even Crook for all his ebullience would appreciate that the first step would be to prove that she did know.

Then another consideration occurred to him. He remembered Crook saying, "Suppose this wasn't premeditated, but a spur-of-the-minute crime?" Miss Twiss might have thought she'd take advantage of circumstances and go on the prowl round old Lady B.'s room at a time when the house was virtually empty. Opening the drawer, since most of the room seemed under lock and key, she might have seen a letter from the Liverpool inquiry agent, read it, realized that her next abode would be either a prison cell or the asylum, and, seeing the sleeping-powders, worked out her neat spontaneous plan to put the old lady where she couldn't do any more harm. The letter, naturally, she would have destroyed; it was improbable that she would speak of the matter to anyone else. And the obvious conclusion would be that the old lady had taken an overdose.

"All the same, Crook's setting himself something outsize in problems if he thinks he's going to prove that," Bill told himself grimly.

CHAPTER NINETEEN

"AND NOW, I suppose," said Bill, having completed his report to Crook, "you know exactly what happened."

"Now I've got all the pieces and I simply have to make out the pattern," corrected Crook. "Not that I ever had any doubt after I heard the Colonel's story."

"You didn't think it might be boloney?"

"It might, of course, though I'd have been more inclined to think that if it had been Bro. Joseph's version. No, I think the Colonel told us all he knew, and without his evidence I don't see how we'd ever have solved the problem. Now all I want is a certain letter."

Bill looked at him woodenly. "A letter?"

"Yes. And I'll have that by tonight or my name's not Arthur Crook. Then I'm goin' down to the house to clear everythin' up. We've been long enough on the job as it is, and I don't like to think of that girl waitin' in chokey, wonderin' how long it'll be before she's weighed and measured for the hangman's benefit."

"Are you," inquired Bill, "hoping to get this tied up without another murder?"

"Hoping," said Crook, 'but not as sure as I'd like to be. Now I'd better get in touch with the old gentleman and warn him to expect me. Don't want him thinkin' me a masked marauder and drawin' a pistol as I come round the corner of the house."

"I've had a letter from that fellow, Crook," announced Joseph Anstruther to his brother and niece. (The Colonel had intimated that he would prefer correspondence to be between Crook and

Joseph, who seemed better able to tackle so robust a vulgarian.) "It seems he's got the rest of the evidence he wants and hopes to be down to get everything settled."

"Why here?" demanded the Colonel.

Joseph looked surprised. "The murder was done here, wasn't it?"

"I should have expected him, if he really has his evidence, to go direct to the police."

Joseph looked at the letter again. "When I say he's got it, what I actually mean is that he will have it by tomorrow night."

"What an extraordinary feller he is! You can't order evidence like tea from a grocer."

"No knowing what that chap might do. Anyway, it'll be something to have the matter settled. By the way, he seems to think your evidence is the turning-point in the case."

"I wish to God it was all over," said the Colonel. "I don't like this sort of thing hanging over me. Besides—deliberate murder! You can't get away from it, and if he's right and the girl isn't responsible, then the real murderer is still under our roof."

He looked up, but Rose was staring out of the window. Joseph was watching him intently, and the eyes of the two brothers met, but their faces remained impassive. If either knew more than he chose to tell, you wouldn't guess it from their expressions.

"Does he say what time he's coming?" inquired Rose.

Again Joseph referred to the letter. " 'Shall be glad if you can have all the household, both sides and the kitchen'—I take it, that means ourselves and our guests—'on the premises. I promise not to keep 'em long, but I have a little experiment to make.' "

"I don't like this at all," objected the Colonel. "Suppose someone else gets killed during his little experiment. Does he say anything else?"

"Just to tell everyone he's expected, so that they'll be available."

"Or give the guilty person a chance to get away?"

"Confession of guilt," said Joseph laconically. He laid the letter down. "He's coming as soon as he can manage after dinner."

"Tonight?"

"Yes."

"It's Gladys' afternoon off," murmured Rose.

"Then she'll have to change it for once. Tell her she's likely to get more entertainment by staying at home than at the local pictures."

Rose was still frowning. "Do you suppose he means he wants to be put up? He can hardly go back to London at that hour, and the local hotels are probably all packed."

"Perhaps he'll sleep in that red abomination of his. I wouldn't put it past him. You'd better let the household know, Rose. It 'ud be just like Mrs. Hunter to be going to the Brightlingstone Palais de Danse tonight."

"She'd stay if she thought Crook was coming," returned the Colonel grimly. He looked out of the window. "Blowing up for a storm. I don't like the electricity in the air."

All through the day the tension increased. At The Downs everyone felt ill-at-ease, people started to speak, then stopped half-way, as though the simplest observation might be dangerous at this stage. In mid-afternoon the storm broke, the rain sweeping in clouds across the Downs, blotting out the horizon and drumming against the glass—like an army trying to get in, said Mrs. Hunter interestedly.

"I must say I'm sorry for poor Mr. Crook if he's going to motor down in an open car in this weather," she added, looking hopefully at Miss Twiss. But Miss Twiss didn't seem to have heard. "I wonder which of us is going to have a nasty shock tonight," continued Mrs. Hunter in a very loud voice, and at that Miss Twiss did look up and say, "Shock? Oh, are you subject to electricity in the atmosphere? My Aunt Millie..."

"Have you taken it in that Mr. Crook is coming down tonight to tell us who really killed old Lady B.?" bawled Mrs. Hunter, to which Miss Twiss replied equably, "I wonder how he found out. But perhaps he doesn't really know."

"He says he does. That is, he's going to make an experiment. Mr. Joseph told us."

"He doesn't say what sort of an experiment, does he?" demanded Miss Twiss sharply. "Oh dear, how warm it is." She pushed the blue shawl off her shoulders. "Perhaps this weather will stop him, I should think he mightn't come till tomorrow."

"Pooh!" said Mrs. Hunter to that. "If I was going to solve a murder I wouldn't let a drop of rain stop me."

"Perhaps it'll interfere with his experiment, whatever that may be."

"He said something about a letter, Mr. Joseph told me."

"A letter?" Miss Twiss's tone was as wooden as Bill's had been. "Who from?"

"He's not likely to tell us that, of course. But he seems to think it ties up the case."

Miss Twiss looked as though she were going to say more, then returned to her game of patience.

"If he's right," continued Winifred Hunter, still at the top of her voice, "someone in this house must be feeling very uncomfortable."

"I am for one," said Miss Twiss instantly. "I don't like all these upsets. I don't pretend I liked Lady Bate, but murder's not nice, even if the person who's murdered is a trial to everybody. I'm glad I couldn't give any evidence."

Mrs. Hunter's eyes were round with amazement. "What a thing to say! I'd have loved it—only, of course, I hadn't got anything to tell, nothing that mattered, I mean." She got up and walked over to the window. A flash of lightning zigzagged between the near-by trees. "If one of them is struck it might hit the house," she reflected. "Oh well, roll, bowl or pitch, every time a blood-orange or a good see-gar."

"That's what Mr. Crook said," contributed Miss Twiss suddenly.

"You seem to have heard a good deal of what Mr. Crook said." It was unlike Mrs. Hunter to be catty and Miss Twiss looked surprised, but she only said, "Because he speaks up so. I don't know what's the matter with most people, they mumble so. Aunt Millie used to say it was people whose teeth didn't fit properly, but some of these people have their own teeth. It's as if they were afraid of opening their mouths. Now I hear you when you take the trouble to speak up, but I could never hear Lady Bate—or hardly ever. Only when she shouted."

"You didn't miss much," said Mrs. Hunter frankly. "All her talk was about herself, and for all her money I never met a less interesting woman."

"It's queer how some people don't begin to be interesting till they're dead."

"You should have met Alfred," confided Mrs. Hunter, and at the memory of her lost husband her voice automatically sank. Because he was still so real to her that she didn't need an audience when she talked about him. Miss Twiss didn't mind. She went on with her interminable patience and her own thoughts.

All the afternoon the rain came down; the ditches were filling up, the roads were churned into mud paths and still there seemed no cessation in the fury of the storm. Inside the house the electricity of the atmosphere seemed to have affected everyone. Even Miss Twiss couldn't keep her mind on her cards, Mrs. Mack forgot to salt the potatoes, Jock kept muttering to himself.

"What on earth are you saying, Jock?" Mrs. Mack asked him.

"I'd put a curse on yon felly if I could," said Jock vindictively. "Upsetting Miss Rose this way."

"Maybe he can't help it," said Mrs. Mack. "After all, he doesn't want the young lady to hang."

"You'd think he suspected one of us," said Jock, and Gladys, who had passed from her original sulkiness at the cancelling of her afternoon out to a morbid delight at the prospect of the evening's visitor, inquired pertly, "Who's your bet, Jock? Though it seems all wrong to me that anyone's got to pay for putting that old so-and-so where she belongs—in the grave-yard."

"You'll hang yourself with that tongue of yours one of these days, my girl," Jock warned her. "And don't be so free with your elders. I'm having no bets on this. Truth's truth and in our law-courts truth prevails and don't you forget it."

"What's the good of telling her that?" inquired Mrs. Mack scornfully. "Her and truth couldn't shake hands."

Gladys tossed her head. "There's one thing, they can't pin it on me. It was my afternoon off, though, mind you, I wouldn't have minded doing the old crone in . . ."

"Haud your tongue," stormed Jock. "Can ye never think of your betters? This is a nice thing to happen in a house like this, with the Colonel and Miss Rose."

"I dare say Mr. Joseph's enjoying it," remarked the unrepentant Gladys.

But Mrs. Mack said severely, "Not him. These things are very nice to read about with your feet up and a cigarette in your mouth, but when they come home to roost they're not so comfortable by a long chalk."

In the dining-room a slow paralysis was descending on the Anstruthers. Each anticipated Crook's impending arrival with a different dread. And gradually the spirit spread throughout the house. The guilty thought, what does he know? The innocent, how will this evening's work end? Hearts bound by affection beat passionately for the loved one's safety, doubt crept in like a tunneling worm, glances were more acute, eyes were gradually veiled, but words were increasingly spare. By eight o'clock, with no word of Crook's arrival and no sign of him and his atrocious little car, the old gentlemen began to consider the probability of the experiment, whatever it might be, being postponed till morning. And the prospect of that delay weighed heavy on every heart.

Joseph, looking across the table at his brother, thought: How much does he know? What does he guess? How much will he tell? And the Colonel met his eye implacably, while similar considerations disturbed his own breast.

At eight-fifteen it was decided to dine, and shortly before the nine o'clock news Rose said simply, "I think we might ask the others to join us for coffee tonight. We're all in this together, and in a way I feel responsible, because it's our house, when all's said and done."

The Colonel frowned at the suggestion—the thin end of the wedge, he called it—but Joseph said hurriedly, "That's a very kind thought, Rose. I'll tell the others myself."

"And I'll tell Jock." The pair departed, leaving the Colonel to frown and speculate. His thoughts, whatever they were, could hardly have been pleasant ones, but he wiped the look of anxiety from his face as Rose came back, saying, "They're coming now. I can hear Mrs. Hunter's voice."

He put a hand on her arm. "Not much longer, my dear."

Rose drew a deep breath. "I always hated suspense. And I don't like this storm. It's a portent."

Jock came in with the coffee and she hurried over and began to pour it into the little blue and gold Minton cups. Joseph, who could be ceremonious enough when he pleased, carried them round and offered sugar with a grave assurance that there was plenty. Mrs. Hunter said affably, "Well, I'm sure I don't know how you manage. I'm a sweet-tooth and I can't deny it. It was very kind of you to ask us over," she continued, turning to Rose. "I must say my nerves are beginning to be a bit shaken. It's not that I mind storms, and Alfred used to love them—said they put men in their proper place. . . ." She hesitated a moment, biting off the end of a chuckle, remembering what else Alfred had said, but deciding you couldn't repeat a thing like that in this arid atmosphere. "But this waiting about—do you think Mr. Crook could have been struck by lightning?"

"He might at all events let us know," said the Colonel testily, but Joseph said, "I dare say half the telegraph wires are down. Not his fault."

"Mr. Joseph." (It was the irrepressible Mrs. Hunter again and Joseph winced at the address.) "Do you know what this extraordinary experiment is, and how it's going to affect all of us?"

Joseph said he'd no notion. He said he supposed it depended on the letter, but he didn't really know anything about that either.

"If you ask me," said Mrs. Hunter shrewdly, "he's not too sure of his onions, but he thinks he can make one of us give ourselves away when we see his precious document."

Conversation flagged, spurted up again as the Colonel recalled his duties as a host, and then died down. Shortly before ten the telephone rang, and Crook's voice asked for Joseph Anstruther.

"Sorry about the delay, Major," he said heartily. "Didn't

allow for the storm. Nearly swept the road away in places. But I'm on my way."

"Do you still propose to carry out your experiment tonight?" inquired Joseph coldly, and Crook said in reluctant tones he supposed it *was* a bit late, but added cheerfully that he'd got the letter and everything was now hunky-dory.

"I hope," said Joseph in a sharp voice, "you will restrict your experiment, whatever it may be, as far as you can. I would remind you we have ladies here who have endured considerable strain during the past weeks, and they are all in a highly nervous state."

"You gave them my message?" said Crook, and Joseph agreed coldly that he had.

"Hold everything," shouted Crook cheerfully. "I'll be coming."

"Have you any idea what time?" Joseph sounded more glacial than the rain.

"That's a notion." Crook never paid any attention to clocks. He worked when work was there and as opportunity offered. "Well, say, it might be as well not to lock your front door tonight, but put the key under the mat."

"Jock will sit up," said Joseph, but Crook was so heartily opposed to that you could almost hear him shaking his head over the wires.

"Not on your life. I mean that, Major. Jock's to go to bed. Got that? No, don't ask for explanations now. Just leave it to Arthur Crook. I'll do all the lockin' up that's necessary, but it would worry me a heap if I thought I was keepin' the household away from their beauty-sleep. Seriously, Major, I want everyone on their toes in the mornin'. If you're afraid of burglars I'll report to you on my way up. How about that? Matter of fact, and in strict confidence, it won't do me any harm to find the place unpopulated when I come."

"I wish you could give me some idea of the nature of your plan," interjected Joseph, but Crook said no, there were some chances only a fool would take and he'd be along about midnight. Just before he rang off he said again, in a very earnest voice, "I wasn't stringin' you, Major, when I said I'd like to find the coast clear when I come down. If anyone is hangin' about waitin' for me, he might get a nasty shock. Only fair to warn you. This storm's altered things a bit, but I think we can catch up if you'll do as I say."

The Colonel was anything but pleased when he got the message. "Why can't the fellow put up at a hotel for the night and come along like a Christian in the morning?"

"Seeing he's coming to hamstring one of us," suggested Mrs. Hunter in her sprightly way, "you couldn't expect him to feel very Christian!"

The long moments dragged on. Mrs. Mack and Gladys, having been told what to expect, went dispiritedly to bed. "And if I catch you prowling around in your godless pajamas after your light's out," Mrs. Mack warned the girl, "you'll know what it would have been like to have a mother."

Jock locked up the rest of the house, Miss Twiss excused herself, Winnie Hunter reluctantly followed her a little later, and at last Rose stood up, saying, "I believe I'm tired. It's the strain of waiting, and it certainly won't please Mr. Crook to arrive and find a row of sleeping dummies. But I must confess I wish the ordeal were over."

"Never knew such a theatrical beggar," grumbled the Colonel. "Why can't he do everything straight and above-board? All these tricks and posturings. . . ."

"Do the fellow justice, James," protested his brother. "Murder isn't a straight, above-board affair. It's damned crooked—I beg your pardon, my dear—and I dare say you do have to go down on all fours to get things straightened out."

He crossed the room to open the door for Rose, who passed out saying, "Good night, Uncle Joseph. You're more comfort to me than you know," and then the Colonel made the final rounds as he did every night of his life to be sure Jock hadn't overlooked anything, and soon after the clocks had chimed eleven all lights were extinguished, voices had died down and darkness descended on the house.

At about ten minutes to twelve, when Crook was speeding doggedly through the night, a bedroom door opened and a figure stole noiselessly on to the landing. It was disguised in some black garment that concealed it, rendering it almost invisible in that unlighted house, and it carried something in its hand. Rigid as a post it stood, listening intently, then began its slow dangerous journey down the stairs. Now and again it paused, as though anticipating interruption, but when none came it continued its downward steps. Within and without, the darkness was complete. The figure approached the front door, lifted the latch, stole forth. Thanks to the discussion in the drawing-room, there could be no question as to the whereabouts of the key, and it used this to close the door from the outside. Its simple preparations were soon complete, and it settled itself to wait. Although it was so dark there were still sounds to distinguish life from death. An owl hooted dismally, trees creaked in the cold damp wind that had followed the end of the rain, there was everywhere the up-rush of scent and the covert whispers that are the hallmark of night.

The watcher in the shadows shivered and strained for the sound of an approaching car.

CHAPTER TWENTY

It was not only at The Downs that the sense of tension was abroad. Crook, making the best pace he could in the atrocious weather—more than one familiar road was blocked and he had to make a number of diversions—was exceedingly dubious as to the welcome he was likely to receive when he reached The Downs. He was accustomed (as Mrs. Hunter would have put it) to dicing with death, but he knew that, since you can't hang twice, and he had made it plain that he intended to name the real murderer, he himself need anticipate short shrift.

He drove for the most part in silence, bending his uncanny eyesight to distinguishing the road ahead, but now and again he made an observation aloud and his words came echoing back to him from the swaying trees and echoing woodlands.

"What is this mad experiment of yours?" Bill had demanded some time earlier, but Crook retorted, "It's experiment enough for me to put my head into that nest of murderers without goin' into exact details."

Bill, though he never displayed an atom of feeling, was secretly anxious. Crook took the craziest risks and it would be no consolation for the murderer either to swing or to die by his own hand if it meant putting out Crook's light as well.

The little red car ate up the soggy miles; now and again on the horizon a light burned to show that life was still extant, but for the most part it was like driving through a deserted world. Even Crook, who boasted he had no imagination, began to feel the spell. There was an illustration he had seen once by a chap called Rackham, a queer, haunted affair, that returned to trouble him now. And he recalled a macabre programme they had sometimes on the radio called Appointment with Fear—change one word and make it Appointment with Death and it might be a first-class caption to the picture. The wheels of the Scourge seemed to move in a definite rhythm—Appointment-with-death, ap-point-ment-with-death—round and round and on and on. Once he nearly drove into the hedge as a white ghostly apparition appeared on his left, hanging just out of reach.

"I'm losing my nerve in my old age," decided Crook, righting the car just in time. "It's nothing but a damned great owl."

But for the moment it had been as startling as a light seen suddenly in the black-out in the middle of a raid. The bird hung there a moment, then drifted slowly away to the left.

"So you're out for prey, too," muttered Crook. "And likely to be luckier than me." Because a field-mouse or mole or whatever sort of provender owls procured for their young—Crook's knowledge of natural history was practically nil—might escape its would-be executioner but certainly could do no lethal damage.

There was no sound now but the hiss of the water round the wheels and the steady noise of the engine—round and round, on and on.

At last he came within sight of The Downs, a deeper patch of blackness in a black world.

"Zero hour," he muttered, bringing the car to a standstill by the gate and opening the door.

He was standing on the road, locking it (since he sincerely believed half London and all the country was anxious to rob him of the little monstrosity) when a terrible shriek came pealing through the trees, filling the night with clamor.

Crook threw back his head when that shocking sound smote his ears. He muttered a word or two, then lowered his bullet-head and went hot-foot up the path. He had reached the porch, and in another instant would have stooped to fumble for the key, when something thin and taut caught him round the knees. Instinctively he flung out his hand to save his face and came crashing down in front of the austerely handsome door. In a flash something moved in the darkness and some substance, thick and stifling, covered his head and face, so that he was left struggling, with a deplorable lack of dignity, to free himself. The hand holding this thing, whatever it was, twisted it closer and a voice hissed, "The letter. Give me the letter." Feeling like a trussed fowl, Crook felt blindly for the envelope in his breast-pocket; the next instant it was snatched from him, a minute gleam of light shone out, and extinguished again. Crook, who had fallen with some force, suddenly went limp. The hand cautiously relaxed its pressure, though he still remained half-choked and made no attempt to move. It was too late for that. Nerveless, he lay like a fallen dog. "I hope I'll get through without another murder," he had said to Bill, "but I'm not too sure." If any of his enemies had been there they might have taunted him with his own boast—Crook always gets his man. Somebody at last, it seemed, had got Arthur Crook.

The killer was wasting no time. Crook felt a hand on his wrist, the sleeve of his coat was pushed up, fingers pinched up his skin. Now he knew what to expect, and still he made no movement. All this time the house was still as death, still as the death that lurked in the dark porch, and in the blackness the diabolical agency methodically went about its horrid, ruthless work. There was a second momentary flash of the torch, darkness again—and yet—and yet there were faint sounds close at hand, so faint that they eluded the ear of the one who had watched and waited so patiently in that cold, bleak night. (Or perhaps deafness accounted for its utter absorption, its momentary inattention that was to prove its undoing.) At all events, as the needle was about to strike home, something shot like a flash of the departed lightning out of the dark, fastened on the thin wrist, there was a smothered cry, a jerk, and then the sound of an electric bell went pealing, pealing through the silent house.

"None of that," said a voice, speaking low and hard. "Haven't you enough crimes on your conscience as it is?"

It was Jock who came in reply to the summons, Jock buttoning a dressing-gown over hurriedly-donned trousers, his normally neat hair dishevelled, his pace hurried.

"Whatever are ye after waking the hoose at this hour?" he

began indignantly. But his voice died as abruptly as it had begun as, in the roar of light that followed his pressing of the switch, he took in the details of the scene at his feet.

Short, stout, ridiculous, his head enveloped in the blue-gray shawl that had played so momentous a part in this drama involving so much tragedy and terror, Mr. Crook lay, while behind him, like a guardian angel, his thin face impassive, yet marked by a certain ruined grandeur, stood Bill Parsons, his fingers still fastened like a vice on the wrist of the last person Jock had expected to see, a furious defeated figure, the fatal syringe still clasped in its helpless predatory hand.

The identity of the murderer came as a shock to them all.

"But, Rose," protested an appalled and stupefied Joseph Anstruther, "it seems impossible it should have been you. Even if that old harridan had got a hold over you—murder's not a game."

There wasn't an atom of pity or remorse in Rose's pale, sculptured face.

"That was precisely the nature of her hold over me. Not that I meant to murder her when I went into her room that day. I went for the diary. She kept taunting me with it, told me it contained damning facts, facts that would ruin me if they became known."

"She couldn't have done anything," Joseph protested.

"Oh, Uncle Joseph, you don't really mean that. Imagine it— she wouldn't have said anything, I dare say, but she had only to leave that book unlocked in the sitting-room when she was out and Mrs. Hunter wasn't, and the whole story would have become public property. How could I have stayed here after that? And this was the only refuge I had left in the world. It became an obsession with me, to get that book. I was so patient. I knew I had to wait for a time when no one would see me go into her room. More than that, when no one would even see me on that side of the house. If Caroline Bate and her aunt were out of the way, then Mrs. Hunter would be fussing around. In the morning Gladys might come in at any moment. In fact, I ruled out the mornings altogether; but in the afternoons Lady Bate stayed indoors, resting, and though she seldom came upstairs she might send her niece up at any moment. Then there was Miss Twiss to consider. She was always in in the afternoon. And all the time my position was getting more desperate. There seemed no end to the demands Lady Bate was making. Her last one was for a private sitting-room, and she knew I daren't refuse. It wasn't really that she needed one, she'd been living in hotels for so long she must have got used to a communal parlor, but she wanted to assert her right to be in our part of the house. Once she was established there she'd never rest till she practically ordered the whole household. I couldn't bear it. I thought once of killing myself, but I wouldn't allow her to defeat me.

"Then I heard she was going to London for the day. The morning was still unsafe, but in the afternoon Mrs. Hunter and the girl went out, the servants never came upstairs then, and only Miss Twiss was left. I had heard Jock say that she always listened to the radio in the afternoon, and he added, 'She'll be no trouble to us. There's some rubbishing play on of a Wednesday—Wednesday Matinee, they call it—and she wouldn't miss it for all the sunshine of an English summer.' It seemed to me I should never have a better opportunity. I looked at *The Times* and saw that the play started at four o'clock and the programme didn't end till five. That would be all the time I needed. True, tea was served at a quarter-past four and I didn't want to arouse speculation by being late, but a quarter of an hour would be sufficient for me to find out if the diary was available. You and father would be playing chess and you wouldn't move till Jock or I made you. Naturally, I wanted to play as safe as possible. I stole into the guests' part of the house to make sure the wireless really was on and I could hear it blaring away like a mad bull. As I was turning away I noticed the big blue-gray shawl hanging on the hat-stand, and I remembered Jock telling me Miss Twiss always wore it about the house. It was just luck that it was a warm afternoon and she had discarded it for once. It seemed to me that if I put that on and went up the guests' staircase it wouldn't matter if I was seen. Everyone would assume I was Miss Twiss. Mind you, at that time I had no thought of doing Lady Bate any harm."

"It might have been precious uncomfortable for the old lady" (he meant Miss Twiss) "if anyone had spotted her going into Lady Bate's room."

"I've told you, the servants are never in that part of the house after lunch." Rose sounded impatient. "I only had to consider the thousand-to-one chance of you or father seeing me. You didn't know which room belonged to which guest in any case, so if, as actually happened, either of you saw a shawled figure opening a door, it wouldn't occur to you there was anything wrong."

"Give you that," agreed Joseph after an instant's consideration. "All the same, Rose, what on earth . . . ?"

"I'm coming to that. Do you remember my telling you that, when I shot Gerald, it was what they call an unpremeditated crime? Nobody could have been further from the thought of murder than I was that night when I went to the villa. And it was the same when I stole into Lady Bate's room. It wasn't till I had opened the drawer and seen the sleeping-tablets and realized how dangerous they were, and yet, so far as I could see, how safe from my point of view, that the notion entered my brain. In that instant I had precisely the same impulse as I'd known nearly twenty years earlier—here was my opportunity. I didn't even hesitate. I saw this as my chance and I took it in a flash. I didn't think about anyone else being blamed. I didn't get as far as looking into the future. Anyway, just as Gerald had been supposed to shoot himself, so, I decided, it would be assumed that Lady Bate had taken an overdose."

"But you didn't know how often she took the tablets," Joseph objected.

"Don't you see, that didn't matter. It was perfectly obvious from the label on the box of salts that she took a regular nightly dose, and anyway she appears to have broadcasted her habits with a singular lack of delicacy. Even Jock knew about them. I thought, there will be no evidence against anyone. I couldn't know about the will. That was the unforeseeable thing that wrecked my plan. You see," she smiled in an odd, grim way that nearly broke Joseph's heart, "she was cleverer than I was.

I over-estimated my strength or under-estimated hers. She's defeated me, each time."

"It wasn't her, it was that chap, Crook. You could hardly expect to get the better of a tough nut like that."

"Uncle Joseph, how did he *know*?"

"He's got his wits about him all right. He remembered that Miss Twiss would be listening in at four o'clock—Jock would have told him—and he knew, too, that she wasn't giving false evidence because there was some change in the cast of the first play, and she couldn't have known that if she hadn't been sitting with her ear glued to the receiver at four o'clock. And it was four o'clock when someone went into Lady Bate's room. Your father gave him that bit of information, by noticing the chiming of the clock. It wasn't Mrs. Mack—you couldn't mistake her, wrapped in half a dozen shawls, the girl was out, Mrs. Hunter and Caroline Bate had their alibi as tight as a drum, there was no one left but you. And then Miss Twiss had said something about not wanting the shawl that day, it being so warm—later on she lent it to Lady Bate, who had twisted her ankle. . . . And beyond all that there was the clock."

Rose looked puzzled. "I don't see where the clock comes in."

"Think a minute. It struck four and the woman in the shawl heard it and started. According to Charles, she nearly jumped out of her skin. *But Miss Twiss wouldn't have heard it.* She's much too deaf. That was the last link in Crook's chain."

"Yes." Rose looked surprised. "I never thought of that. But then I never thought of anyone like Crook. He was the unknown factor no one could have guarded against."

She waited a little, then said, "I suppose this is the end. It seems a pity after so much trouble."

Joseph looked more uncomfortable than she. "You did mean to do for him, Rose," he pointed out. "It's incomprehensible."

She laid a hand on his arm. "You may find it difficult to believe this, Uncle Joseph, but by that stage of the proceedings I was absolutely convinced in my own mind that I had a right to defend myself against him in any way I could. I didn't think of it as murder. It was simply self-defense. He was out to convict me if he could."

"Did you realize from the beginning that it was you he was after?"

"I don't know when he began to suspect me, but—one of the papers described me as absolutely ruthless. Have you noticed that people on the winning side never have that sort of adjective applied to them? And yet he was just as ruthless as I. My life was nothing to him, he'd have taken it as casually as he'd have blown out a match, but no one thinks him inhuman for that. I didn't want to kill him, but—murder's like sliding downhill. There comes a time when you can't stop yourself even though you know there's an abyss ahead. Even if you want to save yourself, it's too late. It was like that with me. I didn't want to kill Gerald, but when the moment came my action slid into place like—like a note in music."

Joseph looked up with a gleam of hope. If she talked like this in the witness box no jury would dare send her to the gallows. Guilty but insane, they'd say, and he began to wonder if that mightn't be the juster verdict.

"It was the same with Lady Bate," Rose continued. "The thought of killing her—but I've explained that. Then I heard that Crook was coming down, that he had proof—a letter. I didn't know what letter. Of course, it was nothing. That was just the story he told. He knew that if he could catch the culprit red-handed, in possession of the letter, he needn't look any further. That crime I did plan. But he drove me to it, Uncle. As an individual I wished him no harm at all. But he wouldn't leave me alone. He challenged me, pitted himself against me. Only— he was too clever. He got an inside witness on his side. That was Jock. Oh, Jock would have lied for me, if he could, but he hadn't a chance. There were Crook and that partner of his on the step, and Jock in the doorway, and I still holding father's syringe loaded with a fatal dose of morphia. What was the good of protesting any more? I would have killed him if I could, and the authorities could have suspected whom they chose." She drew a deep breath. "Didn't you tell me once that the greatest mistake of military strategy is to under-estimate your opponent's strength, and the general who does that deserves to lose the battle? That was my blunder. I couldn't believe that such a creature could defeat me, and when I saw he was ruthless I thought I could be more ruthless still. Vanity, I suppose." Her lovely mouth twisted. "I'd been so successful to date. Gerald. And Lady Bate. No one thought of me—not the police or the coroner or the doctor. . . ."

"But, Rose," protested Joseph, asking the question he could not any longer contain, "suppose a court of law had found that girl guilty, sentenced her to death, you'd have spoken then, you wouldn't have let her hang?" The other crimes to which she had confessed seemed to him relatively unimportant, if only he could have her assurance that she wouldn't have permitted this final outrage.

But Mrs. Anstruther was staring at him in genuine amazement. "You mean, would I have come forward and said I had done it? What would have been the sense of that? I should have found myself in her place in a prison cell, and I'd been fighting all this time for immunity."

Joseph passed a shaking hand over his forehead. "I can't believe it, Rose. All the rest, perhaps, but not that."

But Rose's face was hard as iron. "Uncle Joseph," she said, "you've fought in battles?"

"Well?"

"And I suppose sometimes your enemy was younger, less experienced than you? Did that make any difference to your outlook? When things come to the last ditch it's your life against your adversary's. Would you ever have hesitated to preserve yourself, even if it meant some young lad must die?"

"You can't argue along those lines," Joseph protested.

"Yet that's the way it is. It was her or me. The same with Crook. Him or me. It's absurd to ask whether I thought Caroline Bate or Crook more important than myself. What I had to preserve was my own life." She laughed suddenly, hard, immovable. "It seems so ridiculous that you should even have considered such an action on my part. Of course I wouldn't have intervened. And if my plan had gone right this time—I had it all worked out—I meant to go up to Miss Twiss's room when everything was over and put the empty envelope and the syringe there. . . ."

"You were counting a good deal on her deafness," protested her uncle.

"You've forgotten the coffee. I put some of my harmless sleeping mixture into the sugar, and it kept everyone quiet. I couldn't take any risks. Didn't it occur to you to wonder why no one heard me call out to bring Crook at the run up the drive? I made quite sure—oh, I thought of everything. The servants slept the other side of the house, they wouldn't hear. Only—he'd thought of everything, too. My one fear was that someone would refuse sugar, but no one did. And I didn't do them any harm," she added quickly. "I simply ensured that everyone got a good night's rest. There's nothing criminal about that."

Joseph was looking at her in a sort of horror. For years they'd been living side by side, he had been so proud of her, so fond of her, even after he knew the truth about her husband's death his affection hadn't altered. But now—now she seemed to him some monstrous stranger, utterly callous, prepared to put anyone to death who stood in her way. She'd missed her period, of course. As a Borgia, even as a Queen of England in the Middle Ages, her behavior would have seemed justified—plenty of people had died at the stake and on the rack in the name of religion and patriotism. But in 1945 she was an anachronism. But he couldn't hope a police force would acknowledge that point of view. Crook, it seemed, had rushed into danger with his eyes wide open, if you could employ such an expression, remembering the darkness of that fateful night. He'd known that probable death awaited him, and, having taken all possible precautions, had taken a fifty-to-one chance. Everything had depended on perfect timing. If Bill Parsons had intervened an instant too late, it would have been the end for Arthur Crook, because Joseph didn't attempt to hide from himself the truth that his lovely Rose would have put an end to the improbable little lawyer's existence as coolly as she had shot her husband or poisoned Lady Bate. And what was worse, for he could in some degree condone Gerald's death and even find some excuse for her removal of Lady Bate, she would have stood by and seen that slightly demented female, Arabella Twiss, condemned for a crime in which she had no part and which she could not possibly have conceived.

215

On the whole, he reflected, his brother, James, was lucky to be out of it. For James, on hearing the facts, had had a sudden stroke and had never recovered consciousness sufficiently to appreciate the appalling situation.

As for Jock, Joseph shuddered to remember his face of twisted fury and his matching voice as he said, "If I'd dreamed yon felly was going to bring this trouble upon us all, I'd have knocked him on the head before ever I let him inside the house." And then with an expression of scorn that went beyond all words, "Socialism! The equality of man! You'd only to see him to know he'd no notion of how to behave to the gentry. Why couldn't he stick to London and his own kind? If that's the sort of thing we're coming to, then I'm glad my time's drawing on."

CHAPTER TWENTY-ONE

As SOON as the arrest had been made, Crook and Bill Parsons left The Downs, traveling back to London in the indomitable Scourge.

"Of course," remarked Bill as they left the house behind them, "you were expectin' that to happen, weren't you?"

"I'd have been damn' disappointed if it hadn't," said Crook. "Well, stands to reason she had to take a pot at me, and she planned it damn' well."

"You ran it damn' fine," Bill complained crossly. "Another second and . . ."

"Earth hath one guardian soul the less, Heaven one angel more," intoned Crook. "Well, if a chap can't rely on his buddy. . . . Besides, we had to get the evidence. I will say for the dame she thought it up very neatly. Another time I'd be glad to have her on my side."

Bill's eyebrows climbed. "Another time?" he murmured.

"No. You're right. There won't be no other time for her. She'll swing for this. A democratic Home Secretary won't dare reprieve her. Though it's lucky she confessed to puttin' the old lady out of the way," he added. "I doubt whether we could have proved it even now."

"There was her dead set at you," Bill reminded him. "Can't say that was a spur-of-the-minute murder, whatever the others may have been."

"Have a heart," protested Crook. "You can't go on committing murders on the spur of the minute all your life."

"Well, I've had enough of these women," announced Bill decisively. "Give me toughs every time. You do know where you are with them."

Crook chuckled suddenly. The sound caused an elderly cow that was looking over the hedge to leap like the mountains of the psalmist. "Pity it was so dark and time was so short," he explained. "I'd like to have seen her face when she saw the contents of that envelope. She must have wondered what on earth I had. Of course, I had nothing, but it brought her on to the top step at a run." He chuckled again. There was no bitterness in the note. Murder was just a thing to him, not an affair for hard feelings.

> "Smile awhile,
> And while you smile another smiles,
> And soon there's miles and miles of smiles,
> And life's worth while
> Because you smile."

"That's all it was. Neat, don't you think?"

"She'd probably have thought it was a code," Bill murmured gloomily.

"Oh, she might," agreed Crook in a voice that said you could believe anything of a woman. "Of course, her notion was to leave me cold on the doormat, and then shove the blame on poor Arabella. Did you notice how cunningly she'd twisted a shred or two of the shawl round the wire she used to trip me up? She didn't forget much, that dame. Well, she'd bamboozled the police twice in two different countries. She'd a right to think something of herself."

He hauled his great turnip watch out of his pocket. He beamed. He put on speed.

"They're open," he said, "and the Henpecked Rooster at Barnham has as good beer as you can find anywhere these days —though that ain't saying a lot. Still, the first ten years of peace are the worst and we're half-way through the second one already."

THE END

⟩⟩ If you've enjoyed this book and would like to discover more great vintage crime and thriller titles, as well as the most exciting crime and thriller authors writing today, visit: **⟩⟩**

The Murder Room
Where Criminal Minds Meet

themurderroom.com

www.ingramcontent.com/pod-product-compliance
Ingram Content Group UK Ltd.
Pitfield, Milton Keynes, MK11 3LW, UK
UKHW040435280225
455666UK00003B/76